The Aurora Stone

The Orea Chronicles
Book I

The Aurora Stone
Published by © Cosmic Unicorn Press
authoralanagreig.com
The moral right of the author has been asserted.
This is a work of fiction.

Any references to historical events, real people, or real places are used fictitiously. Other names, characters, places, and events are products of the author's imagination, and any resemblance to actual events or places or persons, living or dead, is entirely coincidental.

© Copyright by Alana Greig 2017
All rights reserved.

No part of this publication may be reproduced, stored in a retrieval system, or transmitted, in any form or by any means, nor be circulated in any form of binding or cover other than that in which it is published and without a similar condition including this condition being imposed on the subsequent purchaser.

Cover design © Marmaduke The Spy Productions
Editing by Sally Orchard

The Aurora Stone: 1st ed.
ISBN 9781548434465

This book is dedicated to
My dad, my hero
My husband, my rock
My boys Finley and Oscar. You two are my greatest adventure.

Acknowledgments

So many people have helped me realise this moment.
Thank you, Beverley Hollowed, for pushing me to do this. Your belief that I could has always surpassed mine. Your constant support and guidance mean the world to me.
Thanks to my sister Aimee Price for reading every chapter as I wrote it and shortening my sentences. (Sorry)
Thank you to Erin Lee for helping me make sense of the self-publishing world and bringing your unique sense of humour into every conversation.
A big thank you to my husband Fraser. I know I have hidden away a lot while writing. Thanks for the endless cups of tea and the reminders to take breaks and for finding your hidden talent for cover design, who knew!
I couldn't have done any of this if it wasn't for my dad. He passed away before this was even a idea. He shared his passion for reading with me from a very young age. He also taught me that if you want it badly enough you will fight for it. I hope I did you proud dad.
The last thank you is to you, (yes you reading this right now) my Chosen, my readers. You make this worthwhile, thank you for believing in fairy tales and for reading mine.

Chapter One

It was, indeed, the most beautiful day, a very special day for Evangeline; today was her eighteenth birthday. For the elvish people, turning eighteen was a special time. This was the day each elf discovered what their extra ability would be. Evangeline, however, would rather have stayed by the stream reading than attending the big ceremony that accompanied this milestone birthday.

It's just such a long and dull ceremony, all the standing and then sitting, just to stand again! I would rather just receive a letter from the wise ones. Sighing, she gathered up her book and the flowers she had picked for her mother. With one last look at the dappled light dancing on the sparkling waters of the stream, Evangeline turned for home.

"HAPPY BIRTHDAY, SWEETHEART."

"Thank you, Mother. Here, I picked these for you. They are the last of the season."

Gwen smiled at her child. How beautiful she had become, the envy of many of the local girls; it broke her heart to think of what she must reveal to her later that day.

"Are you alright, Mother? You seem sad. Can I get you some fern tea? That always seems to make things better." Evangeline moved to the kitchen to prepare tea for them both.

I will miss her. The sadness was almost too much for Gwen to bear. They sat and enjoyed their tea until it was time to get ready for the ceremony. Mother and daughter left to change into their best clothes. Eve had a new dress made by her mother; the material was exquisite, soft as silk with the lustre of moonstone. Eve turned in front of the mirror admiring Gwen's talent with needle and thread.

Here we go. Not able to delay the inevitable, she picked up her shoes and went downstairs.

"TODAY IS MIDSUMMERS Day, a day full of beauty and promise..."

Eve was tuning out the extremely long-winded prelude to her gifting ceremony. Her mind drifted back to the stream glittering like diamonds, the cool water lapping at her toes.

"Eve. Evangeline!"

Eve was suddenly pulled from her daydream by a rather cross-looking elder.

Great.

"Please take your place on the circle of souls and close your eyes."

Eve walked to the circle and stood in the centre. She glanced at her mother before closing her eyes as the Elder had instructed.

"Ready or not," she whispered to herself.

The Elder began the chant that would gift Evangeline with her extra ability. The circle began to glow, first blue, then purple, before finally settling into a brilliant indigo. The Zephyrs caused her hair to fly and her skirts to ripple in a shimmery dance. The chanting faded away, and a hush fell over the congregation. Eve stayed perfectly still, waiting for the instruction to move off the circle and re-join her mother. She felt no different, which was disappointing.

"Evangeline, you may step off the circle of souls. You are no longer a child; whatever gifts the souls have bestowed upon you are unique to you."

"Thank you, Elder."

Eve took a breath and opened her eyes to re-join her mother. There was a gasp; a murmur ran through the gathered elves like a ripple in a pond, the sound growing in volume as it travelled through the crowd. Eve looked down at herself. Nothing was amiss. She glanced at the Elder, who was looking at her in wonder, a slight crease formed between his brows. Disconcerted, Eve returned to her mother's side. Gwen moved her head towards her daughter and whispered,

"It is your eyes, my love, they are no longer the brown of a doe's; they are the green-gold of the first leaves of autumn."

The walk home was a quiet affair. Once in the house, Evangeline went as casually as she could manage to the nearest mirror.

Oh, oh my!

Looking back at her was the face she knew, but it was also very different. Her skin was still the peaches and cream it had always been. Her lips were still soft and with the hint of a smile playing at the corners. But her eyes, they were, indeed, a brilliant green-gold, and they appeared to be lit from within, their depths full of a mystery that had not been present when she had awoken this morning.

"These are going to take some getting used to."

Eve headed downstairs for dinner. After the events of the day, all she wanted was to have a nice warm meal, then to curl up in her reading chair and finish her latest book.

"Something smells wonderful, I really am quite hungry," Eve said, entering the kitchen.

"Sit down. It will only be a minute," Gwen called through from the kitchen. Eve took a seat at the table and waited, anticipating the soothing warmth of her mother's cooking. It always made her feel warm and comforted. After a rather delicious stew, Eve left the table to collect her book. When she entered the snug, her mother was already in there. This was nothing unusual, however, tonight she seemed on edge. Gwen had a small box in front of her on the occasional table.

"Come and have a seat, sweetheart. There are some things I need to tell you."

A sense of foreboding settled over Evangeline. Taking cautious steps, she walked over to the chair opposite her mother and sat on the very edge, mirroring Gwen's pose. Taking a deep breath, Gwen looked into her daughters' strange new eyes and began the task of revealing the truth.

"Eve, I am not your birth mother."

Before Eve could absorb this earth-shattering news, another shocking piece of information was thrown into the already charged atmosphere.

"You had a brother, a twin. His name was Eli."

The room began to spin; Eve felt suddenly sick and far too hot. Before Gwen could stop her, she bolted from the snug and out into to the night. Eve ran to the bottom of the garden; she had her sanctuary there: a treehouse that her father, well the man she had called Father for thirteen years of her life, had built for her when she was six. Eve climbed the ladder that was still as strong as the day it was made. When she reached the top, Eve opened the trunk she kept there, pulled out her blanket to wrap herself in, sat in the pile of cushions in the corner, and cried herself to sleep.

"EVE. EVE, ARE YOU UP there?"

The sound of someone calling her name roused her from sleep. Eve grumbled as she disentangled herself from the blanket. Why was she in the tree house anyway? It then all came flooding back: the ceremony, her eyes, and the revelations.

Who am I?

"Evangeline, please come back to the house. We have to talk... Please."

Gwen stood at the foot of the ladder John had made so long ago. *I wish he were here*, a tear rolled down her cheek. Thoughts of her husband always brought tears to her eyes. *He would know what to do*. Admitting defeat, Gwen stroked the ladder rung one last time and headed back to the house.

Eve found her mother where she had left her the night before. Though she looked tired and had clearly been crying, there was also a look of defeat about her. Gwen had lost her sparkle.

"Hello, Mother, just let me change out of this dress, and then I will listen to whatever it is you have to say."

A pot of freshly-made tea waited for Eve on her return to the snug, along with some toast slathered in honey, just how she liked it.

"I thought you might be hungry."

"Thank you."

Eve took a seat, picked up her plate of food and braced herself.

"I am so sorry about last night, sweetheart; I know it was a terrible shock. The truth is, your birth parents vanished when you and your brother were just six months old. No one knows where they went. They were just... gone. We found you in your cradle."

"My brother, why did you only take me and not Eli?"

She couldn't help but interrupt; anger had bubbled up at the thought of her twin just left behind.

"Eli wasn't there, my love. We searched for him all over the house. We thought that another family must have found him in a different room and taken him in. We asked everyone we met that day if they knew what had happened to Eli. No one had seen your brother. I'm so sorry."

Tears rolled down Gwen's face.

"Please don't hate me, Eve. We searched for him, we really did. Your father even went out into the surrounding woodland to see if he had somehow been left outside. He searched every day for three weeks."

Eve put her plate down again, with only a single bite taken from one slice. It tasted like ashes. *My brother is lost, or at worse - dead! And I never knew. I wish I had a picture of him.* Eve couldn't cry. The tears wouldn't come; everything was too raw.

"Here."

Gwen had opened the box. Holding a small frame out to her, Eve reached out with trembling hands and received the object. Taking a deep breath, she quickly flipped over the frame and gazed at the photo within. Two tiny children sitting beside a dog smiled out at her. There was a red-haired girl with brown doe eyes, and next to her, holding a rattle and the dog's tail, was a fair-haired boy with eyes the colour of bluebells, a beautiful piercing blue.

"Eli," she whispered while reaching out a finger and stroking the boy's image.

"I will find you, I promise."

Evangeline looked at her mother and waited for her to continue. She had a feeling there was more, a lot more, to come.

Gwen picked up the small box and handed it over. It was a small wooden box adorned with typical elvish craftsmanship. Taking a hold of her emotions, Eve lifted the lid to reveal the contents that were sure to change her life even more. Inside the box was another photo; this one was larger and not framed.

My parents!

Staring at the image before her. They looked so happy. Putting it aside, she reached back into the box and drew out a very old and tatty piece of parchment, the kind the elves of generations past would have made. Careful not to damage it, Eve very gently peeled back the folds until it lay open on the table.

"It's a map... but not a map like I have ever seen before."

Eve looked closer at the map, hoping to see something she recognised. "There is Hermoria, the land of the Elves. But where are these places?" Gwen came to sit beside her daughter, and she too looked down at the map.

"I know of Clear Water Valley, the land of the Witches. They are our allies. It is the witches who spin the beautiful yarns we use to make our clothes. In return, we trade our lush grasses and some of the herbs that only grow in our lands, and it has been this way for hundreds of years. The other lands... I don't know."

"I think it would be best to seek out Reena, Mother. She will know the answers." Eve was all ready to go out in search of the wise old elf when she noticed something wedged into the lid of the box. Careful not to damage it, she removed a piece of moonstone. It was just larger than her palm, a quarter of an inch thick, and so very beautiful. Stroking it with the very tips of her fingers, Eve suddenly felt a warm tingle rush up her fingers and settle in her chest.

"That is a seeing stone; they are extremely rare," Gwen whispered in an awed voice. "They can only be activated by an elf that has wisdom and the sight. We need to find Reena." Eve looked up from the stone with a puzzled expression.

"Hold on, a seeing stone? Those are a thing of elvish legend. It's a story dad used to tell me at bedtime." She looked disbelievingly from the stone to her mother's face and back again. "Right?"

Gwen gazed upon her beautiful child - in all but blood - knowing what this stone meant and how much it was about to change Eve's life. Whether the change would be for better or worse was not yet clear. One thing was for certain, the only elf who could glean the message from the stone was Reena.

"Let's go find Reena, sweetheart. She will have the answer. Bring the map, maybe she can enlighten us about these other lands as well." Gwen moved towards Eve and put the map and stone back in the wooden box.

"Come, the sooner we find her, the sooner you will have answers."

REENA, THE WISE WOMAN gifted with the sight, or so many believed, lived away from other elves. She chose to live deep in the forest, and her home was truly beautiful. She never felt the need to venture far; everything she needed was right on her doorstep. It came as no great surprise to see Gwen and Evangeline approaching that day. The change in the child's eyes only the day before was enough to know that something very special lay in the destiny of young Eve.

GWEN RAISED HER TEA cup to her lips; only Reena could make the perfect rosehip tea. Looking across at the two of them pouring over the map, she couldn't help but feel fearful for her precious child. *She is grown now; I cannot always protect her.*

"The map shows the five realms of Orea, including our own. You know of the witch's realm, Clear Water Valley. There is also Mieron, the realm of the vampires, Gloria, the realm of the Fae. Tricky folk, the Fae." Reena ran her gnarled fingers over the areas as she named them.

"Now, let me see. Ah yes, and Olia, the realm of the owl riders." Reena finished pointing to the realms on the map and then looked at Eve expectantly.

"There is also this. It was hidden in the lid of the box; Mother says it is a seeing stone. But I thought they were just a legend." Eve finished in a rush. She did not wish to be seen as foolish. Reena took the cool stone from Eve and turned it over in her hands.

It is as I thought. This child is meant for great things. Keeping her thoughts to herself, she looked Eve in the eye.

"Yes child, your Mother is quite correct. This is, indeed, a seeing stone. A stone of prophecy."

"Wait. What?"

Eve was clearly hearing things. She was sure Reena has just said *a stone of prophecy*.

"What does that mean, Reena?" Not sure she really wanted to know the answer, Eve took a step away from the stone, suddenly not as fond of its lustre as she had been a moment ago.

"It means, Evangeline, that this stone holds your destiny. However, you do have a choice. I can activate the stone to read the prophecy hidden within, or I can hand it back to you. Only you can choose which path to take; I cannot help you, nor can your mother," Reena explained.

"You must look inside yourself and choose your path. The prophecy is as old as time. We do not know who made the stones; maybe the Goddess herself. The fact remains, this stone was meant for you. A stone of prophecy is guarded by mystical forces, and only the one who is meant to fulfil the prophecy will find the stone, or so the legend reads. Make your choice. Look within yourself; the answer is there for you to find."

This is madness! Yesterday I was just Eve, a normal girl with a normal family. Today I have luminous eyes, a missing brother, and now this! Why me? Looking at Reena and her loving mother, she knew what had to be done. The stone had called to her the very first time she had stroked its surface.

"Alright, let's find out what the stone has been keeping secret."

Reena took the stone in her left hand and took Eve's hand in her right. She then began to chant. The sound of it reminded Eve of water flowing over pebbles by the stream; it soothed her. After a few moments, enchanted elvish script appeared on the surface. Reena read it and then relayed the prophecy she had been waiting her whole life to hear.

"Eve, this knowledge was kept from you until eighteen years after your birth. This is your prophecy. Only you can fulfil it."

Reena proceeded to read the prophecy aloud.

"An Elvish girl with changeable eyes will lose her family through the void. Three companions she will travel with. They will be identified by their gems. To get back what was lost, the Aurora stone must return to its home. In no more than a year and four days must this quest be completed, or the realms will be pulled into the void and lost."

Chapter Two

Eve considered the revelation of the prophecy for two days. Everything she had believed to be true had been torn to shreds. Her sense of self was now as fragile as a butterfly's wing. One touch and it would come apart, never to be the same again.

"Why is this all happening at once?" Eve moaned into her soft pillow, taking the meagre amount of comfort given by its delicate scent of honeysuckle. Peeking over the top of her soft haven, Eve once again gazed upon the faces of the family she was born to but, until three days ago, never knew existed.

I must try. It may help me discover what became of my brother. However, remote this chance may be, if I do not at least try, then regret will surely haunt me for the rest of my days. Having resolved this internal dilemma, Evangeline now had another difficult task. *I have to tell Mother.*

After an hour and a half of pacing across her room and practicing different deliveries in front of the mirror, Eve was resigned to the fact that however the words left her, it was still going to cause her mother pain. With leaden steps and a heavy heart, she headed downstairs.

Gwen was pruning her roses when Eve appeared at her side. A look of sadness marred her pretty countenance, yet a spark of determination was also evident in her new luminous eyes. *She is leaving.* Gwen thought her heart would surely break without her daughter. Gwen knew that once her Evangeline had set her mind to something, there was no swaying her.

Eve had prepared herself as best she could for the inevitable. She took a deep breath.

"Mother I..."

"You have decided to take up the quest," Gwen interrupted her. "I could tell just by looking at you, Sweetheart; you have always been easy to read." Eve opened her mouth, then closed it again, taken completely aback. For a few moments, all she was capable of doing was staring at her mother.

"How did you... I" Eve was speechless. "I'm sorry to leave you and our home, but truthfully, to not take up the quest that the prophecy has set before me when there could be a chance, however small, that it could shed some light on the disappearance of my...other family, my brother. Mother, please understand, I must try."

"You are strong-willed just like your father. He would be so very proud of the woman you have become, and so am I, though I will worry every second and miss you more than I can express. Darling, you must follow your heart wherever it may lead you." Tears glistening in her grey eyes, Gwen held her daughter in an embrace that she hoped conveyed all the love she was unable to express eloquently in words. Holding her beloved Eve at arm's length, she put on her best reassuring smile.

"Come on, I will help you prepare."

Together they packed a large leather satchel with everything one could possibly need on a quest. This included the wooden box Gwen had given her a few days previously. Its contents had been returned to it. Gwen also added some food, some money, and some herbs to make simple medicines. Her father had shown her how to prepare them before he died. Eve also had her toughest shoes ready and her warmest cloak.

I am as ready as I'll ever be. Glancing around her room, sadness enveloped her heart. This room, this house, was all she had ever known. Though she felt melancholy, Eve's sense of adventure was fighting to burst to the surface. After all, it wasn't every day one got to fulfil an ancient prophecy.

Gwen was determined that their final dinner together for a while - she refused to believe it was forever - should be a memorable one. She had carefully prepared their favourite dishes, even baking a glorious cake decorated with sugared rose petals that had been picked from her own blooms. Lastly, she retrieved the silk wrapped gift she had for Eve and placed it to the right of her plate. Gwen stepped back to admire her efforts, pleased with what she had achieved. It was time to call Eve down.

WHEN EVE SAW THE EFFORT her mother had gone to, it was difficult of hold back the tears. Everything looked so beautiful. Taking her usual place at the table, Gwen placed a delicate china plate before her.

"Purple carrot and pomegranate salad. Your favourite," she beamed.

Eve laughed, "Thank you, Mother, it looks delicious." Picking up her cutlery that had been crafted by her great-grandfather, she began her meal.

After two fabulous courses, Gwen carried through the cake. Eve knew that her mother had a great talent for baking. She anticipated the richness of the sponge, the tartness of the huckleberry jelly that was sure to be liberally smeared in the centre, and, finally, the lightness of the meringue frosting. It was fluffy as a cloud - pure decadence for the palate.

"I cannot imagine a more fitting finale to such a feast than the masterpiece you have created Mother. Please, may I have a very large piece?" exclaimed Eve, cake fork already in hand. A huge smile was in place that lit up her whole face. Seeing her daughter's expectant expression, Gwen was transported back thirteen years to Eve's fifth birthday. Such a day it had been. John had made the chest that still sat at the end of Eve's bed. Back then it was for her toys, now it stored her most precious memories. Gwen had baked a cake that day as she did every birthday. That year stuck in her mind, maybe because the image of her husband and daughter laughing together was still so fresh in her memory, like it had happened yesterday. Then, like today, the wonder on Eve's face was so innocent. Gwen suddenly felt fearful. *What if she never returns? What if something happens? This could be the last time we ever spend together.* Holding back the tears that threatened, she placed the cake centre stage, smiling down at her.

Gwen replied, "Of course, you can, darling. I will never know where you put such a slice. Like your father, you can eat enough to feed a household and still be slim and strong. Many an elfin maid would love to have such luck!"

Laughing together, they enjoyed their desert. Once Eve was finished, Gwen picked up the gift she had placed by her right hand earlier. Getting up, she passed the token to Eve. Looking at the purple silk wrapping, Eve understood that, whatever this contained, it was sure to be important, a keepsake to treasure. They were not, as a rule, the type of family to frequently give gifts.

"I hope you like it."

Evangeline carefully removed the silken sheath to reveal the secret within. A large locket the size of a chicken's egg sat nestled within the folds. It was exquisitely engraved. She lovingly caressed the surface.

"Open it," Gwen urged her. Very gently, Eve squeezed the sides to open it. Inside was a revelation: a miniature photo album, each one as thin and delicate as a spider's web. Taking care, she turned each frame to reveal the portrait hidden behind its predecessor. There were six in total: one of her mother, one of her father, and one of her as a child of five. The next three were of her birth family, copies of the pictures now safely stored in the bag.

"So, wherever you travel, you will carry us with you. I know we are not your birth parents, but you are, and always will be, our beloved Evangeline." Quickly closing the locket so her tears wouldn't damage the delicate treasures within, Eve got up from her place and embraced her mother.

"No matter who gave birth to me, you and dad will always be my parents, and I love you so very much." Kissing and hugging each other, they allowed a few moments for tears.

"Let me put it on you; I bought the silk especially." Eve moved her russet mane so the silver clasp on the emerald silk necklace could be fastened. The locket sat perfectly just below the hollow of her throat.

"Turn around so I can look at you. Ah, yes, the colour really brings out your eyes and sets your hair aflame," Gwen gushed. Looking in the mirror, Eve, too, admired her appearance. Though not a vain person, she was not ignorant of her beauty.

"Thank you, Mother, it truly is a beautiful keepsake. I shall never take it off."

After clearing the table, they retired to the snug. Gwen picked up some sewing, while Eve took this final opportunity to sit in her favourite chair with a book and become lost in a hero's adventure. Tomorrow, she would be embarking on her own.

AFTER A RESTLESS NIGHT, Eve prepared to leave. She was pretty sure a Kaleidoscope of rather large butterflies had taken up residence in her stomach. Heading downstairs, she was relieved to see some ginger and chamomile tea waiting for her.

"I wasn't sure what you would want to eat. I thought some tea would be palatable...?" Gwen placed the honey pot on the table, knowing Eve liked to add it to her tea.

"Thank you, I really don't feel like eating just now. I will take some bread and an apple for later," Eve mumbled while absentmindedly adding a spoon of honey to her drink. They sat in silence, neither one knowing what to say, though both extremely aware that the time to say anything at all was fast expiring. After her second cup of honeyed tea, Eve stood.

I must not cry, Gwen admonished herself. *Plenty of time for tears later. Right now, I must be strong for my daughter. She must be terrified; I know that I would be.* Moving towards the front door, Gwen helped Eve with her things, carefully rolling her cloak and securing it to her bag.

"Here is your food for later. I have wrapped a piece of cheese in nettle leaves as well; it should stay fresh for a day or so." After adding the food parcel to her bag, Eve was out of things to do; their time was up. Looking around her, she desperately wanted to stay, but she knew that if she were to surrender to this feeling, regret would plague her forever.

"Well... I guess this is it," she stammered.

"I guess it is," replied Gwen. Embracing for what could be the last time, they held on tight to each other.

"I love you," they said in unison. Eyes once again glinting with unshed tears, they both put on a smile to try and comfort the other.

"I will be back before you know it, and what stories I shall have to tell!"

"You will, my sweet girl, and I shall make a cake to celebrate your return!" Opening the front door, Eve walked to the front gate. The sun was shining in the pearl-coloured sky, and the sound of finches chattering reached her on the slight breeze. It was a beautiful, peaceful morning to embark on an adventure. Turning back to look at her mother standing in the doorway, she smiled her best smile and raised her hand in farewell.

"Go east, Eve. That is the road to Clear Water Valley. It would make sense to pass through the realm of our allies first."

Nodding, Eve opened the gate and took the first step of her journey. Reaching back to close the gate, she wanted to turn to see her mother's gentle expression once more.

"Don't look back again, child; your path is east. Only look forward now. I shall be here on your return!" Gwen called, not wanting Eve to see the tears that were now sliding down her cheeks in silent streams of sorrow.

Squaring her shoulders and trying to quell the swarm of what now appeared to be very angry butterflies, she turned her face to the morning sun and headed east towards Clear Water Valley; the realm of witches.

EVE ENJOYED HER MORNING walk through the eastern lands of Hermoria; it was not somewhere she frequented often. The flowers here were in full bloom, even her mother's favourite orange fire lilies. *I will have to remember this when I return.*

As she was wondering about how the flowers were still blooming - since the season for them had passed - Eve noticed an Elder coming along the road on the left. Even from her vantage point, she could see that he appeared to be muttering to himself. *Probably going over his address for tonight's gathering*, Eve thought. She was suddenly relieved that she would not have to attend; having everyone stare at her again was not something she wished to repeat.

"Good Morning, Elder," Eve called out with a wave and a ready smile. It was not the 'done' thing to be so open with an elder. However, Evangeline seemed to get away with it. As the elder drew closer, Eve recognised him as the Elder who had performed her gifting.

"Good morning, young Evangeline, and what are you doing out so early, on what I must say is a most beautiful day?" The Elder smiled down at her. He had now reached her on the road; for an old Elf, he sure moved fast! Unsure if she should tell him her reason for being on the road so early, she decided that a half-truth would be sufficient.

"It is, indeed, a most glorious morning, Elder. I am on my way to meet with a Witch. My Mother wishes me to give her some herbs." Opening her pack, Eve showed the Elder the herbs and grasses. Worried that he would question her further, and not being an accomplished liar, Eve gave him her best smile.

"I will wish you a good day, Elder and thank you for performing my gifting a few days past."

Drawing himself up to his full height, the Elder looked rather pleased to have been thanked. With a smile playing at the corners of his mouth, he nodded to Eve and once again bid her a good morning. Continuing on her way. Evangeline felt guilty for not confiding in the Elder. She was not by nature a dishonest person, yet something had held her back.

"I must follow my heart, like Reena instructed." Eve murmured. Feeling better about not being completely honest, she began once again to ponder about the prophecy.

THE SUN WAS PAST ITS highest point when Eve decided that she could no longer ignore her grumbling stomach. Wary of the now mildly irritated butterflies that seemed to have taken up residence permanently in her stomach, she delicately nibbled at a piece of bread. Once she had finished and felt slightly fuller, Eve looked about for a stream from which to have a drink and refill her water bottle. Not far from the road she saw a twinkling through the long grass. When she reached the stream, Eve had a refreshing drink and filled her bottle, drying the canister on her skirts. Eve glanced up to see a doe taking a drink on the opposite side of the stream.

"How beautiful you are," she whispered.

The doe's ears pricked as though it had heard her. Then, to Eve's amazement, the doe looked her in the eye and bowed. Evangeline was flabbergasted; never in her whole life had she witnessed or even heard of an encounter like this. The doe seemed to recognise her, or so she felt. They continued to gaze at each other, the afternoon sun warming the animal's coat to a glorious chestnut with flecks of amber and gold. A flock of black jays suddenly took flight from the trees behind the doe, startling it, and just like that, the magical moment was lost.

Completely entranced by the event, Eve did not immediately notice the thundering sound that was carried to her on the balmy breeze. Shaking herself, she followed the bank towards the sound. After few miles, the stream widened into a river. The thundering had grown progressively louder, and as she navigated through some rather robust long grass, she saw the source of the sound: a magnificent waterfall, cascading over what looked like the edge of the world. Eve was in awe of such beauty.

I will always remember this view for as long as I live, she promised herself. Walking to the edge of the cliff to fully admire the wild beauty of nature, it suddenly dawned on her; she was very high up.

"If this is a cliff, how on earth do I reach the lands beyond it?" Eve muttered. Looking out and down from her vantage point, Eve could clearly see golden hills and the continuation of the river meandering its way through the lush vista below.

"You must be invited in," said a musical voice just behind Eve.

Chapter Three

"OH, MY GODDESS!"

Feeling quite sure her heart was going to burst from her chest, Eve whipped around, drawing the small dagger she carried from her belt as she went. Now facing her would-be attacker, ready to defend herself, she was surprised to see a rather tiny woman standing before her. In fact, she was a full head and shoulders shorter than Eve. Seemingly unfazed by the dagger, the woman repeated herself.

"You must be invited in." Smiling up at Eve, she reached her hand out in welcome. Feeling slightly foolish for being afraid of such a tiny unarmed woman, Eve sheathed her weapon and took the woman's hand in greeting.

"I am Evangeline, daughter of Gwen. I am on a journey to Clear Water Valley." Finishing her introduction, Eve wondered if she should have disclosed so much.

"A pleasure to meet you, Evangeline, I am Violet, Keeper of the gate," Violet replied with a smile.

Before Eve could ask what exactly a keeper of the gate was and where the gate led to, Violet had moved to stand before two willow trees a few meters from the cliff edge. Intrigued, Eve followed.

"Please stay there," Violet called over her shoulder when Eve was twenty paces away. Not sure what was to happen next, she did as she was bid. Violet raised her arms over her head, muttered a few words, and as the last word left her lips, she brought her hands down in front of her as if in prayer. Then, palms facing outwards, she drew her slender arms apart as if parting a pair of curtains to let in the morning sun.

Before her, the forest that nestled in-between the two majestic willow trees rippled and sparkled. Eve watched in wonder as the woodland dissolved into a million glittering fragments. Now, in its place, was a road.

"As I said, I am the keeper of the gate," Violet repeated as she beckoned Eve forward. Eyes like saucers, Eve walked towards Violet and the road that just a second ago definitely had not been there.

"Wow!" was all she could manage to articulate. Laughing, Violet took Eve's hand and passed between the willows and onto the road.

"I guess you have never met a witch before?" Violet inquired while trying not to allow amusement to creep into her voice. Eyes dancing, she continued to smile at the beautiful elfin girl before her.

"A witch? But that means... I made it... I made it to Clear Water Valley!" Eve whooped and did an impromptu jig, twirling and laughing. Violet was amazed to be witnessing such a bizarre reaction. Noticing Violet once again, Eve blushed as red as her hair.

"Sorry," she mumbled.

Not passing comment, Violet just began to walk. Eve quickened her pace and caught up with her. For someone with much shorter legs, Violet could sure move fast! They walked in silence. Eve, still embarrassed by her childish behaviour, took in her new surroundings. The road was a buttery gold colour and seemed to be almost like clay. Making a note to investigate its texture later, knowing that later would need to be a return trip, she continued to peruse the landscape. The trees were much more delicate than back home, with wispy green leaves that looked a lot like feathers, and their bark was a silver-white.

Hmmm... like an elvish ash tree, Eve mused.

"A bit, though the bark is vermilion when it peels," Violet informed her. Eve was sure she had not spoken her musings aloud, but not wanting to make a fool of herself again, she held her tongue.

Glancing sideways at her walking companion, Eve noticed the differences between them. Violet was very slight in build with willowy limbs and a mane of blue-black hair that fell to her waist in a ripple of silk. She wore a short green dress of good heavy cotton, picked out at the collar and cuffs with yellow embroidery. Her face was beautiful with a rosebud mouth and large violet-coloured eyes that seemed to take up half her face. She noticed Eve's scrutiny of her. Wrinkling her nose, she turned to Evangeline and asked in an exasperated tone, "Is there something on my face? You have been gaping at me for at least ten minutes, and I am becoming irritated by your lack of manners."

Blushing once again, Eve looked at the floor. "No! There's nothing at all wrong with your face; it's lovely. I have never met a witch before, and I was noticing the differences between us, that's all." She rushed her words, quite sure Violet must think her stupid, rude, or both.

"Hmm... well, we are different, that's true; however, I suggest you don't stare at every witch you meet." Violet advised. Nodding, Eve felt she might be remembering this leg of her quest for all the wrong reasons.

About an hour later, Evangeline got her very first glimpse of Clear Water Valley. They had just reached the crest of what felt like a very steep hill.

"Welcome to the heart of Clear Water Valley!" Violet exclaimed, throwing her arms out wide as if to embrace the view before them.

"It is a lovely view, very picturesque," Eve replied, smiling. The valley was beautiful, with dove grey houses. Their cheerful orange and yellow roofs caught the light, making them look more like copper and gold. Eve's stomach chose that moment to let out a rather monstrous growl. Cheeks aflame, she quickly began to dig about in her bag. Hastily, she began searching for a snack before the next guttural protest and managed to knock her lump of cheese to the ground in her embarrassment. Moving swiftly, she tried to save it from becoming spoiled. To her amazement, the cheese never made contact with the butter yellow ground. Even more astounding was that it seemed to be rising upwards.

"How...is my cheese flying?" Eve squeaked. Chuckling, Violet opened her hand and received the nettle wrapped lump.

"It wasn't flying; it was just a simple levitation charm," she replied breezily. Handing the morsel back to Eve, Violet began heading down the hill towards the houses. Eve eyed her cheese and decided that floating food was not something she was ready to experience. She carefully placed it back into her bag under her apple in case it started to levitate again and hurried after Violet's quickly retreating back.

It soon became clear that Eve was going to have to get used to objects – and, indeed, people - behaving in ways that they usually did not.

Now in the Square, the large open area in the centre of town where markets and festivals were held, Eve saw many things that would be hard to forget.

"Close your mouth, for goodness sake! You look like you have been cursed," Violet admonished. Rolling her eyes, Violet headed for a charming house with a bright pink front door. "Come on, before you really do get cursed by an over-sensitive witch!"

Opening the door, she hurried Evangeline inside before any more witches noticed her staring.

"I am so sorry, but that gentleman was holding fire in his hand, and it was green!" Eve babbled. Sighing loudly from a room at the end of the hallway, Violet began to make tea and a light supper, with perhaps more force than the crockery deserved. Eve made her way towards the commotion. Feeling foolish, she kept her head bowed as he entered the kitchen.

"I'm sorry," Eve mumbled, still looking at the floor. Sighing, Violet thumped two plates of sandwiches and fruit down on the table.

"Forget it; just eat," she replied, sitting herself down as she waited for Eve to do the same.

After a rather quiet meal, which Eve enjoyed despite her embarrassment, Violet showed her into the snug. Cosy with soft inviting sofas, a wood burning stove, and best of all, a book shelf positively bursting with books, it was a room Eve could be content in for hours.

"So, Evangeline of Hermoria, what brings you to the realm of witches?" Violet inquired, as she gracefully folded herself into one of the armchairs, by the crackling wood burner.

Taking the chair opposite Violet, Eve perched on the edge, not sure where to begin, or how much to divulge. "The witches are our allies. It has been this way for hundreds of years." The words of her mother floated through her memory. She had decided that sooner or later she was going to have to surrender some information, or she may never find her brother or fulfil the prophecy.

"I am searching for answers," Eve explained. Looking at her, Violet knew there was more to it than she was likely to discover now. She waited patiently for Eve to continue. "I am searching for my brother. We were separated as babies; I want to discover what became of him," she added a few moments later.

"Why come here, though? There aren't any elvish living here, only witches," Violet asked. To her, this seemed a strange place to begin the search. Her mentor would remind her that every path had its twists and turns. Inwardly rolling her eyes at the thought, she continued to wait for Eve to disclose more.

"I was sent here by a wise elf who has the sight and my mother. As you are our closest allies, they believed that I would be granted safe passage through this realm," Eve concluded.

Feeling a little disappointed at the complete lack of detail, Violet gave up and offered Eve a bed for the night. After being shown to her room, Eve took a bath and changed out of her clothes. Violet had offered to clean them for her. Eve couldn't thank her enough, as she had no idea when the opportunity to have them cleaned would come again. Taking out her book and pencil, she wrote down her experiences of the quest so far.

WAKING WITH A START, Eve fell off the bed, landing on the striped floorboards. Rubbing her sore shoulder, Eve was sure that this was yet another experience she was not overly keen on repeating. After getting to her feet, Eve began wondering what had woken her so suddenly. Then she heard it: rain beating against the cottage. Moving to the window, she pulled the curtains back to gaze out at the storm. Lightning flashed, illuminating the valley in a harsh, white light. Following the jagged fingers of lightning, the thunder struck. A colossal booming reverberated around the valley. Awestruck by the power of nature, Eve stood at her window, mesmerised. Suddenly, the bedroom door burst open, and a bedraggled Violet tumbled in.

"What happened?" Eve exclaimed, rushing to Violet's side. Violet groaned as Eve helped her onto the bed.

"The square... the tower was hit, and two houses have been crushed. Many more are ablaze." Trying to rise from the bed, Eve pushed her gently back down.

"You have done enough. Stay and rest; I will go and do what I can." Dressing quickly, Eve rushed into the night.

Bedlam was the only way to describe what Eve found upon reaching the square. Witches were everywhere and children were screaming. It was a wonder more people had not been injured. Running towards a group of young witches, she bellowed over the storm.

"What's happening? Why is everyone panicking? You are witches... use your magic!"

It was painful to see them just standing there, looks of complete confusion on their faces. "We can't use magic; we are not allowed to interfere with the will of nature!" Screamed one of the group. Not quite believing what she had just heard, Eve left the group and ran to a lone man. When she got closer, she noticed the girl in his arms. The girl was covered in soot, and even from a distance, Eve could tell that she wasn't moving. Arriving at the man's side a moment later, she took the girl gently from his arms and laid her on the grass a few feet away. She hoped she could help at least one person here.

Eve felt for her pulse, hoping there was one. This girl was only a child, no more than five years old.

"Please live, little one," Eve begged. Finding no sign of the child's heartbeat, Eve felt tears prickle her closed lids. Leaning forward, she kissed the child on the cheek, "May you find your ancestors across the golden sea. May you find peace there," she whispered to the child, placing her hand on the child's chest.

She was about to leave her and find others that could be helped, when Eve felt movement under her palm. Checking again for a heartbeat, Eve was relieved to find one. "You are tough, little one." She praised the unconscious child while she stroked her hair. Leaving her for just a moment, Eve ran back to fetch the man who had been holding her. "The child, she lives! You must come, she is not yet conscious, but it would be best to have someone she knows with her," Eve rushed. The man's eyes lit up, and he ran to where the child lay. Eve watched as he picked up the small form and hugged her close, tears streaming down his face.

Happy that at least one life had been saved, Eve went in search of a witch with the authority to end this madness of not messing with natural disasters, as nature was sure having no trouble messing with them. After dodging a falling sapling and being knocked to the ground by scared children, Evangeline finally found a group of adults. They had congregated around the well and seemed to be in deep conversation.

"Excuse me... Excuse me!" Eve yelled as she ran towards the group. Looking up, they were stunned to behold an elfin maid running toward them, russet hair flying and with such a determined look on her beautiful face. Lighting cut across the sky, illuminating Eve. The witches gasped as her eyes flashed with green-gold fire.

"So it is true," the youngest member of the gathering whispered.

"Please, use your magic to end the suffering," Eve begged, skidding to a stop before the group. She looked each member in the eye, hoping that one would see the folly in abstaining from magic while their Kin were dying.

"We never interfere with nature's course, young elf," snapped a witch whose hair was the colour of iron despite the fact that her face was plump with youth.

"People are dying!" countered Eve, completely enraged that these people would not act, knowing they could. "You are cowards! Children are dying! People are losing everything. And you stand back, feeling no guilt because you won't interfere with nature's course! I am very sorry, we may be allies, but no Elf would stand by and let their kin die, and I will not stand back and let these people die now." Eve blasted.

Turning to the well, she began to draw the pail up, *if only to slow the inferno and give them a chance to get away*, she thought. Unhooking the bucket from the chain, she ran to the flames closest and soaked the wall to its left. She continued this for what seemed like forever. The witches looked on with expressionless faces and hands behind their backs.

It was dawn before the rain began helping to douse the flames. Eve had worked tirelessly all through the night, and no one had helped her. The anger and disappointment she felt towards these people were swallowing her whole. Returning the pail to its chains, she slumped down, resting her back against the rough stone of the well. Closing her eyes for just a moment, she was bone-weary and filthy. *Violet*, was Eve's last thought before she drifted into exhausted oblivion.

Chapter Four

Two days later, Eve was reading in Violet's snug. A steaming cup of sage and honey tea was on the table beside her. Coughing, she placed her book down and took a sip of the savoury-sweet brew.

"Ugh, I don't think this will ever be one of my favourites," she grimaced.

"Maybe not, but it will make you feel better," Violet assured her. Taking the chair opposite Eve, Violet looked at the elf with new eyes. That terrible night when the storm had hit, Eve had made a stand and had helped people she had never met, risking her very life for others and for a town she had no ties to.

"Thank you for everything. I cannot begin to express the gratitude I feel," Violet said. Looking at the painting her great-grandmother had left her, she continued, "The fire, the blood... I couldn't be near the blood," she admitted sadly. Eve placed the unpalatable tea back on its saucer.

"That is nothing to be ashamed of; many folks cannot bear the sight of blood. Indeed, my mother turns a wonderful shade of green if she gets so much as a paper cut. There is also no need to thank me. What I did that night was what I was able to, nothing more," she stated.

Getting up, Evangeline stretched. Then, deciding that a walk was just what she needed, she headed for the hall to retrieve her cloak and shoes. Opening the front door, Eve stepped out into the late overcast morning. Halfway down the main avenue, she heard feet pounding against the road, a muted *thud, thud, thud* gaining on her fairly quickly. Eve stepped aside to let whoever it was past.

"Thank the Goddess, you stopped! I haven't run like that since being chased by an angry goose four years past." Eve turned to see a young man doubled over, clutching his side. He seemed familiar to her; most likely she had seen him the night of the storm.

"Can I be of some assistance to you?" she inquired.

Straightening up, the man looked down into her mysterious eyes. "I just wanted to meet the woman who stood up for what she believed, and look, once again, into your extraordinary eyes," he complimented. Unsure whether this witch was trying to court her or just had a funny way of saying thank you, Eve smiled and responded politely.

"I did only what I could. I will be on my way now if that is all; I feel the need for a walk." Eve turned and was about to continue on her way when a hand gently touched her forearm. Turning back, she once again looked up into the young man's eyes.

"Please, I would very much like to walk with you, if you are not averse to this?" he asked. It was only now that she noticed that this witch had eyes as extraordinary as her own. His were blue, but not just any blue. They were the blue of the sea with flecks of silver that seemed to swirl like the crest of a wave breaking on the rocks.

"If you like, my name is Eve. It is a pleasure you meet you," Eve introduced herself and offered her hand in greeting. Taking her hand, all the time looking into her eyes, the witch replied.

"It is my pleasure, Eve. I am Caleb."

They walked for a while, Caleb telling Eve about Clear Water Valley, pointing out historical landmarks and introducing her to any witch that passed them. After about an hour, Eve was feeling a bit tired. Though she would never admit it to Violet, she was still feeling a bit run down. The chill she had caught the night of the storm had almost gone, but it had left her drained of energy. Heading back towards Violets' home, Caleb became aware of the sickly pallor of Eve's skin.

"Are you feeling alright, Eve? You are looking a little pale."

"I am just tired. A sit-down and more of Violet's awful sage tea shall set me right, I am sure," she replied wearily. Not liking the colour of her skin, the light sheen of perspiration that followed her hairline, or the way she swayed as she walked, Caleb made a suggestion.

"My home is close by. My father is there and my sister. I will take you there, make you some tea, and you can rest for a moment. I will escort you home after you have some colour return to your cheeks. How does that sound?" Caleb coaxed.

"I think that may be a very good idea, Caleb. Thank you," Eve said weakly and swooned. Panicked, Caleb caught Eve and lifted her into his arms. He ran the remaining quarter-mile to his home.

"I am so sorry, Caleb. I am not making a very good impression here," moaned Eve, as she sat drinking a cool glass of apple juice. She had come around as Caleb had entered the cottage.

"Oh, I don't know, you have made quite an impression on my family," he smiled. A small girl skipped into the room. When she caught sight of Eve on the sofa, she began hopping up and down,

"My angel! Daddy, Daddy, my angel is on the sofa talking to Caleb!" she squealed. Eve was quite sure she was not an angel, but the child seemed so pleased to see her. Then it came to her... the girl covered in soot without a pulse. Could it be her? This child was beautiful with blond hair that caught the light, shining in golden tendrils around her face, eyes as green as emeralds, and the most glorious smile Eve had ever seen.

Her inner musings were confirmed when the girl's father entered the room. "Hello, my name is Robert, and this is my daughter, Grace. I see you have already met my son," Robert smiled. Eve was speechless for a few moments. Then, remembering her manners, she rose to her feet and held out her hand.

"A pleasure to meet you. My name is Eve. I am so very glad to see you both again... and under happier circumstances," she beamed at them.

After finishing her juice and having to promise to come back and see Grace again, Caleb and Eve left for Violet's house.

"Why didn't you tell me you already knew who I was?" asked Eve, fiddling with the hem of her cloak.

"Well, for one thing, you would have thought that I only wanted to thank you for saving my sister. Also, I am not proud of our first encounter, so I hoped that if we met and you were unaware of the connection we already had, that I might be able to make a better second impression," Caleb hurried. Puzzled by this, Evangeline took a moment to think where she had seen Caleb and how it could have been a negative encounter. Then it came to her - the gathering by the well.

"You were the young man with the group of cowards at the well," she responded, an accusatory tone entering her voice.

Looking her in the eye, Caleb answered. "Yes, I was there, having the same argument as you had with them."

"Then why didn't you speak up while I was making a complete fool of myself?" Eve countered.

"I couldn't. I was busy trying to stop a tree from falling onto the Mathews house, four houses down from where we were standing, which is not easy when you are...never mind." Not wanting to have an argument about this on the street or say more than he should about certain things, Caleb took Eve's hand and hurried her up to Violet's door. Once they were sitting in the sung and very sure that Violet was out, Eve wanted answers.

"You were doing magic to save other witches, but that is forbidden. Your kin made that perfectly clear," she spat, the accusation twisting her expression. His face blank, Caleb waited for Eve to calm down.

"Yes, I was trying to use magic against the rules; however, I do not regret it," he stated, stony-faced, eyes burning with indignation. Not sure what he meant by 'trying to use magic,' and not wanting to question him about it, as it was clearly a touchy subject, Eve remained silent. After a few minutes, Caleb got to his feet.

"I'm sorry you think badly of me. I was doing what I could, just as you did." Sighing, he headed to the front door. Eve got up and followed him.

"Wait, please don't go. I feel terrible about my reaction."

Hand on the doorknob ready to leave, Caleb turned back to face her. "It's fine, I am not mad with you, far from it. You saved my sister," he said, smiling down at her. Caleb opened the door and stepped out into the dusk. "I will call on you tomorrow, if that's ok. I would like to talk some more."

Looking up, Eve could not deny that Caleb looked breath-taking with the blush colours of the dusk behind him. He stood at six foot two with sea blue eyes and chiselled features, and although he was wearing a jacket, it was clear that he was muscular and strong. Remembering that Violet had said not to stare, Eve looked past his left ear, noticing the way his blond hair curled on his collar.

"Yes, I would like that," Eve replied. Smiling once more, Caleb turned and headed in the direction of his home. Eve was still staring after him when Violet returned with supper.

Eve and Caleb spent every day thereafter together. Sometimes Violet would tag along and they would have a picnic by the river, Eve had come to think of them as her friends. This worried her, as she knew that staying here was not an option. There were other realms to venture through and a prophecy to fulfil. On her eighth day in the valley, Evangeline decided it was time to leave. Grace was becoming attached to her, and she did not wish to cause the child pain. Violet, she was sure, would be pleased to have her house back. Then there was Caleb. He had become a close friend in such a short space of time. It would be difficult to say goodbye.

Packing her bag up the next day was hard. She was truly sad to be leaving. Eve hoped to return after her quest, with stories to tell Grace and a new book for Violet. Gathering up her bag, she headed for the snug to bid Violet farewell and continue on her adventure. Violet was waiting for her and so was Caleb.

"I didn't expect to see you here, Caleb. We said goodbye yesterday," Eve murmured.

"So we did. However, it occurred to me this morning that a gentleman would escort a lady to wherever it is she was headed, to make sure she arrived safely," he replied with a bow. Suppressing a giggle, Eve smiled and replied.

"Indeed, it would be. However, I don't know exactly where it is I am heading, or how long it will take to get there. You would miss your dinner for certain." *This,* she thought, *would seal the deal,* as Caleb really loved to eat. She had no idea where he put it all. Looking rather pleased with himself, Caleb stood to his full height and produced a backpack from beside the chair.

"All present and correct," he laughed. Now she was out of bluffs. Eve was going to have to tell them the truth. Just as she was about to, she noticed a lump under the collar of Caleb's black t-shirt, and it was... humming! She was sure only she could hear it. Yes it... yes, the hum seemed to be emanating from the hidden item around Caleb's neck. Walking towards him, she touched the lump. It moved; the humming reached a crescendo.

"What's this?" she asked, eyes still on the lump. It was no bigger than her little finger. Reaching under his shirt, Caleb withdrew a chain. Suspended from it was a smooth point of stone. It was all the colours of the sea combined, grey and green with flecks of electric blue. It seemed to change colour when viewed from different angles.

"Oh, it was my grandmother's; it has been passed down forever. It's a gem called labradorite."

I have found one of the three, was Eve's first thought. Suddenly realising that he had to come with her, she grabbed his hand and smiled. "I would love for you to escort me at least to the border of the realm," Eve gushed. Picking up his backpack and Eve's bag, he headed for the door, leaving Eve to say her goodbyes to Violet. "Thank you for allowing me to stay with you. I am so pleased to have met you." Eve embraced Violet and kissed her cheek. Violet replied rather gruffly.

"Don't mention it. Maybe next time you will be better behaved." Smiling at her friend, Eve put on her cloak and headed to the door. Taking her bag from Caleb, she slipped it over her head and checked her belt for her purse and knife; she was ready.

"Come on then, Caleb, lead the way," Eve chuckled. Knowing that she was going to have to reveal some pretty amazing things to him shortly, Eve wanted to keep the atmosphere light until they were away from the town.

"Let's get this show on the road!" Caleb all but sang.

Oh boy, are you in for a surprise, Eve thought as they headed up the main avenue that lead out of Clear Water Valley.

When they were four miles outside of the town, Eve explained to Caleb all that she knew of her quest - the prophecy and his part in it. To his credit, Caleb listened to her all the way through before he uttered a single word. Once Eve was done, he took a moment to compose himself. Caleb had known there was something about Eve the night he saw her eyes flash in the lightning. Now he understood, the legends were real. Glancing at Eve, he saw how anxious she looked, waiting for his reaction. Taking a breath, Caleb smiled at her and responded with confidence.

"Well, I guess you have a travelling companion, Evangeline, and I do believe the next realm is Olia, the realm of the owl riders."

THE AURORA STONE

WATCHING THE ELF AND the witch make their way north to Olia through the swirling mists of the crystal, the malevolent being licked its dripping maw. Placing a claw onto the crystal over the image of the elfin maid, the creature let out a chilling cackle. "Soon you will be mine, young one. Your light must be extinguished, and I look forward to that time immensely."

Moving away from the crystal, the creature gazed out the window of its lair. The sight of the broken souls in the pits below caused it to shiver with glee. Not even hope could survive here, and there was far worse to come.

"Chashoc!" screeched the creature. A moment later, a grotesque form appeared, covered in purple skin that seemed to be charred in places, with a spine so curved, that patches of its long, lank black hair grazed the floor. Looking up into his master's face with black eyes, Chashoc spoke in a gravelly voice, putrid yellow saliva dripping from his fangs.

"You called, Great Master."

"I wish you to follow the Elf and Witch," the Creature ordered. Bowing, Chashoc began backing out of the room.

"It shall be done, Master; I shall take great care not to be seen," he assured.

"Oh, I know you will, Chashoc, for if you are indeed seen, I shall cast you into the void myself!" The creature bellowed, its red eyes flashing with malicious intent.

"Ye... yes, master, I shall not fail you," Chashoc whimpered as he lumbered from the room. Smiling, the creature reclined on its throne, knowing that is was only a matter of time now. The creature's cackle filled the chamber with the eerie sound of evil madness.

Chapter Five

Eve and Caleb walked for the entire day, only stopping to eat. By nightfall, they were still nowhere near the northern border. They made camp under some pine trees. Caleb produced a tent and a sleeping bag for each of them, which astounded Eve until she reminded herself, *Caleb is a witch. Of course his bag was enchanted*. Once everything was set up, Eve made a small fire to cook the fish they had caught earlier. When both were full and snuggled into their sleeping bags, Caleb turned to Eve and asked her all about Hermoria - the landscape, what the people were like and, of course, the food. Eve told him all about her home and the lovely house she shared with her mother. How she ached to see her beloved mother. It had only been a week or so since she had left, but it felt so much longer.

"I think by tomorrow we should reach the border," reassured Caleb as he repositioned his folded jacket he was utilizing as a pillow.

"Do you know much about Olia?" Eve inquired, turning to face Caleb.

"No. The owl riders are a bit of a mystery to us. There was a time, long ago, when they used to steal star shine roots from our lands. My Grandfather said that there was a great battle, but neither side claimed the victory. Since then, Witches and riders haven't really mixed. I still think it an odd thing to fall out over." Eve pondered over this revelation. Snuggling down into her bag, she drifted off to sleep, her dreams filled with owls with large jewel-like eyes and masked riders brandishing spears tipped with silver.

A few meters away, Chashoc crouched in the branches of a pine tree, the saliva dripping from his fangs scorched the bark where it landed. He scanned the camp the two companions had made. The only weapon he had seen was the dagger the Elf carried on her belt.

"Time for some fun," he chuckled. Cupping his claws, he howled into the night. After a few moments, another howl could be heard on the wind... and then another. Smiling, Chashoc moved to a tree slightly closer the pair. "Let us see how you fare against werewolves, young ones."

To the west of the camp, six sets of yellow eyes appeared in the dark. Rubbing his claws together in anticipation, Chashoc prepared to watch the scene unfold.

Caleb was woken by a growl. Suddenly very alert, he sprang from his sleeping bag. Grabbing the pan they had cooked supper in, he turned towards the menacing sound. A huge beast stood before him, eight feet long with paws the size of dinner plates and extremely long claws that glinted in the moonlight. Intelligent yellow eyes assessed him. Caleb, however, was most concerned with the size and amount of razor sharp teeth the beast had in its open, salivating jaws.

"WEREWOLF!" Caleb bellowed just as the beast leaped at him. Knocking him to the floor, Caleb was momentarily winded. The wolf snarled as it brought its jaws down to rip out Caleb's throat. A loud clang rang out as the cooking pan connected with the beast's skull. Caleb used this moment to look for Eve, hoping she had not been harmed.

He saw her then, dagger in hand, blood dripping from its blade. A wolf circled her, fangs bared and snarling; it had a large gash down its left flank and was missing an eye. The wolf sprang, claws extended, ready to peel flesh from bone. If he hadn't seen it happen, Caleb would never have believed what took place next. Eve's eyes flashed with golden fire. She leapt straight up at least six feet into the air. Turning a graceful summersault, she slit the beast's throat as it reared up to claw her. Landing on the balls of her feet, just behind the now dead wolf, she looked magnificent. Her hair cascaded over her shoulders and rippled like wildfire. Eve then moved onto the next wolf and then the next. Like a graceful angel of death, she seemed to almost dance with her attackers before cleanly dispatching them.

Caleb, who had been staring at Eve for the past few moments needed to snap out of it. He had problems of his own; the wolf he had successfully concussed was out cold on top of him. Unable to move, he was easy prey for any remaining beasts. Wiggling was futile; the animal must have weighed at least seven hundred pounds. Not wanting to ask a girl for help - he had his pride, after all - he muttered a levitation charm. The huge bulk rose a few inches off him, which was all Caleb needed to extract himself. Ready to bludgeon the beast to death, he raised the pan above his head. Just as he was about to bring it down on the wolf's skull, Eve grabbed his arm.

"No! It is unconscious and of no threat now. Let's gather our things and leave this place," she urged.

"It tried to kill me!" Caleb spluttered.

"There is no honour in the killing of an unarmed opponent. Come on, Cal, let's go," Eve begged, pulling on his arm. They packed up quickly, then hand in hand they disappeared into the forest.

Chashoc sat stunned on his branch overlooking the scene below. Four dead wolves, all killed by the elf! One was unconscious, and the sixth pack member had retreated. Master was not going to like this, especially since Chashoc had been instructed to follow and nothing more. Feeling decidedly sick at the thought of the possible punishments that he was sure to have earned himself, he took out an amulet of onyx and uttered a spell in his guttural voice. A portal appeared in the tree trunk. Taking one last regretful look at the carnage below, Chashoc leapt into the vortex and vanished.

The sky was turning the pearl colours of the dawn when they finally stopped running. Reaching yet another stream to wade across, the pair decided a well-earned rest was in order. Flopping down on the bank, Caleb dug about in his pack for some food. Finding some apples, he washed them in the stream, then tossed one to Eve. She caught it and bit into its crisp rosy skin. Enjoying the crunch of the fruit's flesh and the sharp tang of the juice, Eve was transported back to a different stream, where the light danced through the canopy of leaves and the comforting embrace of ancient tree roots cradled her.

"It's a shame we don't have any cheese," moaned Caleb. "These would taste even better with a bit of my uncle's homemade orange cheddar, or ruby skin yaks cheese." He sighed, looking at the remains of his apple. Rolling her eyes at how desolate he sounded, Eve opened her own pack and produced the famous floating cheese. It had been in the pack for some time, so she wasn't holding out much hope that is would even still be edible. Getting up and handing the slightly squashed lump to Caleb, Eve smiled at him.

"Here, if it's not green with fungus and mould, you are welcome to it," she laughed. Caleb unwrapped the cheese; it had indeed seen better days, though surprisingly, it was still fresh- looking. Smiling like he had just received the best gift ever, Caleb tucked into the soft, creamy offering.

"Oh, my Goddess, this is amazing!" he exclaimed through a rather full mouth. Eve went to the stream to wash her hands and face while Caleb finished up his meal.

"How much further is it to the border?" Eve asked Caleb once they were ready to go. The sky was now the palest of blues, almost white.

"I am not sure; it can't be too far." At least that's what he hoped. Caleb had left out one tiny detail about the border. He didn't know exactly where it was located. Deciding now was not the best time to divulge this rather inflammatory piece of information, Caleb put on his most charming smile.

"Come on then; the day is young, and I want to reach Olia before tea time," he bolstered.

"YOU HAVE NO IDEA WHERE we are going, do you?" Eve seethed. It was now twilight, and they still hadn't reached the border. She was so angry right now, bone weary and dirty with a combination of sweat, wolf blood, and forest derby smeared all over her. She was ready for a bath and clean clothes.

"Not exactly...no," admitted a sheepish Caleb. Keeping his eyes on his shoes, he didn't dare look Eve in the face. "I know we are on the right track; Olia is north. I just don't know exactly how far north," he stammered.

"Wonderful, that's just great Cal. WELL I AM NOT STAYING ANOTHER NIGHT IN THIS FOREST!" Eve screamed. Oh, how wonderful it felt to scream. She had hated killing those wolves - not that she had a lot of choice in the matter. What was really bothering her was that she was sure there had been a creature watching from one of the pines by their camp.

Storming off, Eve picked up a few stones and began throwing them into the forest ahead of her. She could hear Cal running to catch her up. Still mad at his dishonesty, she didn't slow her pace. It was almost too dark to continue, and she was not looking forward to the prospect of another night in this forest. Eve threw her last stone as hard as she could. Sighing, she was about to declare that they would have to camp here when something hit her hard on the forearm.

Instantly alert, Eve reached for her dagger. Looking for what had hit her, she was surprised to see the stone she had just thrown sitting by her right shoe. Confused, she picked it up and was about to throw it again when Caleb stopped her.

"Wait, someone is using magic nearby," he told her.

"You can sense it?" Eve asked, slightly astonished that this was even possible, but then she wasn't a witch, why would she know about such things? Nodding, Caleb took the stone and threw it ahead of them, with a lot less force than Eve had used. This time, Eve's keen hearing picked up a slight popping and then a hum. A few seconds later, the stone landed about a foot away.

"Interesting," Eve murmured as she went to retrieve the stone.

Curiosity getting the better of her, she moved further into the forest. Caleb caught up with her, putting a finger over his lips. They moved stealthily through the trees, the moist loam underfoot aiding them. Soon they were facing a rather impressive wall. It was made of tree trunks that had been tied together with the thickest vines they had ever seen.

"The border," they uttered in unison. Pleased to have finally reached their destination, Eve walked forward to see if there was a gate nearby.

"Eve don't go any...." Caleb warned, but it was too late. When Eve was a meter from the wall, she hit an invisible barrier. She was momentarily held in place, then there was a loud pop, and Eve found herself being repelled from the wall at high speed. Caleb made a grab for her and got winded for his trouble.

"Ooof!" he gasped. Eve quickly got off him.

"What on earth was that?" she wondered, slightly shaken.

"Magic.... force field.... powerful...." Caleb coughed. Eve helped him to his feet, and they once again approached the wall. "There must be a gate somewhere," she assumed.

They walked along the wall, keeping at least three metres' distance. Suddenly, up ahead they could see the flickering of torches. Quickening their pace, they arrived before a rather grand set of gates carved from the same type of tree as the wall. They were a masterpiece of filigree and embedded with polished stones.

"How do we get in?" Caleb muttered to himself. He tried a couple of charms, but these just caused the force field to shimmer and crackle. They tried calling and waving their arms frantically. Then, in a last-ditch attempt, they threw stones, but this resulted in Caleb getting a black eye. "Let's just call it a night," he grumbled, rubbing his eye. Moving out of direct sight of the gate, they made camp. Eve worked quietly over a bowl near the campfire while Caleb went off in search of something to eat. He returned an hour later with a cut arm and two fish. Throwing them down, he asked if he could borrow Eve's dagger to gut them.

"It's ok, Cal. I'll cook. Here, put this over your eye. It will help with the swelling," Caleb took the bowl Eve had been working over. It was full of green paste, which he applied to his eye. Instantly he felt some relief as the cooling effect soothed his swollen skin. A sigh escaped his lips.

"You are full of surprises, Evangeline. A warrior and now a healer, not to mention a great cook," Caleb complemented. Smiling, she packed up her herbs and began gutting the fish.

"My dad taught me how to make simple remedies when I was small," she told him.

"Well I am very grateful that he passed on the knowledge," he praised. After their meal, they curled up in their bags, and deciding to try to gain entry again at first light, they drifted off to sleep.

It was, however, not a restful night for either of them. Every woodland sound caused them to wake. The small creatures of the forest sounded large and dangerous in the hush of the forest, and in the early hours, a deer walked by the camp, causing them such a start that they decided that they would take turns to keep watch for the rest of the night.

Eve had known another night in this forest was a bad idea. Upon opening her eyes, she was greeted with the sight of several sword blades and a couple of spear tips all pointing at her. It wasn't quite what she was expecting, but she wasn't terribly surprised. Careful not to make any sudden movements, she asked her captors, "Where is my friend?" No answer was given. Instead, large paw-like hands reached for her. She was pulled roughly to her feet. "I would very much like to know what has happened to my friend," Eve asked once again.

"No more talk; you answer only our questions!" shrilled one of her captors, "Who are you, and why did you spend an intolerable amount of time disrupting our force field?" Understanding that these, whatever they were, must be the owl riders, Eve began to raise her head to look at the creatures surrounding her.

Speaking in a neutral tone and moving slowly, she answered. "My name is Evangeline of Hermoria. I am travelling with a friend. He is a witch called Caleb. On our behalf, I would like to apologize for causing a disturbance last night. We merely wished to seek shelter. The night before, we were attacked by a pack of werewolves and were rather anxious not to spend another night in the forest." The creatures took a moment, talking in hushed tones amongst themselves.

Eve now had her chance to get a look at them. To her amazement, she found herself gazing at very large and extremely muscular *mice*! However, they were clearly not the usual kind she found in the larder at home; these creatures stood at five feet tall with tails as thick as her forearm. They wore leather chaps but no shoes, leather vests, and some kind of strange hat that appeared to have tinted glasses attached to it. Their paws were more like hands, though the feet still resembled those of a mouse. Each one carried a weapon.

Turning back to their captive, one of the creatures gripped her arm and began escorting Eve towards the now open gates.

"We have decided to allow you entrance, but do not mistake this for weakness, girl. We merely want to hear more about how you came to be at our border and what you and your witch truly want within our realm."

THE CAT O' NINE TAILS came down on Chashocs' blooded flesh for the sixteenth lash. Knowing that screaming would not lessen the pain, he did his best to stay silent. However, this seemed to enrage his master more.

"You disobeyed me! How dare you!" the creature bellowed, taking several more swings with its chosen weapon. Chashoc finally let out a piercing scream and slumped forward, hanging by the shackles at his wrists, his back slashed to a bloody mess.

Leaving the dungeon, the creature slunk along darkened corridors. The slaves visibly shook and cowered as their master swept past. Reaching the throne room, it moved to the great tome open on the reading stand, flicking through the vellum pages made from the skin of the ancient, dammed, and enslaved and bound together with their blood and hair. The book was truly a thing constructed of pure evil. Finding the page it wanted, the creature chuckled.

"Yes, this will be most enjoyable, most enjoyable...for me!" The creature's manic laughter echoed through the castle.

The creature began constructing its new plan for the two companions. It worked tirelessly. The only sounds were its murmurs and the screams and desolate moans from the pits drifting up through the open windows. Finally, it was ready.

"Grimmer!" yelled the creature. A huge beast appeared before its master, kneeling in respect. Grimmer was more humanoid in form but horribly disfigured. Large scars covered his entire body, giving him the appearance of a melted wax candle. The creature approached its minion. Holding out a vial to Grimmer, it commanded, "Make sure this is consumed by the elf and that witch. Once they have ingested it, return to me, and unless you wish to meet the same fate as Chashoc, I suggest you do only as I command."

Grimmer stowed the vial in his belt pouch and bowed to his master.

"It shall be as you order." Taking his leave, Grimmer left for the portal chamber, a malicious grin transforming his scared countenance into something from a nightmare.

Chapter Six

The owl riders escorted Eve rather roughly through the open gates. What she saw was so beautiful that she was convinced it must be a dream. All she could see were treetops, the leaves turning the shades of autumn. The colours ranged from gold-green, that matched her eyes, to warm coppers and rich reds. From her vantage point, Eve thought the autumnal tree tops looked like a rippling sea of fire. Her eyes travelled away from the swaying treetops to the horizon, to where purple mountains, their mauve faces warmed by the morning sun, stood like sentinels. The sky was clear, so she was able to see the snowy caps that would certainly vanish on a cloudy day.

Dragging her eyes away from possibly the most beautiful vista she had ever had the pleasure to see, Eve began to study her position. She was standing on a gangway that was six feet wide and ran for as far as she could see. At regular intervals along the gangway, there were large gaps in the barrier. Looking over the edge, Eve noted that the gaps were just that, holes in the fence. If anyone were to fall, they would crash through the canopy of fiery leaves and surely meet their end on the forest floor. Gulping, she turned to her captors and asked, "How do we get down?"

Snickering, the leader of the group looked at her like she was crazy and replied, "Down…Why would we want to go down?"

Confused by the mouse-like creature's response, Eve decided to keep her mouth closed for the time being. Noticing a movement to her left, Eve turned to see what her captor was doing. He had taken a strange looking curled reed from inside his vest. Putting it to his lips, he blew through the reed in three quick puffs, then paused and concluded with two shorter puffs and one long one. Eve hadn't heard a sound.

She was about to ask what that was all about when suddenly two things happened. The first was that the whole gangway seemed to move clockwise. Eve felt like she might fall, so she lunged for one of the posts that made up the fence and held on tight, looking the way she was traveling so as not to feel nauseous. Eve saw that a few metres ahead the atmosphere seemed to thicken; the very air seemed to become opaque. Suddenly, the world around her became blurred. The section of gangway she was on had passed into the strange atmosphere. Becoming scared, Eve closed her eyes. Unsure if she was able to breathe within this heavy and strangely jelly-like air, she began to panic as she was fast running out of oxygen. Then, with a slight squelching sound, she found that they had passed through the viscous atmosphere. Eve took a deep lungful of air and then another while the mice-like creatures chuckled at her. Opening her eyes, she was confused to see that it was dark.

I am losing my mind, she thought.

It was then the owls appeared, and like the mice, they were not normal-sized. These owls were huge, with jewel-coloured eyes that flashed in the starlight. There were three approaching them; two were white with silver wing and tail feathers. The third was bronze in colour; its wing and tail feathers were blue-black.

"Beautiful," Eve sighed.

The owls landed on the posts that were a few feet away from the opening in the gangway. Eve watched as the Owls extended their left wings to bridge the gap.

"Come, let us find your friend. Then we can begin our discussion," the leader said as he placed a paw on the small of Eve's back and guided her towards the bronze owl's wing. Hesitating, Eve tried to back up. An exasperated sound came from behind her, and then she found herself lifted around the middle and carried along the wing to be deposited on the owl's back. Heart pounding in her ears, Eve frantically looked around for something to hold onto. The mouse who had carried her sat in front of her. "Hold onto me," he instructed. She didn't need telling twice; she wrapped her arms in a death grip around his middle. The owl then seemed to fall off the perch. Eve screamed, convinced she was about to die. The owl swooped upwards, then began gliding towards the horizon.

After a while, Eve took her face away from the rider's back and looked into the night. The view was beautiful. The moon, full and fat, illuminated their path, lighting a highway across the lake they were soaring over. In the distance, she could make out hundreds of tiny specks of light. Assuming that this was their destination, she settled into a more comfortable position and kept her eyes on the lights glowing in the distance.

"We are about to do a bit of fancy flying, so hold on tight to me," the rider instructed over his shoulder. Once again, Eve tightened her grip and buried her face in his back; she felt, rather than heard, his chuckle. The owl swooped down, then banked left, right, then left again, before soaring straight up. Eve could feel her panic rising.

"I can do this, it will be over soon," she told herself over and over again. The owl landed gracefully on another perch and extended its right wing to allow its passengers to alight from its back.

"Thank you for the ride," the mouse murmured. The great bird gazed at them both for a second with its huge eyes, the colour of smoky quartz, and then took off, disappearing into the night. They were now standing on yet another gangway. This one, however, led to another - more solid - path. Gasping, Eve took in her new surroundings. She was looking out at a town in the sky. Many gangways led to cosy-looking dwellings, some made within the trunks of the trees. Following the line of dwellings, Eve noticed stairs that wound themselves around the tree trunks. Looking up, she saw yet more illuminated windows and many more mice going about their business.

"Amazing," she breathed.

"THIS IS WHERE YOU WILL be staying; your friend will be brought here as well," her escort announced at the door of one of the dwellings on the higher levels. It was mostly built into the tree trunk, but they had added a cheerfully rounded extension in which the front door sat pride of place.

"Thank you, this is a truly lovely house," Eve remarked, turning to her escort.

"They are not called houses here in Olia. These are called burrows," came the gruff reply. Keeping her thoughts to herself, Eve had a feeling that offending these creatures would be a very bad idea. She twisted the carved doorknob and entered her accommodation, very aware that she had no idea how long she might be there.

"Eve! Oh, thank the Goddess you are alright!" Caleb almost sobbed as he rushed through the front door a short while later. Holding each other close, Caleb looked down into Eve's face. Smiling up into his blue eyes - that always reminded Eve of the sea - she reassured him.

"I'm fine, Cal; the owl riders have been very good to me." Moving out of the embrace, Eve went through to the kitchen; Caleb followed, shaking his head at how completely calm she seemed.

"Girls," he muttered under his breath, with a slight smile playing at the corners of his lips.

After some sandwiches and tea, Eve gave Caleb a tour of the house. She had taken the bedroom which didn't have a view but a beautiful stained glass, irregularly shaped window that had been made to fit into a split in the tree's bark. There were other 'windows' - for lack of a better name. Eve liked to think of them as 'light' veins.

These were very thin splits and cracks in the tree's bark that the mice had glazed to keep draughts out and allow as much light as possible into the room. She wondered how the veins would look when the sun came up.

All the furniture was built into the tree. The owl riders had excellent design skills, and the rooms were cosy and light but also totally functional. Caleb's room had a large window that overlooked the gangway network and the other burrows on this level. Heading back down the spiral staircase to collect his bag, Caleb was surprised to see two of the riders standing outside the open front door.

"May we come in?" the taller of the two asked.

"It's your house, I mean burrow," Caleb replied. On entering the burrow, the riders wiped their paws and stood by the front window. Unsure what to do, Caleb began to flounder. Then Eve appeared on the bottom stairs.

"Hello again, how may we help you?" she inquired.

"We have come to escort you both to our leader's home for the talk I mentioned on your arrival here." Opening the front door, the rider made the common gesture for ladies first. Sighing, Eve made her way to the door. Slipping on her shoes, she waited for the riders and Caleb to exit.

"This way, please." The riders guided them through several levels before arriving at their leader's burrow. Knocking on the door, the company waited for admittance. A small female opened the door. Like the males of her kind, her paws were more like hands, and she wore attire similar to her male counterparts. "Erica, we are here to see Maximus," explained the taller rider. *He definitely seems to out-rank his companion,* Eve thought.

Opening the door wider, Erica allowed the party to enter.

"You will find him in his study. Remember to knock this time, Jericho. I have only just finished cleaning up the glass from the last projectile that was nearly embedded in your skull," she pleaded.

Chuckling, the tall rider called Jericho nodded in agreement. Taking one last look at the visitors, Erica headed back the way they had come.

Reaching the end of the corridor, Jericho stopped outside a heavily carved door. "Upon entering this room, you will be respectful at all times, and only speak when spoken to, is that clear?" he asked the two friends. After Eve and Caleb had nodded their agreement, Jericho raised his fist and knocked on the door.

"ENTER!" shouted a deep voice from within.

THEY HAD BEEN IN MAXIMUS'S study for hours, and, so far, he had thrown two inkwells and a heavy candlestick at no one in particular. These outbursts were due to his dislike of the answers given to his many questions.

"Girl, for the last time, why are you here?" Maximus yelled, his eyes wide and ears pulled back. Once again, Eve gave the only answer she could: that they only wished to pass through his lands and to experience the wonders of the cities in the tree tops. Though the flattery went some way to calm him, it did not totally appease the angry rodent. Deciding that he was getting nowhere with his line of questioning, Maximus decided to play the slow game of interrogation. "Fine. If that is why you are here, I shall say no more about it for now." Changing tack, he continued his questioning, "I understand there has been some werewolf activity in the woods close to our border... How many attacked you?" Surprised by the sudden change in the questioning, Eve was momentarily lost.

"That would be six, Sir," Caleb answered. Making a mental note to thank Cal later, Eve stayed quiet and allowed Caleb to explain the attack.

"Hmmm, this is worrying news, indeed," Maximus murmured once Caleb had told his tale.

"Please, Sir, if we could just rest for a day or so and maybe wash our clothes? We will then leave your lands in peace," Eve said as she looked the fierce mouse right in the eyes.

"You may stay for a few days. Jericho and Dexter here will be your guides for the duration of your stay. But mark my words, if you turn out to be spies, you will be very sorry indeed!" He warned them, though Eve hadn't failed to notice that when Maximus had commented about the possibility of them being spies, he was looking only at Caleb. Making another mental note to find out more of the history between the witches and riders, she stood with the others waiting to leave.

"Thank you, Sir," they mumbled like a pair of naughty children and made for the door, which Dexter was holding open.

"Jericho, a moment please," Maximus called after them. Returning to the study, Jericho stood before his leader. Leaning in close, his black eyes were fixed on his subordinate. Maximus uttered in hushed tones, "Watch them carefully, especially the witch." Nodding, Jericho turned and left, closing the door with a muted click behind him.

Chapter Seven

It had been nine days since Maximus had spoken to them, and during this time Eve and Caleb had explored the tree-top city. There had only been one incident in which Caleb had managed to become an unwilling participant in a fight with a rather scary-looking resident by the name of Nex. Caleb was still nursing some bruised ribs and three broken fingers from that encounter. It turned out that the riders did not like being referred to as 'mice.' Not only had Caleb been beaten up by a giant rodent, it had also been an extremely public spectacle. The incident had taken place in the Dome. A covered area where the food market and other trades were based, the Dome was located on the mid-level of the City. It was the only part of this sprawling treetop metropolis that was always full of activity.

Caleb had been waiting in line for lunch at one of the most popular stalls in the Dome when he'd managed to accidently stand on the tail of a female waiting in line ahead of him. Unfortunately for Caleb, this had happened to be Nex's little sister Zoe. Nex was well known for his short temper and violent outbursts. He was the kind to lash out at the slightest of misdemeanours, some of which were his own perceptions and not actual slights against him. As on every occasion where there was a possibility for Nex to dish out some punishment, he had demanded that as part of his apology, Caleb purchase Zoe's lunch for her, which Caleb had agreed to. It all would have ended there had Caleb not muttered, "This mouse is touchy; too much cheese before bedtime." Nex had heard him. The next thing Caleb knew, he had been being tackled to the ground by a very angry, three-hundred-pound rodent. "We...are...not...mice...ignorant...witch!" Each bellowed word had been punctuated with a kick to Caleb's ribs. Picking Cal up by his collar, Nex had held him up so that his feet were off the floor. The enraged rider had glared into Caleb's bloodied face and snarled. "We are Miscurts, fearless aerial warriors, death dealers from above. You would do well to remember that, witch."

That had been three days ago. Today, Eve was going to visit the Owls, or Protectors, as Jericho had informed her they preferred to be called. Preparing to make her way to the lake, she was buzzing with excitement. Since her first and rather a scary ride, she had learned that the protectors were not pets of the Miscurts; they were a race in their own right. Jericho had spent an entire afternoon with Eve in the city library explaining the history and alliances with the protectors. It answered many of her questions but also created plenty more.

"So, why did you steal the star shine roots from Clear Water Valley?" Eve asked Jericho, as they sat in the library. "Caleb said there was a great battle many years ago." Eve couldn't help it, the question just popped out. Laughing a hearty belly laugh, Jericho wiped the tears of mirth from his black eyes and answered the inquisitive young maid.

"There was no battle, Eve. That is the story the witches tell their young to keep us, the monsters, and them away from our borders. We came to an agreement to stop digging up the roots in exchange for our own crop." Eve was confused.

"Yes, but why did you want the roots in the first place. Are they magical?"

Jericho had wandered away from her to return the volume they had been looking through.

"No, they just taste nice," he answered over his shoulder. It was all too much for Eve; she burst out laughing. She couldn't wait to tell Cal.

"GOOD MORNING, EVANGELINE!" called Dexter as he exited the healer's quarters. He had taken a fist to the snout when trying to get Nex off of Caleb, and it was still a bit swollen and red.

Waving as she passed, Eve called to him, "Hello Dexter! Your nose is looking a bit better. I'm off to meet Jericho. He is introducing me to the protectors." Eve skipped down the last staircase and ran the short distance to the edge of the lake, where she could see Jericho waiting.

"Finally!" Jericho grunted. It felt like he had been waiting for half the morning. Eve arrived at his side, eyes sparkling like she hadn't a care in the world. "I was wondering where you had gotten to," he stated. Smiling sheepishly and fiddling with the ties of her new leather chaps, Eve apologised.

"I am sorry, Jericho. I was up late last night reading." Huffing, he retrieved his curled reed to alert the Protectors that they were needed. A few moments passed, and then Jericho raised his paw in greeting. Eve looked in the direction he was waving and saw two Protectors gliding over the lake. They landed before them, the morning sun bringing lustre to their feathers and fire to their jewel-like eyes. Keisha, the Protector Eve had met before -as she had been the owl Eve had ridden on her journey here - observed Eve with her Smoky quartz eyes. Then, spreading her bronze wings, her midnight blue primary feathers catching the light, Keisha bowed gracefully. Amazed that yet another creature was welcoming her in this manner, Eve curtsied to the majestic bird.

Clearing his throat and hoping that none of the shock he was feeling came through in his voice, Jericho gestured to the other owl that had accompanied Keisha. Eve turned her attention to the other Protector waiting quietly on the shore. This owl was white with black flecks on her breast. Its feathers were not as striking as Keisha's, but then Eve looked into the bird's eyes. They were sapphire blue. Never had she seen any creature with eyes such as these.

"This is Sapphire," Jericho introduced the Protector.

"Named for her eyes, no doubt," Eve whispered, stepping to stand in front of the snowy owl. Eve looked up into her blue eyes, smiled, and dropped into a curtsy. Sapphire clicked her beak, and instead of bowing, as Eve had expected, she brought her snowy head down and placed her forehead against Eve's.

As soon as the contact was made, Eve experienced a rush of images: a house, her brother, and her birth parents. The house must have been her home with them. Then the darkness appeared. It slithered into the house in the dead of night. The darkness entered her room but shied away when it touched her. Eve then saw it enter her brother's room and do the same. When it reached her parent's room, it began to circle their bed faster and faster, until it was a blur of black. Her mother woke, and just as she opened her mouth to scream, both her parents and the darkness vanished.

Eve could feel tears rolling down her cheeks, upset by the images she had just witnessed. She tried to pull away, but a gentle voice that came from within her head whispered. *You must see it all, dear one.*

Eve knew it was Sapphire she had heard. Taking a breath, she prepared herself for the rest.

It was the early hours of the same night. Eve was asleep in her crib, thumb in her mouth. Eli was crying in the room next door, but no one came to soothe him. Just as the sky changed to the pearly colours of pre-dawn, two men entered the house. They looked much like Caleb, though their features were more pointed and they had gossamer wings folded against their backs. They entered Eli's room, picked him up, and left as quickly as they had arrived.

"Nooooo!" Eve moaned as she dropped to her knees, the connection lost. Jericho just stood there, not understanding at all what had just taken place.

"I know where my brother is. Jericho, I need to find Caleb." She rushed her words, tears still streaming down her face. Confused, he picked her up, and was about to run back to the city when Eve reached out to Sapphire. Taking her closer, Jericho watched as the great bird rested her head on Eve's hand and watched a large tear fall from the owl's beautiful eye.

"Thank you, dear friend. Please wait for me to return. I won't be long," Eve whispered to her new friend. Sapphire nodded her head in an assurance that she would, indeed, wait.

"Amazing!" Jericho breathed.

They were back at the lake ten minutes later. Eve was running and Jericho carried Caleb, much to his displeasure. On arriving, Eve very quickly explained to Caleb what had happened. Caleb stood and listened until Eve was finished before he spoke.

"So the owl..." There was an angry screech from behind Caleb. "Sorry! I mean Sapphire, shared this information with you?" Eve nodded, while Jericho was becoming even more confused. Eve then explained her quest and the prophecy she was destined to fulfil.

"So let me get this straight. You are on a quest to find this Aurora Stone and your long-lost brother? Caleb is one of your three companions, and you can communicate with Sapphire? Wow! I need a moment." Jericho moved away from the group and sat on a boulder, looking out onto the tranquil lake. Eve turned to Caleb,

"We are going to have to explain at least part of this to Maximus; it will look really suspicious if we suddenly have a pressing urge to leave." Not happy but knowing that sneaking off would never work, Caleb agreed. Though he also made it clear that Jericho was to be there as well.

WHOOSH! A LARGE BOOK missed Eve by a hair. Maximus was enraged. He had known there was more to these two than he had

been told. Picking up a glass paperweight, he launched it across the room. The orb ricocheted off the bookcase and embedded itself in a rather large portrait of his grandfather.

"DECEIVERS! I KNEW YOU WERE LYING TO ME!" he bellowed, the pinks of his ears turning purple.

"I can prove what I am telling you to be true, just please calm down," Eve pleaded from behind Jericho. This seemed to cause Maximus to reach new heights of fury. His breathing was becoming shallow and fast, eyes wide and ears flat.

"You shouldn't have told him to calm down," moaned Jericho as he watched his leader knock over three chairs and tear up a large map.

Eve stepped back and reached for the door handle. If she could just get to her room, she could retrieve the box and hopefully begin to prove her story to be true. Unfortunately, the Miscurt leader saw her. Picking up the cane that a moment ago had supported his prized cheese plant, he came crashing towards her.

"Where do you think you're going?" Raising the cane, Maximus was about to bring it down on Eve's shoulder when he caught his foot on the rumpled rug and fell. Miscurt and cane flew in opposite directions. Maximus came to land with a thud against the end of his desk with the wind knocked out of him. He was about to spring to his feet when the ink blotter that had been on the edge of his desk fell off and struck him between the eyes, knocking him unconscious and leaving a smudge of blue ink in its wake. Caleb, who had been watching from the chair he had been too scared to vacate, looked at the now still Maximus.

"Is he...dead?" Caleb whispered, eyes wide. Rushing to his side, Eve placed her ear to the mighty rodent's chest.

"No, just knocked out. He will be alright. I will make him something for the pain." Leaving the room, she asked that Jericho bring Maximus to her burrow as discreetly as possible. Sighing, he went towards the great leader and hauled him over his shoulder.

"I hope you know what you are doing, Eve; Maximus is not going to like this when he wakes up." However, he found that he was addressing a closed door, as she had already left.

It was a tense few moments when Maximus came around. At first, he was ready to tear the burrow apart and throttle the lot of them. However, realising this was physically not possible and that Eve had been tending to his extremely sore head, Maximus did something he had not managed since he was a child, Maximus listened.

"I have never seen a stone of prophecy in all my years; you must guard it well, there are those who would destroy it," Maximus warned Eve, as he carefully handed back the slab of moonstone.

"Destroy it? What good would that do? The prophecy has been heard," Caleb interjected. Maximus, trying hard to keep his temper, explained that the stone was also a key, and without it, the prophecy could not be completed. This was news to Eve; Reena had not mentioned anything more about the stone, apart from advising her to keep it safe right after it was activated.

Finally, they made it back to the shore. Keisha had returned home, but Sapphire was still there, her beautiful snowy head tucked under her wing. Cautiously, Eve made her way to her new friend and reached out a hand to touch her soft feathers and rouse her.

"I don't think you should be touching a sleeping giant bird, Eve. It might not be too happy about it," cautioned Caleb, from the brave position behind Jericho. Sapphire must have heard; she was now awake and extending her wings in what looked like a post-nap stretch.

"Dear Sapphire, we need to visit Gloria. Could you please take us there?" Eve asked the owl tenderly. Her blue gaze never leaving Eve's green-gold one, she nodded. Sapphire then looked at Jericho and Caleb, making a move with her talons, she scratched two lines in the dirt. Jericho was the first to understand.

"She can only carry two of us; we need another owl, or one of us must stay behind." Eve knew that she could not leave Caleb behind, and she needed Sapphire to guide them to the border of the realm of the Fae: Gloria.

"I cannot leave Caleb or Sapphire, nor can we involve another protector. It is wrong to demand that of them," she explained. Jericho knew he was the logical choice to stay, but Maximus had ordered that he accompany them, and never having gone against a direct order, he was not about to start now.

"Then we will have to all walk and allow the protector to lead us from the sky. Maximus ordered that I go with you; at least allow me to follow my orders. I will come as far as the border." Shaking her head, Sapphire let out two long hoots. Keisha reappeared a moment later. Seeing how worried Eve looked, Sapphire leaned her forehead against hers and explained that it had already been decided, but she thanked her for not having ordered another protector to come.

"Thank you," Eve murmured. "Our travelling obstacle has been resolved; let us make haste. I would like to reach the border before dark." Walking up the Owl's snowy wing, Eve suddenly felt confident; circumstances were changing for the better. Jericho assisted Caleb onto Keisha, and then they were flying. The direction was unimportant to Eve, this time. She knew her friend would guide them true.

"I am coming, Eli." She whispered her promise to the wind.

Chapter Eight

The view was spectacular. Eve was desperate for some paints to capture the russet landscape; the trees ruffled by the wind still reminded her of fire. Every so often, Sapphire would bank slightly, drawing Eve's attention to another beautiful view that the land had to offer. Glancing over at Keisha, Eve waved to Caleb and Jericho. It was a truly surreal method of travel; the Protectors seemed to float. Their massive wings moved fluidly, hardly causing any disturbance to the riders. Eve found the motion so very soothing. Combined with the warmth of Sapphire's back, she soon found herself drifting off to sleep.

Sapphire let out a gentle hoot; Eve heard someone calling her name as if from far away.

It is time to wake up, Dear one; we are halfway to the border. Eve knew that it was Sapphire she could hear. She thought to herself how extraordinary it was that even in sleep, she was able to hear the protector's soothing voice. Eve stirred but did not fully awaken.

I know you are tired. Once we have made camp, you can return to your slumber. However, now you must wake up, Sapphire crooned. Sighing, Eve opened her eyes; she had fallen forward and was lying with her face resting against the soft snowy feathers of Sapphire's neck. Sitting up, she stretched and took in the new vista. A magnificent sunset painted the skies with fiery scarlets, hot pinks, and deep oranges.

"IT IS TRULY A BEAUTIFUL SIGHT TO BEHOLD!" shouted Jericho from a short distance away. Kashia had glided closer now. Her bronze plumage was giving the effect of being molten, as if lit on fire with the warm glow of the sun's last rays. Jericho seemed to puff up with pride at the view. This was his homeland; his heart was here, and it showed. Caleb was too busy clutching handfuls of feathers in his fists. Eve was sure his knuckles must be white with tension. Giggling to herself, she called to her companions.

"Sapphire says it is time to make camp. We should try and find a sheltered spot by the river." Nodding his agreement, Jericho gestured for Eve to go first. Sapphire took her queue and began the gentle descent to the forest floor.

They had found a wonderful spot to make camp for the night. There was a small glade a few hundred feet from the river where the trees were less dense, so they would be able to watch the fiery sky turn into the inky blue of twilight and await the stars. The two owls flew off to collect wood for a small cooking fire while Jericho disappeared into the water to gather a surprise for their supper. The fact that he had said 'gather' and not 'catch' had Eve intrigued, to say the least. Caleb, on the other hand, was still a rather spectacular shade of green. His hands were stiff from the death grip he had forced on them directly after take-off earlier in the day. Keisha had a rather interesting spiky section of plumage which she had attempted to groom into place before accompanying Sapphire. The look she had given Cal had been one of equal measures of despair and irritation.

Shaking her head, Eve went over to her friend. Taking his left hand, she massaged it to help relieve the tension. Starting at the fingertips, she soothed the stiffness out of the joints, allowing them to relax back into their natural state so they were no longer claw-like and sore. Looking up, she watched as Caleb's shoulders dropped as some of the tension left his body. By the time Eve had administered the same care to his right hand, Caleb had lost some of his sickly tinge and was definitely more relaxed.

"Mmm...thank you so much. I thought my hands would remain like that for the rest of my life," he sighed. Flexing his fingers, he heard the small joints crack. Smiling, he took Eve's hands in his and kissed her palms. "You are a marvel; I am truly honoured to name you amongst my friends." Blushing slightly, Eve removed her hands and busied herself with arranging sleeping areas for the three of them.

Jericho arrived at the camp a short while later dripping wet with a huge grin on his face and clutching something black and slimy looking. Dropping to his knees, he began peeling his acquirement. Under the black outer layer lay a peach-coloured substance that reminded both Eve and Caleb of a milk pudding. Fascinated, they watched as Jericho finished peeling and placed the 'pudding' into the cooking pot.

"Excellent! Once the girls get back from gathering the wood, we shall have a feast indeed!" Jericho beamed. At the thought of food, Caleb seemed to perk up.

"What is that you have brought to eat? I have never seen anything like this that did not require milk from one of the animals," Eve asked, drawing closer to the pot.

"It is custard weed. It can be found in most rivers, though you need to be a strong swimmer and able to hold your breath for a while," Jericho explained. "The plant grows at the very bottom of the river. Only the very tips of the plant can be seen above the sandy floor." Picking up the black outer cases, he showed them the part that they would see, if they ever chose to go looking for it.

A rustling came from the trees; the owls had returned. Sapphire had a beak full of dry twigs while Keisha had dry leaves and kindling. Once they deposited their burdens, they immediately took flight again. "Off in search of their own supper," remarked Jericho as he built the fire. Reaching into a pouch at his hip, he removed his flint, and within a few moments, a fire crackled merrily, throwing shadows out around them.

"It smells wonderful, like my mother's vanilla pudding," sighed Eve, her stomach rumbling. Her mother would say that she was a slave to her sweet tooth, and at that moment, with the appetising smell of the custard weed drifting to her on the breeze, she was inclined to agree with her.

"Mm...hmm, this is going to be a treat for you both!" Jericho announced, handing Eve, then Caleb a bowl. Taking a spoon, Caleb tucked in. His eyes widened, and then with a groan he savoured his first mouthful.

"It tastes like my Auntie Heather's raspberry pie," he mumbled through a creamy mouthful. Smiling, Jericho continued to eat his portion. Confused as to how it could possibly taste anything like raspberries, Eve raised her spoon and had her first taste. No, definitely not raspberry. However, it also didn't taste anything like vanilla pudding as she had expected, given the tantalizing smell.

"It tastes wonderful, like chocolate with pomegranate and toffee ice-cream!" she exclaimed, spooning more of the weed pulp into her mouth. Grinning at them both, Jericho licked his lips and took the kerchief from around his neck to wipe his whiskers.

"Yes, it is rather tasty. Though, to me it tastes of peaches and cheese fruit. This weed is a chameleon plant; it changes to suit the tastes of the eater. Maybe next time you sample it, it will taste of something different," Jericho explained. Looking both amazed and incredibly tired, Eve finished the most interesting meal she had ever eaten. Taking her bowl to the river she washed it and then her face. Lastly, she took a drink of the refreshing waters before making her way back to camp.

"Right, gentlemen. I am rather tired, so I bid you a goodnight." Yawning, she headed for her sleeping bag. The witch and the Miscurt regarded each other across the campfire. Even though they had been in close quarters for over a week, they both sensed the animosity that radiated off the other. The nocturnal creatures were creating a symphony of their own, which was both eerie and soothing. Despite this, the silence that hung between the two males was deafening. Becoming uncomfortable with Jericho's piercing black eyes boring into him, Caleb decided to call it a night, too.

Mumbling what sounded like goodnight, he retreated to his sleeping area. Jericho remained by the fireside; he was aware of the witch's unease around him. No doubt this had a lot to do with the bad blood he believed existed between their two races. Eve clearly had not had a chance to enlighten him on that subject. As he watched the gentle rise and fall of the elf's sleeping form, Jericho realised he had respect for her. She was so brave and compassionate: a warrior. After all, she had cleanly dispatched several werewolves. The burden she carried was huge, and yet Eve still managed to help others and enjoy the simple pleasures of life.

"I will go with them," Jericho whispered to himself. He also decided to put Caleb out of his misery and reveal the truth about the past. As tensions within a travelling party were always a risk, this was one that could easily be rectified with some truth telling and a handshake between men. Stamping on the dying embers of the fire, Jericho walked the camp perimeter. Not finding anything out of the ordinary, he returned to the camp. Just as he was climbing into his sleeping bag, he saw the two protectors land a few meters away. "Goodnight, girls," he whispered. The two owls looked over, the moonlight reflected in their enormous eyes. Smiling, he rolled over and fell asleep knowing they would not be disturbed, not with the protectors so close.

THE MORNING'S JOURNEY was eventful, to say the least. Caleb had to be physically put onto Keisha. It seemed that his fear of flying was deeply ingrained. Unfortunately, all of Eve's and Jericho's reassurances sounded hollow when, after twenty miles, they hit a snow storm.

"HOLD ON, THIS COULD GET ROUGH!" Jericho bellowed, his words snatched by the wind. Securing her hands deeper in Sapphire's feathers, Eve leaned into the bird's neck and prepared to conserve as much body heat as possible. The cold was biting, Eve had never experienced snow before. She had read about it in books, and it always seemed such a magical thing, floating down to kiss one's nose and cheeks, each flake a unique work of art, individual crystals of dancing lacework. This, however, was not the experience Eve had read about. The wind howled, whipping her hair about her. The snow fell in an aggressive deluge, the flakes small, and when they made contact with any exposed part of her, it felt like being pricked by a thousand needles. Her skin both burned and felt numb. It was unclear how long it would take to pass through the storm; she hoped it would be soon. Looking to her left, Eve tried to spot Keisha, Jericho, and Caleb through the swirling white. It was futile since the snow was falling in such quantities. It was a white out.

Do not fret, dear one, they are there. Keisha is keeping them safe, though she wishes Caleb would stop screaming about dying. It's becoming tiresome. Sapphire implanted the message into Eve's head. Knowing that her protector would not lie to her, Eve re-adjusted her seat and hunkered down once again.

"How much further? I am so very cold now," Eve asked. She was still surprised by her unique connection with Sapphire. A telepathic link was certainly an advantage, especially in this weather.

Not for much longer. I can feel the warmer air currents coming from the west; we shall leave the storm soon, Sapphire replied in her soothing tone. Feeling glad that they would soon leave this penetrating cold, Eve closed her eyes and weaved tunes with the howling wind.

They landed on a rocky outcrop an hour or so later; Keisha was already there. Sapphire clicked her beak and shook her head, Eve gasped when she saw the build-up of ice on the bird's wings. She was about to start brushing it away when a bedraggled Jericho appeared from behind the boulders off to the left. His coat was wet, making the fur on his head stand up at odd angles. He did not look happy.

"Don't fret about the ice, they will sort themselves out. I suggest you come and talk to your friend." Rolling his eyes, Jericho retraced his steps and disappeared. Knowing that Caleb must be trying the Miscurt's patience, Eve hurried to follow him. Caleb was red and pacing, his hair a wet mop of blond waves that fell into his eyes. The way he pushed it back off his forehead showed Eve how upset he really was. He was trying to shout, though the cold had caused him to lose his voice somewhat, so it sounded more like a rasp.

"I will not get back on that infernal bird! Never in my life have I been so scared! I swear she was banking like that just to hear me scream and hoping I would fall to my death!" Caleb raged, his strangled vocal cords protesting and his face scarlet.

"Cal, will you please calm down? No one is making you get on Keisha. We are all wet, cold, and in need of a warm drink at the very least," soothed Eve. She began to dig about in her bag, glad that it was water-proofed, and that its contents were still in perfect order. Removing some sage, lemon grass, and a small wax sealed jar of honey, she turned to Jericho.

"Could you please start a small fire? I will make us some warming tea." She looked into the Miscurt's black eyes and smiled sweetly. Huffing, he nodded and retreated to the far side of the outcrop where a few trees and bushes grew. Walking over to Caleb, Eve gave him a quick hug and then moved on to dig through his backpack in search of the kettle and mugs she knew were in there. Finding the items she needed, Eve returned to her bag, sat down, and began to make the tea.

"Ah, thank you. My poor throat feels raw; this tea is a balm indeed." Caleb sighed in-between sips of the steaming hot brew. Pouring himself another mug full, Jericho reclined against the boulder and drank in silence.

"How far are we from the border? It's already afternoon," Eve noted, as she packed away the herbs. Though she would never admit it, she was not feeling her best and would give anything for dry, clean clothes. Finishing his tea, Jericho motioned for Eve to join him.

"You see the river winding its way towards the hills in the distance? The border is on the other side of those hills, no more than four hours' ride. If the protectors are agreeable, we could be there by tea time." The thought of being back on an owl was too much for Caleb; he choked on his mouthful and began to cough. Running over to his side, Eve began to thump him on the back. Eyes watering, Caleb made it extremely clear that nothing was going to get him back on that 'evil flying spawn.'

"If that is how you feel, then so be it; however, be very sure. The walk is long, and the animals here are fierce," Jericho informed him. "You see this?" he pointed to a pile of dark brown lumps. "That is the waste products of the fanged tree cat. I would not want to be anywhere near here when the sun goes down," he concluded, face deadpan. Jericho found it highly amusing to watch the indignant witch ponder over the two choices he had. After a lot of pacing, hand rubbing, and opening and closing his mouth likes a fish out of water, Caleb finally decided that possible death due to plummeting from the sky was preferable to certain death of being ripped apart by a large fanged cat. Chuckling under his breath, Jericho went to check if the protectors felt up to continuing on their journey.

Chapter Nine

Caleb spent the last leg of the journey thinking that he had always known that an adventure awaited him; he just didn't realise that it would come with the possible destruction of the entire world. As he gazed out towards the slowly approaching horizon, he came to the conclusion that he would need to tell Eve what he knew of the prophecy. Reaching down, he withdrew his pendant from beneath his shirt. In the afternoon sun, it flashed with electric blue. Rubbing it between his thumb and index finger, Caleb made the decision to begin using his 'real' magic; he was no longer within the boundaries of Clear Water Valley and so was not subjected to the consequences of rule breaking. At least, he hoped that was the case.

Jericho, too, was contemplating the future. The young elf was stronger than she appeared. An iron will was hidden beneath her youth and beauty. Yet, he felt protective of her. It had not gone without notice the way her very presence lit up a room. Her smile was infectious, and her compassion seemed to be limitless. Jericho very much wanted to continue with her on this quest. However, he was under orders to return once he had seen the couple to the border. Though he knew there was no way for him to be brought back to the city, Maximus would make his punishment most severe when he did return.

Deciding not to make any solid plans until they reached their destination, Jericho returned to gazing at the breath-taking views of his homeland. He would never become tired of this view, not if he lived to be one hundred.

We will land soon, dear one, please hold on tight, crooned Sapphire. She had become quite attached to the elf, which was not very surprising. They had been destined to find each other. Sapphire was concerned with how little Eve knew about her destiny and how significant her part was. She knew that Eve was strong-willed and intelligent, but what caused her the most concern was her undiscovered gift. Sapphire knew what it was, of course. However, she was unable to reveal it to her companion. *I wonder if it will be too much for her?* she thought, worry clouding her blue eyes. Keeping the telepathic link closed, Sapphire allowed herself a few moments to consider how best to fulfil her role within the prophecy. Even as she pondered this, she knew that whatever she decided, the future was pre-ordained, and there wasn't anything she could do to change it.

THEY WERE ENJOYING a snack of wild berries, tiger lily stems, and pansies. Though they should have arrived at their destination by now, they had not arrived because Caleb had practically begged for a break. They were an interesting party to behold: two giant owls who stood like sentinels, a Miscurt warrior, a witch, and an elf maid. All were a little sore from the long hours spent sitting on the backs of the owls. Each also had much on their minds.

"I have decided to stay with you for a while longer if that is acceptable to you, Eve?" Jericho had made his choice; he felt both relief and dread. Not wanting to see her reaction, he continued with his meal. Eve was quite surprised; she had believed that Jericho found his babysitting duties tiresome and beneath his rank. She wondered why he wanted to accompany them into Gloria. Was it on Maximus's orders? Eve didn't think that was likely. A smile touched her lips at the thought of the cantankerous old rodent.

"I have no reason not to agree to your company, Jericho. Indeed, I haven't the power to prevent you accompanying us even if I disliked

THE AURORA STONE

the idea," she replied smoothly. Keeping her eyes on the Miscurt, she did not notice Caleb. He looked like he would very much like to decline the rodent's request; he did not trust him. Still, he would not be made to look foolish, so held his tongue. Caleb was sure that Jericho would prove himself untrustworthy soon enough.

"Well, it's nice to have an extra pair of hands. Are the protectors...err... coming along as well?" Hoping the answer to his question was no, Caleb tried to look indifferent as he awaited a reply. Smiling at her aero-phobic friend, Eve approached the two protectors, who were busy grooming their lustrous plumage. She waited quietly to be noticed, as she did not wish to interrupt what appeared to be a rather important exercise. After a minute, Keisha looked up. She looked rather cute with her feathers ruffled from her grooming - that is, if you could ever call an oversized owl 'cute.'

Walking up to the beautiful creatures, Eve reached out with her mind and inquired about their status now that their task was almost complete. Her eyes sparkling in the sunlight, Keisha replied, *No, I will return home. I have young that I must attend to. As for Sapphire, I believe she will be staying with you; you two have a bond like nothing I have ever witnessed. You are a part of each other; that much I can tell.* Keisha clicked her beak and leaned forward so that her head touched Eve's. *You have much to overcome, young one. Remember, darkness cannot survive where there is light.*

Unsure what all that meant, Eve lifted her hand and stroked the great bronze bird's cheek. Thanking her for her help and her patience with Caleb, Eve stepped away from her and turned towards her snow-white friend. Taking a moment to admire the powerful beauty and grace that emanated from Sapphire, Eve felt truly blessed to have met this magnificent creature and was honoured to call her a friend. Walking over to her, she was about to ask whether she was to stay with the group when she felt their connection flare.

I will be with you. We are bound together, dear one. There is much more I have to share with you. Sapphire held her gaze as they shared a silent conversation. Eve felt as though they were on the edge of a discovery. So many things were falling into place. Looking up into Sapphire's eyes, it suddenly hit her. The owl's eyes, her name, the prophecy!

Three companions... you will know them by their gems.

There was, of course, the possibility that she was wrong. However, it gave Eve some comfort to believe that she was correct. It meant that the path was set. The elements of the prophecy were coming together. Eve wholeheartedly believed that she was another step closer to finding her brother.

THE FAE, OR 'THE ENLIGHTENED Ones' as they liked to be called, were a flamboyant race. The King and Queen were famed for their outrageous attire and themed balls. Nothing seemed to be taken very seriously in Gloria, with its rainbow waterfalls and lush forests. It was as if a story-book had come to life.

The sentinel guarding the mirror that was the passage into Gloria was bored Jerry was cloaked in invisibility and sat on the fallen tree that was positioned to the right of the mirror. Unless a creature was aware of its existence, the mirror was hard to find. It was an oval, suspended a foot off the ground, nine feet high and four feet wide. One could walk past it and not see it. It had been three months since anyone had discovered this entrance.

"Yet another boring day; here I am sitting alone," Jerry grumbled to himself. He was still sore from the disciplinary action he had received for being found asleep at his post last Tuesday. Sliding off the trunk so he could rest his back against it, Jerry closed his eyes for a nap. He was hoping that if he were caught asleep again, they would give him a job on the Gloria side of the portal. With that thought bringing a smile to his lips, Jerry fell asleep to dream of Sarah.

EVANGELINE AND HER strange company landed in a glade full of bluebells and daisies. Keisha and Sapphire had a short conversation in their unique way, and then, after bowing to Jericho and Caleb, the bronze owl came and rested her forehead against Eve's.

It is time for me to return, young one. Remember what I told you: darkness cannot survive in the light, Keisha projected. Eve promised to remember. Taking one last look at the group and clicking her beak at Caleb just to see him flinch, the great protector gracefully ascended into the cloudy sky and was gone.

Jericho took in his surroundings, and admitted that he had no idea of the exact location of the border. However, he pointed off to the left, explaining that this direction 'felt right.' Not sure how he could not know where the border of his own realm lay, Eve and Caleb exchanged a look.

"Right, so we walk blindly around the Forrest until we find the wall?" Caleb challenged. Ignoring him, Jericho continued towards the tree line. "Unbelievable!" exclaimed Caleb, turning to look at Eve, who in turn shrugged and followed the Miscurt's retreating back. Though reluctant to get lost, Caleb didn't follow right away. After a second, he felt a jab to his back. Jumping forward, he looked over his shoulder to see Sapphire apprising him. Caleb rolled his eyes and made his way after Eve.

"Are you coming then, Sapphire?" he asked as he reached the tree line. She shook her head and took off to soar over the trees. Picking up his pace, Caleb soon caught up with Jericho and Eve. The forest was teeming with life, and even though the trees were tall, they were not heavy with branches, so plenty of daylight reached them. Brown rabbits with fluffy white cotton tails scampered through the mulch and wild flowers. Their feet kicked up clumps of the loam as they played chase.

"It is a wondrous place that you call home, Jericho; I would love to come back and visit some more once my quest is complete," Eve proposed, eyes bright with joy and cheeks flushed with colour. Smiling at her enthusiasm for his homeland, Jericho nodded.

"You will be most welcome, Eve; there are many beautiful areas to explore."

They continued in companionable silence. Sapphire's shadow kissed the ground occasionally, so they knew that she was close by. As beautiful as the forest was, there didn't appear to be a wall, which is what Eve and Caleb had expected since that had been what they had found upon entering Olia. Caleb was about to ask how much further when Eve stopped.

"Jericho, there is a mirror just off to the left of where I am standing. It's a few feet away," Eve whispered, knowing he would hear her and not wanting to draw too much attention to the anomaly in case it was a trap. Walking over to her, Jericho looked in the direction Eve had indicated and saw absolutely nothing. Looking puzzled, he was about to say that maybe they should take a break and eat if she was now seeing things that were not there. Before he got the chance, Eve boldly took his paw and walked to the left, until they were in front of the mirror.

"I am not seeing things, which I know you were about to say. Just look. If that is not a mirror, then how am I both here and there?" she asked, pointing to her reflection.

"Ah..." Jericho replied. Looking up to see where Sapphire was, he was pleased to see that she was already coming into land. "Eve has found a portal," he explained to Caleb and Sapphire once they had reached them. Caleb was a bit put out that he had not been next to Eve when she saw it, but nature had called, and he had dashed into the trees to relieve himself.

Sapphire would not fit through the portal. She would have to fly further and hope the connection she shared with Evangeline would be enough to allow them to meet up at another gate once the business in Gloria was completed. She explained this to Eve, and though her face clouded with sadness that Sapphire could not come with her, she understood, and they agreed to test their link every few hours to make sure it held.

"Sapphire won't be coming with us as she quite clearly won't fit through that portal, so she will meet us at another portal once we are finished searching for Eli," Eve relayed to the others. Secretly pleased, Caleb schooled his expression into one of mild disappointment and concern. Jericho noticed and chuckled as he approached Sapphire to collect the bags she had so kindly carried while they had travelled on foot.

As he passed he whispered to Caleb, "You are a poor actor, witch."

Turning red with indignation, Caleb turned his back on the Miscurt and headed towards Eve to discuss her plan for this next leg of their journey.

Since the portal was magical, it was decided that Caleb would go first to see if he could feel any magical wards protecting the mirror that might prevent them from entering Gloria. Feeling that now was his time to shine - as neither Jericho nor Eve had the first clue about how this mirror portal worked - Caleb finally felt useful. Striding purposefully over to stand before the mirror, he was about to begin the revealing spell to show any wards that might be protecting it, when he felt the hum of a cloaking spell. Moving slowly, he stopped in front of the fallen tree and an unaware Jerry. Knowing that there was someone cloaked there who had not yet attacked them, Caleb gathered that whoever was hiding was not interested in them, so he moved back to the mirror.

"Make this look impressive, Cal," he murmured to himself. Raising his arms over his head, he began moving them in circular motions and chanting quietly. In reality, he was saying random nonsense. There were no spells protecting it. Clearly, the cloaked creature was meant to be guarding the entrance and doing a poor job of it, which was all the better for them. After what Caleb deemed to be long enough, he turned and faced his two companions.

"The portal is clear and ready to pass through," he announced rather grandly.

Looking rather impressed, Eve moved forward to stand beside Caleb. She looked at her friend and wondered how much longer he was going to compete with Jericho. It was something she didn't understand and found both amusing and tiresome.

"How do we pass through, Cal?" Eve asked, anxious to begin their search of Gloria. Caleb looked at the girl beside him and wished he could tell her how he was feeling right then. With the sun muted behind cloud cover, her hair was still flashing with fire, and her mystical eyes were captivating. She was mesmerising, completely open and innocent. Shaking himself, he smiled and pushed his thoughts away. Now was not the time.

"You just step through. I know it looks solid, but it's not. It will feel strange, cold, and wet, but you will remain dry. Once you pass through, wait just on the other side for us," Caleb explained, putting extra emphasis on the waiting part. He knew how impulsive Eve could be.

"Maybe I should pass through before Eve to make sure it is safe," Jericho injected, not liking the idea of Eve wondering through a portal without knowing what waited on the other side.

"You are right; I will go through first," countered Caleb.

Rolling her eyes at the fact that, once again, the two males had begun another testosterone competition, she waited until she was only inches from the mirror and then called to them.

"While you two fight about which of you is the more gentlemanly, I am going through. Feel free to join me once you have finished your disagreement." Smiling at the sight of their comically stunned faces, Eve gracefully leapt forward through the mirror. It rippled like a pond that had had a pebble tossed into its centre and then returned to its original state. Jericho and Caleb looked at the mirror and then at each other.

"Women!" they both muttered and quickly leapt through after Eve, hoping she was waiting for them and had not wandered off.

GRIMMER PUSHED OPEN the heavy iron door to the portal room. It was a wondrous place to behold. Around the octagonal space were opening; within them were what appeared to be holes in the floor. These were the portals: the links to other realms. The master was extremely proud of this network, and it allowed his minions to slip between the realms without being detected.

Grimmer, being a high-ranking demon, carried a crystal around his neck made from a point of hematite. This allowed him to open a portal back to his master's fortress without the need of potions or spells, unlike the unfortunate underling Chashoc who would never again transverse Orea. He approached the portal directly to his right and stood before it. Gloria, the land of the Fae was at the other side of this one. The fuchsia swirls of this cosmic cyclone were nauseating to the demon. Knowing that he could not stay long in this realm, he paused to make his plan. The light alone would burn his skin, and the pureness of their magic would weaken him.

Taking one last look at the vortex at his feet, Grimmer felt for the potion vial his master had given him. Finding it secure, the demon stepped into the portal and vanished.

Chapter Ten

Passing through the portal was both exciting and a little disturbing. The journey was quick and no harm had come to her. However, Eve felt like someone had poured cold water all over her. Rubbing her arms vigorously to rid herself of the phantom chills, Eve glanced around quickly, making sure that no threat was near. Once she was sure of her safety, she waited for Caleb and Jericho to join her.

Can you hear me, Sapphire? Eve thought, projecting her question skywards. She had no idea whether their telepathic bond would hold now that she was in a different realm. After no answer was received, Eve realised that, until Sapphire found another entrance into Gloria, they were on their own.

Jericho and Caleb appeared moments later, both wide-eyed and ready, it seemed, to do battle with any unsuspecting creature that happened to cross their path.

"Stand down, gentlemen. There is, as far as I am able to tell, no immediate threat to us here," she said, trying hard to keep the smirk from her lips. Caleb walked over to the edge of the tree line. It seemed that in some sense, the mirror was just that; this forest looked identical to the one they had just left. He peered through the thick shrubbery, not expecting to behold a thriving village that couldn't have been more than a mile away.

"Look! We can make it to that village by tea time, which I have to say is mighty good news for my tummy. It hasn't shut up complaining in hours!" Caleb grumbled while rubbing his abdomen, which let out a thunderous rumble in protest. Jericho and Eve both had a look at the short distance and agreed that a warm meal, the possibility of a wash, and a clean, comfortable bed would be most welcome indeed.

The village was quaint, with single story cottages snuggled up together, their grey shingle roofs shimmering in the last of the afternoon's muted sunlight. The trio entered the village and headed towards the first fae they saw. Deciding that Evangeline would do all the talking, the two men hung back and kept watch in case of sudden attack. After having a short chat with a lovely fae by the name of Olga, the companions made their way through the village's winding streets until they came to the address Olga had given Eve.

The owner of the home was a rotund female fae with wisps of grey hair that looked as though it was trying to fly away, cheerfully rosy cheeks, and dancing brown eyes. On seeing the odd group at her door, the woman did a double take and then called back into the house.

"Albert! Get yourself to the door. We have visitors!" Turning back to the now concerned trio, she smiled sweetly at them while they all awaited the arrival of Albert. Once he appeared at the door, looking a bit crumpled and rubbing the sleep from his eyes, he addressed them.

"Good af'noon, and what can we be doing for you?" he inquired, peering at each of them in turn. Looking to Eve to answer once again, Jericho and Caleb hung back and kept quiet.

"Good afternoon, Sir, Madam. My friends and I are travelling through Gloria on our way to the Royal city. We have been on the road for some hours." Eve paused to smile at the couple and continued. "We were looking for a place to stay just for tonight; I asked in the village, and Olga said to come here. I hope that we are not imposing." Eve smiled her sweetest smile. Albert and the brown-eyed woman, who Eve assumed to be his wife, exchanged whispered words. Turning back to Eve, Albert confirmed that this was indeed the place to come. Asking them to wait, he disappeared back into the cottage.

"Sorry, I haven't introduced meself. I'm Betty; Albert's me husband. He's just gone to get the key to the guest accommodations," Betty explained. She seemed to bob on the spot as she spoke, which Eve found endearing, although by their muffled coughs and sniggers the men found it amusing. Thinking she would have to remind them of how to behave in public later, Eve returned Betty's smile and complimented her on the lovely flowerpots she had lined against her wall.

"Here we are; follow me please," Albert instructed as he shuffled down the street. Thanking Betty once more, they followed Albert's retreating form. Five doors up, Albert stopped and inserted the brass key into the door, pushing it wide and mumbling 'maidens first.' Eve preceded the men into the cottage. Albert closed the door and explained the house rules to them, and then, handing over the key to Caleb, he left.

"Well that was different," Jericho said as he looked around the sitting room. It was a cosy room with plump chairs and a sofa practically hidden under a mountain of cushions. There were two doors other than the front door. One led to the kitchen at the back of the cottage and the other to a short hallway, off of which there were a bathroom and two bedrooms. Not happy that he would have to share a room with Jericho, Caleb headed back towards the kitchen, hoping he would find a tasty morsel that might satisfy his grumbling stomach. Caleb was most disappointed, finding nothing but veg and some strange bottles of Goddess knew what. He gave up his pursuit for sustenance and made his way back to the sitting room. He flopped down into one of the chairs.

"What on earth is the matter with you, Cal? You have a face like sour milk," Eve remarked as she entered the sitting room. She was wearing a pair of cropped trousers and a tunic she had found in the wardrobe. Thankfully the Fae were not under the misconception that elves were wee folk like the witches had been before the alliance. Combing her fingers through her damp hair, she waited for Caleb to answer her.

"Nothing. Bath any good?" he replied, not really answering her question. Eve nodded. Caleb then got to his feet and headed down the hall to find his room and prepare for a bath.

"He is hungry," Jericho stated, throwing himself down on the sofa.

"How do you know?" Eve was confused as to how being hungry could be a reason for such a sullen mood. Chuckling, Jericho explained that males behaved the same when hungry wherever they were from. Not fully understanding this, but not wanting to offend him, Eve went to the kitchen to find something for their tea.

JERICHO GAVE EVE THE 'I told you so' smirk later that evening when, after two bowls of steaming vegetable soup and bread Eve had found in the larder, Caleb was more himself. Although it was lovely to have a comfortable place to rest for the night, it bothered Jericho how easy it had been to enter Gloria. He knew full well that Caleb had not performed any elaborate spell before the mirror - that it had been an act for Eve's benefit. There should have been a guard or a trap of some kind; the Fae were known for being ultra-careful. He voiced his concerns to Caleb and Eve.

"I did feel someone cloaked by the fallen tree, but whoever it was didn't attack or prevent us from entering," Caleb admitted. Jericho was incensed; it was incredibly foolish to have not shared this information. Regardless of how confident he felt, what if the hidden person had harmed Eve as she approached the mirror? Caleb paled at the thought. He really had not considered the possibility that it was a ruse to get to Eve. After all, they had encountered werewolves already, and Eve had said she felt they were being watched by something or someone that night. Caleb took the lecture with good grace, because, this time, Jericho was undoubtedly right; he had placed everyone in unnecessary danger just to boost his ego.

Eve sat quietly through the whole exchange, feeling bad for Caleb but also understanding that Jericho had a very important point. She made an internal promise not to rush off without them again. Without her, the prophecy could not come to pass, and her brother would be lost forever.

"I think I will head off to bed; we have a fair journey to the Royal city tomorrow. Goodnight Eve, Jericho," Caleb mumbled, as he made his way to his shared bedroom. The door clicked quietly behind him.

"I understand why you admonished him, Jericho. I really think he will be more mindful in the future. It didn't occur to me that I could be endangering both myself and the two of you when I passed through the mirror. I, too, will be more careful, and I will never go anywhere without one of you with me," promised Eve, looking into Jericho's black eyes. Letting out a sigh and pulling on his ears, the mighty Miscurt nodded.

"I think a lesson has been learned today. It would be best if we made it known to Betty and Albert tomorrow about the cloaked creature. It might have been a guard or something more sinister," Jericho suggested. Nodding and hoping it was a sleeping guard rather than a hidden foe, Eve bid Jericho goodnight. Before turning in himself, Jericho checked all the locks on the windows and doors. They might be in a cosy cottage with comfortable beds in which to sleep tonight, but they were also in a foreign land, and the Fae were well known for their trickery. Something told Jericho that their time spent in Gloria was not going to pass without incident.

GRIMMER MADE HIS WAY through the royal city. He already knew that the companions had not arrived yet; this pleased him.

Finding his way into the city park that was overlooked by the castle itself, he cloaked himself in darkness, checking once again for the vial in his pouch. Tomorrow at dusk, they should arrive. Tomorrow he would trick them all and end this quest forever. Grimmer wanted this girl dead; she was more powerful than she could ever imagine, and if she found her brother... He would not allow that to happen.

"I will destroy the prophecy, and before I kill her, she will know how close she came to finding her twin." A sadistic smile spread across his grotesque countenance, causing his scars to distort his features further. "Yes, I shall break her, kill her twice. First I shall kill her soul with the news of her brother, and then I shall give her the poison and watch her agony." Grimmer quickened his pace; he wanted to find cover for the remainder of the night.

The pureness of the land was sickening to him, and if it were to rain, the droplets would feel like tiny daggers piercing his corrupted flesh. Spying a summerhouse just ahead, he vanished and reappeared within its wooden structure. Grimmer extended his cloak of darkness, pushing it out from his body. It flexed like a second skin and slowly expanded. Once it had blocked the light from the moon and stars, he knew there was no chance of his being seen. Walking to the centre of the room, he took out a small orb from his pouch and held it before himself.

"Master, I have arrived in Gloria. They have not yet reached the Royal city," Grimmer spoke to the orb.

"Good, my servant. I await your report on the girl's most horrific demise." The malevolent tones of his master filled the room. After assuring him that his will would be done, Grimmer returned the orb to his pouch. Sitting on the nearest chair, he folded his muscular arms and waited.

EVE WOKE WITH A START. She'd had the most bizarre dream. *She was searching in a place she had never seen, and it was a place of sadness and great evil. Through the high-ceilinged corridors, she searched for the stone... Her brother... She wasn't sure, but knowing that her life depended on it, she continued to run. She came to two huge doors made of copper; they were locked. No matter how much she pushed, the doors would not open. It was then that she felt the hairs on the back of her neck stand on end; a chill ran up her spine. Something was behind her, and it was pure evil.* It was just as the evil being had reached out to touch her shoulder that she had woken up. She knew that this had been a premonition; it had felt far too real to be a simple nightmare. Eve scrambled out of her bed and shot across the room. Flinging open her bedroom door, she threw herself down the short hallway and banged on the other bedroom door.

"Caleb, I need you to get out here! I've had a premonition!" she yelled through the solid wooden door while banging frantically. Seconds later, a wide-eyed Caleb opened the door and found himself clutching Eve as she tumbled through.

"Come on; I need you to extract my dream so we can make sense of it," she rushed. Righting herself and grabbing his hand, she began to drag him back towards her room.

"Hang on; I can't perform that spell. I don't know how," Caleb explained as he tried to pull away from her. For a female, she had a very strong grip. Eve didn't appear to be listening to his protests. Once back in her room, she turned to her friend and explained rather quickly about the premonition. He listened ashen-faced.

"So, you have to try, Cal. I know this is important, but it's already hazy now that I am awake. It is slipping away like leaves caught in the breeze," she pleaded, holding his hands. Her eyes were wide with fear and unshed tears. Caleb knew how to perform this spell, yet, even though he had decided to start using his magic, he still held back.

"I don't know how, Eve. I'm sorry," he lied, letting go of her hands. He went over to the small dressing table, hoping to find writing materials. Maybe if she wrote it down, then they could capture it before Eve lost it to her subconscious. Finding nothing of any use, he was about to head for the sitting room when he felt Eve behind him.

"Please, I need you to try." Eve was doing her best to hold back the tears. The vision had scared her, and even though the vivid images were already fading away, the fear she had felt was still present. Hanging his head, Caleb turned back to face her.

"Okay, I will try, but I cannot promise it will work. We should wait for Jericho to wake, though, how he slept through your banging, I will never know."

Eve wasn't willing to wait for a second longer. She returned to Caleb's room and began banging on the door. Jericho appeared almost instantly. Explaining that he had heard her the first time, but seeing as she was screaming for the witch, he had decided to stay put until he was sure the drama was over or she came looking for him. Eve explained to Jericho what had happened; it came out in a rush. She was desperate to have the vision extracted. When they reached the sitting room, Caleb was ready. He had cleared a space on the floor. There were four candles, each a different colour. There was also a bag of salt and one lit, white candle. On seeing the other two enter, Caleb stepped away from the cleared area. Eve looked at the strange setup and wondered where the candles had come from.

"For a non-practicing witch, you seem to carry the tools of the trade," Jericho commented with a hint or sarcasm. Ignoring him, Caleb reached for Eve's hand and led her to the cleared area between the four candles.

"Are you ready to begin?" he asked. Nodding her head, Eve watched as Caleb bent down and picked up the white candle. Handing it to her, he smiled and asked, "How did you know about an extraction spell?"

Looking him right in the eye, Eve replied. "Violet let me read her books."

Rolling his eyes at the carelessness of the young witch, Caleb picked up the box of salt and made a circle that encompassed them while muttering under his breath.

"Now for the technical bit," he murmured, wondering why he had agreed to this and how he was going to explain it if the binding spell still held this far from Clear Water Valley.

Chapter Eleven

Caleb turned to Eve and explained that once he began the spell, she must not break the circle; it was there for protection. Nodding her head, Eve stood still, holding her candle. Caleb went and stood before the green candle. He then began to call upon the elements.

"All hail the watchtower of the east, the element of air.

I do summon and call you forth, to guard and protect this circle. Be here now."

Eve didn't dare move. As she watched his back, she saw his hair ruffle as if caught by a breeze, which was impossible. They were indoors, and all the windows were closed. Caleb then picked up an anthem that she had not noticed from the floor and drew a five-pointed star over the candle. Once complete, Caleb lit the green candle and moved onto the red candle.

"All hail the watchtower of the south, the element of fire.

I do summon and call you forth, to guard and protect this circle. Be here now."

As Caleb invoked the element of fire, he felt the temperature rise slightly. Feeling relieved that he no longer seemed spellbound - as all witches were, unless members of the council; only simple everyday charms were allowed for normal citizens - he once again drew the pentagram and lit the candle that represented elemental fire. It felt wonderful to feel his magic awaken, like waking from a long sleep and having the most wonderful stretch.

"All hail the watchtower of the west, the element of water.

I do summon you and call you forth, to guard and protect this circle.

Be here now."

Jericho watched from outside the circle. He had felt the change in the atmosphere the moment Caleb had begun calling the elements to him. *He is powerful*, Jericho thought to himself. Miscurts were naturally wary of witches; they did not trust beings that could conjure. They much preferred a fair fight of arms than one of spells and potions. The irony of his current situation was not lost on him, given that he now travelled with a witch and within Gloria.

If he disliked witches, then Jericho *really* disliked the Fae. Their magic was all the more dangerous. They did not need to cast circles or say spells. A fairy could think you tied up and helpless, and you would be. Yes, the sooner they found Eli, the better. As Jericho became lost in his thoughts, Caleb completed invoking the elements.

"All hail the watchtower of the north, the element earth.

I do summon and call you forth, to guard and protect this circle.

Be here now."

As the last element was invoked, Caleb gazed at his handiwork. Forming a barrier around the circle were four bands of coloured light, one representing each element. Now he was ready to perform the extraction spell and collect the premonition from Eve's memory.

"I need you to hold the candle in your left hand and hold my right hand," Caleb instructed Eve. Once she was in the correct position, he rested his hand on her left one so that he, too, was holding the candle, and they formed a circle of sorts with their arms. Asking her to close her eyes, Caleb began the spell.

"Images, now memories, hidden from sight.

Draw towards the candles light.

Show me what has been seen,

What was discovered in a dream,

Reveal yourself to me.

So mote it be."

Eve experienced a slight pulling sensation within her memory, and then she saw a rush of colours and blurred images on her closed lids. As quickly as it had begun, the sensation stopped, and Eve felt lighter.

"You can open your eyes now, Eve. The spell is complete," Caleb whispered. He was trying to stay calm, as the rush of images had come at him after they passed through the candle flame. It was like being hit by lightning, too long he had been without his magic. His heart hammered in his chest, and adrenaline ran rampant through his system. Checking to see if the circle was still protected, Caleb was relieved to see it was. Turning back to Eve, he asked her to concentrate on the white candle they both held.

"I am going to reveal the images now. Are you sure you want to do this?" he asked, looking for any flicker of doubt on her beautiful face. Slowly shaking her head, Eve held firm and returned her gaze to the candle. Grounding himself, Caleb prepared to release the power and project the images onto its smooth wax surface.

"New knowledge I have gained, borrowed from another.

Reveal yourself to us once more, so that we may learn your meaning.

Draw to the candle's pure light and cast your secret upon it.

Reveal yourself for all to see.

So mote it be."

Even though he had braced himself for the release of power, it still made him slightly dizzy. Once he had regained his equilibrium, Caleb focused on the candle's wax. There on the snow-white surface was Eve's vision, swirling and moving in and out of focus. Pleased that it had worked, Caleb uttered the word that would project the images exactly as Eve had seen them out of the candle and into the circle.

"Release."

It was a surreal experience to stand in one's dream with someone else and be objective. They both watched as Eve ran through the dark corridors. When she reached the copper doors, Caleb gasped. The symbols on the doors were ancient and very powerful. Even more disturbing was the glimpse of the creature he saw standing behind the dream Eve. It seemed to waver in and out of substance, darkness so complete, he felt sucked into it. The only solid thing he saw was the gnarled claws reaching out with sharp points for Eve's shoulder. Moments later, the images evaporated.

JERICHO SAT AND LISTENED as Caleb recounted what had taken place in the circle. Eve was taking a nap. The magic had drained her, and she needed to rest before they could make their way to the city. The only part Caleb omitted was about the markings on the copper door. He would need to think more about those and their meaning. Jericho had found the entire spell casting unnerving, even more so when a strange white mist had blocked his view of the pair within the circle.

"That was the images releasing around us. The circle keeps us safe and also acts as a screen when performing these types of spells, to stop unwanted eyes seeing the information," Caleb informed Jericho, an apologetic grimace contorting his expression. Understanding that this could not be helped and grateful that information was being shared with him now, Jericho did not feel the need to make the witch feel any more uncomfortable than he already did.

"So, what does it mean? Where is this place?" Jericho asked as he got up and began pacing. He found that he thought better while moving. Shrugging, Caleb couldn't give him an answer, as he wasn't too sure himself. The only thing they agreed on was that it was definitely some kind of premonition, and wherever this place was, Eve must not enter it.

THE AURORA STONE

IT WAS MID-MORNING before they managed to get out the door. First, they headed back to Betty and Albert's to return the key and thank them for the use of the cottage. Waving away their thanks, Betty handed them a parcel of food, and gave them the use of her pony and trap. If they were surprised at the gift of food and the offer of transportation, that was nothing compared to how they felt when the 'pony' was led from the stable.

"Is that a..." Eve started to speak, but words failed her as she stared at the wondrous creature before her.

"Unicorn. Yes, dear. We call him Bobby," Betty replied to Eve's half-finished question. Walking over to the animal, Betty reached into her apron pocket and pulled out some chunks of apple. Bobby made quick work of them and then stood perfectly still. Eve stayed back, drinking in Bobby's beauty. He was silver-grey, with a mane and tail that were the colour of snow, so white that she could almost see rainbows in them. His horn was magnificent, long and proud, the perfect twist of molten silver crowing his forehead. While Eve gazed adoringly at Bobby, Jericho and Caleb climbed into the trap and were busy securing their belongings.

"Well, go on dear. The day is wasting. If you're worried about him nipping you, don't be. Bobby is a gentle soul, never harmed anything in his life," Betty assured her, giving Eve a shove in the small of her back, which sent her into Bobby's line of sight. The second he saw her, his blue-grey eyes seemed to light with recognition, similar to other animals they had encountered along her way. Just like the animals that had come before, Bobby gracefully bowed to her. Eve was now becoming used to this strange behaviour that animals kept demonstrating whenever she was near and dropped a curtsy in front of the unicorn.

"Well, I never saw him do that before. Clever boy, Bobby," cooed Betty, as she ambled back to her front door. Eve took Jericho's arm and pulled herself up into the trap. It was quite comfortable with her cloak folded up to make a cushion. Eve felt the journey would be a pleasant one, exploring the countryside on their way to the city.

"Thank you, Betty. We will make sure Bobby and the trap are returned in excellent condition," Eve called as Jericho clicked his tongue to get Bobby moving. Eve was about to ask how were they to direct Bobby, as he wasn't wearing a nose strap, when Caleb leaned forward and politely asked the unicorn to take them to the city.

Laughing at her confused expression, Caleb explained, "Bobby is a magical creature. He understands everything we say to him. That's why he hasn't any reins. There is no need for them. As long as we treat him with the respect and kindness his kind deserves, he will be most amenable."

Feeling a little out of her depth, but absolutely ecstatic to be in the company of a real unicorn, Eve settled herself into a comfortable position and watched the village begin to thin, giving way to green fields and the open road.

GRIMMER WAS SUFFERING. The darkness he had cloaked the inside of the summerhouse with was holding, but the sickening pureness of the place was leeching him of his strength. It was only going to get worse. He knew instinctively that the sun had not yet reached its highest point. This, combined with keeping his darkness stretched to guard him against prying eyes, was making him extremely angry. Anger was good; anger fuelled him and made him feel stronger, even as the pureness of Gloria sucked at his strength. The hours would soon pass, and once twilight fell, his mission would be complete. With this thought sustaining him, Gimmer closed his eyes to conserve his energy. He would need it later for the torture he was anxious to administer.

JERRY STOOD BEFORE Theo, his superior. His head was hung in shame. He had only intended to get caught by his opposite nodding on the job, and he had been. However, he had also let three unauthorised creatures through.

"You have been instrumental in allowing these creatures into our land. The royal family may not worry about travellers, but I am head of the border guards, and you, Jerry, are in serious trouble!" Theo bellowed, spittle flying from his lips.

Jerry didn't dare try and defend himself; he knew that several Fae had interacted with the travellers. Indeed, one family had put them up for the night. Theo was fuming. Nothing Jerry could say was going to get him out of this. If only he had just done his job instead of wishing for a different one. Sarah was never going to want to court him now. With this thought crushing his heart, Jerry followed Theo to the cells where he was to spend the night thinking about what he had done, or in this case - not done.

BOBBY KEPT UP A BRISK walk until mid-afternoon. Eve had suggested that, due to the time lost this morning, they eat on the road since Betty had provided a wonderful picnic for them all. She had asked Bobby if he would like to stop for something to eat and rest, but the unicorn had shaken his head, his pure white mane catching rainbows as it rippled with his movement.

Gloria was an unusual land. It was luscious but very flat. They could see for miles ahead of them. The trees and villages that were dotting the landscape seemed almost toy-like until they drew close enough to see clearly. Jericho pointed out that, the closer they got to the city, the more outrageous the villages became.

"Look at that house; it's purple!" gasped Caleb, pointing at rather a small cottage at the end of the village high street they were passing through. Indeed, it was a violent shade of violet with bright pink flowers in boxes adorning the windows and a green front door.

It was at this point that Bobby began to slow. Jericho invited Bobby to choose a place for him to rest. Nodding his head, Bobby kept walking until they reached the outskirts of the village. Jericho helped Eve down from the trap, while Caleb collected their bags. Jericho removed the harness that connected Bobby and the trap. The unicorn then walked into the trees a few meters away and disappeared.

"I hope he comes back," Eve said, worried that they might have just lost Betty's pride and joy in the woods.

"Bobby will return to us. Unicorns are loyal, and I have no doubt that he has gone to find a stream to have a drink from," Jericho assured Eve. Jericho dug about in his bag until he found the apple and pear he had saved from his share of the picnic; he had saved them for Bobby. Hearing Eve laugh, Jericho looked up to see that she was also holding an apple and a small piece of flapjack.

"Bobby shall be returning to a feast," she laughed. Sitting down on the grass, Eve set the fruit to one side and looked towards the town rising out of the landscape a few miles ahead of them. Once Bobby had returned and gently taken the fruit and flapjack that were offered to him, he walked back over to the trap and waited to be reharnessed. It was a marvel to Eve that he was so willing to be used as a common horse, and yet he was so much more.

Caleb suggested that if they wanted to reach the city by nightfall, that they should make a quick stop in the town ahead to get more food. That way, they could once again eat on the road. Jericho thought this a sensible plan, apart from the fact they had no money with which to purchase food or indeed anything else. Caleb smiled and reached into his bag. A moment later, he was holding onto a small sliver disk with a hole through its centre; the disk was hanging from a piece of leather.

"I don't think that will buy us very much, Cal. It's a nice thought, but..." Eve was cut off by Caleb's chuckle.

"I'm not going to try and buy food with this... exactly. Well, I suppose I am, aren't I?" he replied, smiling at the now two confused faces before him.

"Now is not the time for games; we have only a few hours of daylight left," warned Jericho, involuntary flexing his muscles. Still smiling, Caleb placed the disc between his palms and closed his eyes. He heard the collective gasp as he felt his hands slowly begin to move apart. Opening his eyes, he smirked at his two companions. In his hands was a pile of money. Silver slips of paper with purple, pink, and green swirls on them.

"It's a money charm; I can produce money of any kind using this," Caleb boasted, handing each of them a small pile of the notes. Thinking it would be a good idea to get a few other things in the town to aid them in their search for Eli, Eve smiled at Caleb, her eyes dancing with joy and affection.

"This is wonderful! Let's be on our way. The town is not far, and we can be in and out in no time!" she exclaimed, turning to Jericho to give her a boost up into the trap. Eve felt that things were falling into place. She just wished that Sapphire were with them. Eve felt lost without their connection. She knew that Caleb and Jericho were able to protect her, but Sapphire understood her like no other. How she hoped it would not be long until they were reunited.

THE CREATURE SLUNK along the gloomy corridors of its fortress, its heavy black cloak making a hissing sound as it slid along the marble floors. The copper vault was its destination. For a creature of pure darkness, this room was vastly important. This was not an area of the great fortress the creature often visited, but last night while, watching the damned in the pits below from the windows of its chamber, the creature had felt an emotion that unsettled it to the core...fear. The feeling of being observed in some way, like an unwanted presence had been in the fortress, unnerved him.

The elf was still alive; Grimmer had not returned. Therefore, his task had not yet been completed. Upon reaching the great copper doors, it reached out one clawed hand and pressed a discoloured talon into one of the engravings. *This door must never be discovered by the light carrier; Grimmer must succeed*, the creature thought as it checked the doors for signs of weakness. Finding the locking spells still in place, a smile split across the creature's face, exposing its fangs within its lipless maw, blood still clinging to the corners of its almost non-existent lips. No longer concerned about the copper vault, the Darkness vanished, only to re-appear in its chamber. A yell rang out as the creature fully materialized by its throne. Turning to the sound, its eyes fell on the young witch. He was stripped from the waist up. Large scars covered most of his torso. Clearly, he had been beaten into submission when first brought to this place. One of the gashes was new, and his blood trickled from it, dripping onto the marble floor.

Smelling the fresh blood acted like a siren's call. Stalking the witch, the Creature parted its cloak to expose both its clawed hands. The man was now thrashing about the floor. It was a futile act; he was chained to an anchor secured deep within the marble. There was to be no escape. Usually, the Creature did not play with its prey; however, experiencing fear for the first time in millennia had caused it to want to make this witch suffer more than usual and experience extreme pain and fear.

Reaching one clawed hand out, it peeled a slither of skin from the man's chest. The captive's blood-curdling scream echoed around the chamber. The creature shivered in glee as it deposited the ribbon of flesh into its jaws.

"You are going to suffer, witch, for my pleasure." The creature cackled as once again it peeled another ribbon of flesh from the prisoner's chest. Panting through the pain, the witch looked up into the face of pure evil and defilement.

"You will lose, Nimayaorin. No amount of torture is going to change this. Kill me if you wish; rip my body apart. The truth is, you are going to be defeated," the witch declared, all the while looking with defiant eyes into the horrifying countenance that belonged to the creature he called Nimayaorin. Not many knew of the creature's name, and those that did never uttered it. Seeing as he was going to die, the witch used this knowledge to taunt the monster before him.

"You dare to speak my name, you mewling meat sack!" Nimayaorin screeched, enraged that his name was known within the pits. His eyes shining crimson, he removed the hood of his cloak. "Look upon the face of the darkness. It will be the last thing you ever see in this life and will haunt you in your next!"

The witch looked up into the face that had been ravaged for a millennium by hatred, dark magic, and evil. "You used to be one of us; how far you strayed from the path," he whispered. This was too much for Nimayaorin. Moving lightning fast, he dug his claws into the witch's bleeding chest, all thoughts of torture forgotten. Closing his claws around his prey's beating heart, Nimayaorin smiled as he ripped the organ from the chest cavity. Holding the still-beating organ before the witch, he allowing him to watch it beat his life force onto the floor.

"You see, witch, your words mean little. For whom will you tell?"

With his last breath, the witch answered his murderer. "I know what you are, and others will soon know your name. Evil is only feared when it has no name. Think on that, because someday soon you will be no more than a memory. That is what matters, and I wish you to know... my name is Thomas. I guarantee you will never forget...it"

Chapter Twelve

The stop in the town of Hemlock had been short but memorable. They had never seen such an eccentric place in all their lives. Brightly-coloured houses with windows of different shapes and sizes lined the streets; no two were the same. The shops were just as colourful, and so was the produce on offer. Eve would have loved to have stayed and explored, but it was imperative that they reach the city that day. After collecting enough food for themselves and a glut of apples for Bobby, they headed out of Hemlock. Eve thought of Eli as the trap bumped gently along the road, opening her locket she looked at each image, in turn. Pausing at the one of Eli, his adorable smiling face looked out at her. It was bitter-sweet gazing at this picture. How much she wished they had had the childhood their parents had planned for them. The rush of love and hope she felt was so strong knowing he was close by. Eve really believed they would find him here in Gloria. It was like a sixth sense pulling her onwards towards her twin.

The next image was of her mother Gwen. How she missed her! It was heart-breaking knowing how hard it had been for her to reveal the information about Eve's parentage, and then to discover she was destined to fulfil a prophecy. It must have been so awful for her to feel she had lost her daughter twice in a few days. Of course, she would never truly lose Eve, and she hoped with all of her being that Gwen knew this.

Caleb came over to see what was causing the pensive look on Eve's face. The thought of her being in any kind of pain caused him anxiety. It was becoming abundantly clear now that he was falling deeply in love with her; even Jericho had been winking at him the last few days. Caleb realised he was going to have to declare his feelings at some point, along with the knowledge he held. He was not at all sure that either was going to get him a favourable response. However, it had to be done. *I will talk to her once we are free of Gloria and hopefully, have Eli*, he decided.

"You miss your mother very much; I can see the pain in your eyes," Caleb said as he put his arm around Eve's shoulders and looked at the tiny image in her hand. Sighing, she closed the locket and returned it to her neck.

"Here, let me." Caleb offered, seeing Eve struggle with her russet mane and the tiny clasp on the silk. Turning her back to him, she accepted, enjoying the touch of his warm fingertips on her skin. The quickening of her heart whenever he touched her was not exactly unwelcome. She just didn't know what to do with it. One thing Eve was sure of: there was no time for love, not while her brother and the prophecy still lay ahead of her.

The three companions ate on the road, stopping only to offer Bobby some refreshment and the chance to be free from the trap. He took the apples but declined the offer of a rest. Jericho held much respect for the unicorn, knowing that, even as a magical creature, it would still be tiring to pull a trap with three adults aboard.

As the white-blue of the afternoon skies began to darken and the horizon to the west turned a magnificent amber, ribbons of fuchsia and hints of red reached up to capture more of the blue, transforming it into celestial fire. It was a truly striking sight to behold.

"Not far now. We will reach the city within the hour," Jericho stated, and Bobby nodded in agreement. The road gently ascended, so they didn't get their first proper view of the Royal city until reaching the top. It was huge. Large glass buildings glowed in the last of the sunlight, their unusual shapes making the cityscape seem alive with movement and light. Quite out of place, but beautiful in its own right, was the castle that sat on the hill. It seemed to be at the far side of the city. The moment Eve saw it, she knew that was where they needed to go.

"That's the Royal residence, I should think. It would make sense for us to ask for an audience with the King and Queen," Caleb commented as they approached the towering arch that welcomed them to Nemea, Capital City of Gloria.

Once through the arch, the city spread out before them in a breath-taking expanse of silver roads and glass structures. Everything seemed to shine. Though the buildings were glass, they were mirrored in places to allow the occupants some privacy. Other sections they were able to see through, and the sights they saw were extraordinary. There were whole rooms filled with puppies and comfortable sofas, groups of Fae seemed to gather there just to play with the puppies. There was another building with a room that had a stream running through it and a grass floor. This was clearly some kind of workspace, as there seemed to be tables and chairs with writing equipment on them. Nothing had prepared them for the level of eccentricity that was now before them.

"If these are just the workplaces, I wonder how outrageous the living quarters are, or the castle is for that matter!" exclaimed Caleb, his eyes wide as he took in the scene before him. Many of the Fae wandering the streets stopped and admired Bobby as he passed, waving and pointing at the beautiful unicorn.

With the light fading fast, Bobby headed towards the large oval park with ivy-covered gates in the centre of the city, where a sign proclaimed that it was permanently open. From her seat, Eve could see that there was a lake with small boats moored at a jetty, and beautiful trees, which had been artfully trimmed onto woodland creatures dotting the banks. To her, it looked like a truly magical place.

The full moon was now visible in the twilight, cutting a silver path across the surface of the lake. Jericho thought it looked like a highway to the stars and shared his musings with the others. Caleb then told them a story about the Goddess of nature and how her lover lived on the moon. Eve thought it was very romantic and listened as the trap rolled gently along the damp loam paths.

The gates at the end of the park came into view, along with the Royal residence. Everyone was tired and hoping for a warm bed for the night; even Bobby seemed to have slowed his pace a little. Eve was snuggled into Caleb, listening to his steady heartbeat, when, suddenly, a Fae girl came screaming from the woods, her clothes torn and blood dripping from cuts on her arms. Bobby stopped as the girl ran blindly into his path.

"Hey, what happened? Stop! We can help you!" Jericho called, as he vaulted from the driving platform and chased after the girl, who had stumbled and then fallen down the slope towards the lake. Jericho reached her moments before she fell into the water. "I have you. Nothing will harm you now," he soothed. The maiden was hysterical, jabbering about a demon in the summerhouse and how it had tried to eat her. This concerned the Miscurt. He was sure that the girl had indeed been attacked by something. He really hoped it wasn't a demon, since that would mean...no, he would not think of that. First, he had to get everyone to the safety of the castle.

Jericho scooped the girl into his arms and began running back towards the trap. A scream that he knew to be Eve's pierced the night air, making his blood run cold. He practically flew the last few meters up the rise and back to the trap. What he saw was nothing short of horrific. Bobby was loose from his harness. Large gashes ran across his rump, his silver blood running down his legs. Behind him on the floor, also bleeding, was Caleb. From what Jericho summarised in the few seconds he took to analyse the situation, it seemed that Caleb had freed Bobby in the hope of Eve getting away on him. But where was she? Jericho glanced about; he couldn't see Eve anywhere! Panic began to descend over him.

"EVE!" He yelled into the ever-growing darkness. Even the moon had gone into hiding, as if not wishing to bear witness to the horror that had taken place below. Running towards the trap, Jericho put the girl down by one of the large wheels. "Stay here, girl, and do not move. If anything comes back this way, I want you to shout for me. My name is Jericho," he instructed the petrified Fae before he turned and ran towards the tree line.

"EVE!" he shouted again. Once engulfed by greenery, his cries seemed muted by the closeness of the trees, and it was even darker under the leafy canopy. He ran for a few minutes searching for clues as to which direction she may have been taken, and that's when he saw the blood. Whatever had Eve had hurt her. The situation had become desperate; Jericho was now convinced that what the Fae girl had said was true. There was a demon in this park, and it was after Eve. Picking up his pace, Jericho ran through the trees, following the spatters of blood like a trail of gruesome breadcrumbs, hoping he would reach her in time.

Grimmer smiled as he ran through the trees, the elfin maid unconscious over his shoulder. He knew he could simply transport them both back to the summerhouse, but where was the fun in that? Grimmer wanted to be chased. He knew that by the time her would-be rescuer found them, it would be too late.

The summerhouse came into sight as the trees thinned. *Soon*, he thought, *soon the elf will be dead*. His original plan had been to wait for her to find Eli so that he could torture them both. However, the fairy maiden had wandered by, and he was so hungry that he had attacked her without thinking.

Knowing that his master would not allow him to live if he failed in this mission, Grimmer had had to think quickly. It was fortuitous that he had consulted his orb of revelation and found that the traveling party he was waiting for were mercifully close. It had been so easy to take her. The witch was too slow in his efforts to save her and had been slashed across the chest for his trouble. He would be dead soon. The thought made Grimmer smile.

The unicorn could have been a problem, but as luck would have it, the foolish Elf had launched herself at him dagger drawn. It had been easy to disarm and render her unconscious in moments. The cut on her arm was not fatal, and though her bleeding gave him pleasure, the smell of the dormant magic within her blood was making him feel nauseous.

Entering the summerhouse, he dropped Eve onto the floor. There was no time to lose. The shouts of the Miscurt were becoming louder; he would be here soon. Taking the vial from his pouch, Grimmer walked back to Eve and forced her mouth open. Pouring the contents into her mouth, he forced her head back until she involuntary swallowed the poison that would grant his master victory.

The effects were almost instant. Eve began to convulse. The force was enough to move her around the floor. Blood began to trickle from her closed eyelids. Grimmer watched her wither in agony and laughed. He had completed his mission. The witch would die from his wound, so there had been no need to waste the poison on him. It had all gone into this meddlesome elf maiden who, had she lived, would have been the end of his existence.

JERICHO BROKE THROUGH the tree line and saw the summerhouse. His acute hearing picked up the sound of boots hitting the floor. This both gave him hope and worried him. He had found her, but the sound was too fast and erratic.

Flinging the door open, he was just in time to see the demon, his scared face grinning at him manically. Jericho launched himself at Grimmer only to find himself grabbing at thin air. The demon had vanished. A moaning from behind a sofa drew his attention. Eve was behind it on the floor, blood running down her cheeks; her body was convulsing violently. Having no time to check for further danger, Jericho ran to her. Scooping Eve up, he held her in a vice grip against his chest. Exiting the summerhouse, he immediately began running towards the gates that led to the Castle. Eve's only hope now was a healer. Looking down at her, he could see that she was already a deathly white. The skin around her mouth and eyes seemed to be drying out. As he watched, a flake of skin came away from Eve's chin and disappeared into the encroaching night. Jericho knew Eve simply could not die. The prophecy must be fulfilled. Even as he ran, Jericho wondered if he was going to be in time to save her. Pushing the thought from his mind, he ran.

CALEB REGAINED CONSCIOUSNESS. The first thing he noticed was that his chest was burned. Trying to get up, he saw that Bobby was close by. Reaching out a hand, he tugged gently on the unicorn's tail, leaving a bloody smear in his wake. Bobby turned and gazed at Caleb.

He addressed the unicorn, "I know you understand me, and right now I need your help. We must get to the summerhouse that the Fae girl was screaming about, Eve is in great danger." Nodding his head, Bobby folded his legs beneath himself, allowing Caleb to climb onto his back. Moaning as blood oozed from the wound on his chest, he grabbed a handful of mane. Just as Bobby was about to leap forward into the trees, a voice shaking with fear called to them.

"Please don't leave me. The Miscurt said he would be back, and he hasn't returned. I can take you to the summer house, just please don't leave me here alone," the girl sobbed, covering her face with her hands. Caleb really wanted to find Eve, and the girl could be of some use in finding her.

"Come on then, but quickly; we haven't a moment to lose. I just pray the Goddess is looking down on us all tonight," he said as Bobby walked over to the sobbing Fairy. In no time, she was up behind Caleb, holding his shoulders as they raced through the night towards the summerhouse.

"My name is Freya; it is not far to the summerhouse," she sniffed. Caleb was not interested in exchanging pleasantries with her. All his thoughts were consumed with Eve. He needed to find her.

GRIMMER ARRIVED BACK at the fortress of darkness moments later; he had cut it fine to get out of the summerhouse, but it had been worth it. The look on the Miscurts face as he laid eyes on him had been worth almost getting run through for.

Walking briskly from the portal chamber, Grimmer headed for his master's quarters. He could feel his chest swell with pride; his master was going to be pleased. Entering the tower, Grimmer dropped to one knee.

"Master, I come with the news you have be waiting for. The elf is dead, as is the witch," Grimmer proclaimed, eyes still on the marble floor. He couldn't help the smile that spread across his scarred visage. Nimayaorin rose from his throne and approached his most prized minion. *Could it be true?* he thought as he swept across the marble floor.

"I hope you are not lying to me, Grimmer," Nimayaorin cautioned, his tone indicating that to do so would not end well for the demon before him. Reaching down, he put a claw under Glimmer's chin and forced the demon to look at him.

Grimmer felt the Claw pierce his skin and his black blood seep from the wound. Knowing that showing fear would only encourage his master to hurt him further, he reached into his pouch and removed his orb, holding it aloft for inspection.

"Master, here is my orb. I placed a spell upon it so as to capture images of my elimination of the Elf." Glimmer's words were strained and slightly slurred, as he did not wish for the Claw to puncture all the way into his mouth. That would take days to heal and make eating most difficult.

Taking the orb and mercifully removing his now blood-soaked claw from his servant's skin, Nimayaorin slithered over to his larger orb and muttered an incantation. Moments later, the orb was filled with images of the elf girl convulsing and bleeding on the ground. Her pain gave him immense pleasure. The prophecy could not come to pass once this girl was dead.

Nimayaorin turned to the large windows that overlooked the pits and laughed. The sound grew louder, echoing off the vaulted ceiling. Opening the windows, he continued to laugh, the slaves in the pits cowering at the manic sound.

"Hear me! Your light carrier is dead! Nothing can save you now," Nimayaorin shouted down to his slaves. As expected, a cry of deep sorrow rose from the pits as the damned souls below realised their fate was sealed. Smiling maniacally, his scarlet eyes shining, Nimayaorin closed the window and turned back to Grimmer. "As your reward, go to the cells and have your fill of any creature you wish."

The demon did not need telling twice. There was a vampire down there whose blood he was sure, by the smell of her, would be most palatable. Thanking his master, he rose and left the room.

Nimayaorin returned to his throne, the smile still set on his monstrous face. Soon all the realms would fall to the darkness, one by one, swallowed by the void, and he would be Emperor of them all.

Chapter Thirteen

Jericho thought his lungs might burst. The pain from running with Eve in his arms was taking its toll. He could have sobbed when the silver gates of the castle came into view. Like the park, these, too, were open. Glad that he would not have to wait for admittance, he dashed through. Ahead of him was a bridge. He crossed it unchallenged, taking no time to look into the moat and glimpse the Mer-people frolicking in the clear moonlit waters. Reaching the huge silver doors, he placed Eve gently down, and with all his strength he banged on the ornate surface until a guard opened it.

"Please! My friend was attacked by a demon; she needs a healer!" Jericho exclaimed, already bending to pick Eve up. The guard was about to decline, but then he saw the girl in the Miscurts arms. Eyes wide, he stepped back and pulled the door open further.

"Follow me. I will take you to the royal healer," the guard replied, already walking briskly ahead of Jericho to open the door to the left of the grand staircase. Not needing further encouragement, as every second counted, he followed the guard. Eve was looking dangerously close to death. If it wasn't for her shallow breathing, Jericho would have believed she already was.

"Una, are you in there? We are in need of your skills this very minute!" The guard called as he knocked on the door of what Jericho assumed was the healer's quarters. The door opened to reveal a young fairy with bright red hair. She was beautiful. Blue butterfly wings adorned her eyes. Seeing Eve, she stepped back and gestured for Jericho to enter.

"Lay her down on the bed," Una instructed. She then turned back to the guard.

"You must inform the King and Queen. Go now; I will do what I can for her." After closing the door on the retreating guard, Una moved quickly towards Eve and her Miscurt protector. Running her hands over Eve's still form, she asked several questions that Jericho did his best to answer, though, he had not been present when the attack took place. He described the convulsions and pointed out the dried blood on Eve's cheeks.

"Please, you must help her; this girl simply cannot be allowed to die." Jericho pleaded, pulling on his ears, tears pooling in his eyes. Una promised she would do all she could for Eve and then immediately began using her healing magic on the elf.

An hour passed, and Eve was still no closer to being well again. Una feared that she had been poisoned, and without the identity of the concoction it would take days to find the antidote. Eve did not have days, she had hours.

CALEB, FREYA, AND BOBBY arrived at the summer house, only to discover the doors wide open and blood all over the floor. Caleb was distraught. Where were they, and whose blood was all over the floor? Pacing up and down outside the empty house, he winced as his wounds continued to bleed. Feeling light-headed, he slumped to the ground. Freya seemed to have calmed now that she was no longer alone. On seeing Caleb fall to the ground, she rushed to his side.

"You are hurt," she stated. This got her a withering look from the witch. Placing her hands over the wound, Freya closed her eyes. Caleb was surprised to feel a tingling in his chest as the skin healed. Within moments, his chest looked perfect again.

"Thank you," Caleb said as he got to his feet, still feeling light-headed but no longer in pain, Caleb climbed back onto Bobby's back and pulled Freya up behind him. *Where would they go?* he thought, knowing that time was short for one of them - judging by the amount of blood on the floor.

"The castle is where I would go if mortally wounded; the royal healer is the best in all Gloria," Freya offered. Agreeing that it was the best place to start, they headed in the direction Freya gave Bobby at break-neck speed.

UNA WAS EXHAUSTED. She had tried every spell and herb she could think of just to see if they would have an effect, but nothing was working. Eve's breathing was now irregular and coming in short, sharp gasps. Jericho had begged, he had pleaded, and he had even threatened the Fae's life if she did not heal the girl. Una had explained that she was doing all she could. However, it was dark magic that had concocted this poison, and without knowing what she had been given, there was a good chance Eve would die this night.

The door to Una's room swung open with such force that it hit the wall, knocking three books to the floor and smashing a glass vile of something blue. Into the room strode a man and a woman of middle age. Una saw the couple and dropped a curtsy.

"Your Majesties," Una murmured and then turned back to the girl. The King and Queen walked to the bed and looked at the elf lying on the primrose sheets. Jericho was immediately on alert; if the King and Queen had come to see Eve, then they must know who she was, and then he remembered that Una had sent the guard to inform them. The King looked over Jericho with a look of disdain. He did not trust the Miscurt race. *Primitive* was how he thought of them.

"How did you come to be with this elf?" the King asked, his tone slightly suspicious. Trying to stay calm, as insulting the King of the realm would result in him being banished or worse, Jericho answered with as much respect as he could manage, given the situation.

"I have been accompanying the girl and her friend as protection, Your Majesty," Jericho bit out, adding a bow of respect at the end of his explanation. The King was about to launch into a lecture about how this clearly hadn't happened, and that this Miscurt should maybe go back to simple guard duty, when his wife touched his arm.

"Now is not the time, Efrin. The girl is mortally ill; we need to save her," the Queen muttered as she gently squeezed King Efrin's forearm. Sighing, Efrin nodded his head. Smiling at her husband, she moved to Una's side and began speaking with her in frantic hushed tones. The two males paced the room. Time was running out, and they both knew it.

THOUGH HIS INJURIES were severe, Bobby ran as fast as he could. He became a blur of silver-white, streaking through the night like lightning. The castle was not far away, but, to Caleb, it felt like a thousand miles. He was so consumed with shame. Why had he not been able to protect her? Finally, the open gates came into view. *Please let her be alright*, he thought as Bobby practically flew across the bridge to the main doors.

PAIN, SO MUCH PAIN. *I can hear people around me, but I cannot answer. Jericho is here! But where is here?* Eve fought to make sense of the situation she was now in, although the waves of pain made it feel as though every cell of her body was on fire. *The demon! What has happened to him, and where is Caleb? Too many questions and so much pain!* Eve's thoughts calmed as she felt the cool hand of someone touch her forehead. For a few blissful moments, that small area felt wonderful.

"She is so hot, though pale like one already dead," Una muttered as she continued to work on Eve.

I am not dead! Eve wanted to scream, but no sound came from her parched lips. *I must stay awake; I have to fight this for as long as I can so that whoever is caring for me can find a cure.* Trying to move the very tips of her fingers caused so much pain that Eve thought she would surely pass out.

"She cannot die. Please! There must be more that can be done?" Jericho begged as he paced the room.

"Where is she?!" Caleb shouted as he stumbled into the room, two palace guards hot on his heels. Seeing Eve's still form, Caleb rushed to her side, *this cannot not be happening.* Placing his hands over her heart, Caleb grounded himself and drew on the Earth's power, allowing it to flow into Eve. After a full ten minutes, Caleb was totally spent, and Eve's condition had not changed.

"It was a valiant attempt, young witch. Sadly, I believe she is beyond all help," Efrin said as he placed a bejewelled hand on Caleb's shoulder. Dashing the hot tears from his eyes, Caleb stood and turned to leave. Reaching the door, he turned back, looking at Eve's face, still so beautiful even close to death.

"There was so much I had to share with her," he choked out before he fled from the room. Jericho left to find him, knowing that there was nothing more he could do now. Before leaving, he gave instructions that he would return Eve's body to her mother to see she received the ceremony befitting such a brave woman.

Efrin looked to his Queen. This elf's death was indeed a terrible tragedy, one that they could not hope to avoid. Una was the best healer they had, but even she was at a loss. Without the poison's ingredients, there was to be no saving Eve.

"Come, Sophia, let us retire. Una can do no more." Efrin coaxed his wife away from the dying girl and led her to the door.

"You do know who she is, don't you?" Queen Sophia asked as she took Efrin's hand. This elf was the one to save them all, and now she was about to die. This was a dark day for all the realms. Looking down at his beloved wife, Efrin nodded.

"Yes, I know who she is, my love. I fear some hard times are ahead of us all. We should keep the boy away from this wing of the castle."

Agreeing with her husband that it would do their charge more harm than good to discover the truth, they left the dying elf and the promise of being saved from the darkness and slipped away quietly from the healer's quarters.

During all this time, Eve had drifted in and out of consciousness. Fragments of the conversation had flitted to her like leaves tumbling on the breeze. She was pleased to have heard Caleb's voice, yet heartbroken that he was hurting because of her. If only she could wake up. But the fire raged on, her limbs now ablaze. Her very bones felt like they must resemble ashes. *They believe I am to die*, she thought as another wave of heat coursed through her blood. *I will never see my mother again or find my brother.* If she had been able to cry, Eve would have sobbed. Lying there, a prisoner in her own body, she gave into the abyss for the final time.

WHILE EVE SUFFERED through the early hours, up in a plush suite in the east wing, Eli slept, ignorant of the fact that the world as he knew it was about to end. The King and Queen had not lied to him. No, he had always known he was an elf, that he had been rescued when very young. Although he accepted this, Eli also felt like a fundamental part of himself was missing. Sometimes when he dreamed, as he did now, he would glimpse a small chubby hand reaching for his own. Smiling in his sleep, he rolled over, unaware that the owner of that once chubby hand was dying downstairs.

BY SUNRISE, EVE WAS dead. Caleb was inconsolable and refused to leave his opulent guest chamber. Jericho had been in a heated discussion with Una and King Efrin for over an hour; he needed to return Eve to her mother. Unfortunately, the poison that had been administered to Eve was likely to decompose her body before they reached Hermoria. The King was adamant that the only compromise that could be made was for Eve to be cremated as a warrior would be, and her ashes returned to her mother, along with any special keepsakes and belongings she had with her. Unhappy with this, but knowing that he could not simply take Eve, Jericho agreed. The cremation was to be held at sunset.

The ceremony plans were taking shape. Flowers and silver chairs were being brought to the Queen's garden. The plan was to row Eve out to the island that sat in the middle of the lake and shoot burning arrows of purple fire onto the pyre. This was to be a warrior's send off, with the Royal seal of acknowledgment.

Jericho helped with the heavy lifting. Though the Fae could have just used magic to move the heavy logs to the island, they were aware that the Miscurt needed something to do and let him be. While the outdoor arrangements were underway, Eve was being prepared by Queen Sophia and her hand-maidens. They washed her in rose water and dressed her in a beautiful emerald shift that, even in death, made her skin glow and her hair flame with amber fire. The maids wept as they anointed Eve's skin with oils. They, too, knew who she was and what her passing now meant for all of Orea. The future was to be a dark place, and so they wept as they carried out the last honour they could bestow onto their would-be saviour.

NIMAYAORIN WAS ELATED. Oh, how she had suffered! The thought of the Elf trapped, a prisoner in her body, and suffering unimaginable pain, sent shivers down his spine. Grimmer was to be decorated for his instrumental role in the destruction of the light, the only being that could have saved the mewling parasites of Orea from his rule.

Sweeping across his vast chamber, Nimayaorin cast his claws over his orb of sight. His legion of spies should reach Gloria soon, and he intended to have a front row seat for the decimation of that girl's physical form.

CALEB STOOD AT THE lake's edge, tears leaving tracks down his cheeks. Eve was gone and his heart along with her. So many wasted chances, so many opportunities, and now he was out of time. He had seen Eve before she had been taken to the island - how beautiful she had looked. He had kissed her cheek and whispered to her the words he never quite found the right moment to say.

Jericho stood on his left. The Miscurt seemed smaller somehow. He, too, was mourning the loss of a friend. Jericho would not shed tears here. That would be a dishonour to his own race. There would be time for tears later in the privacy of his rooms. They were due to return to Hermoria tomorrow. It was several weeks away, unless they could somehow call Sapphire once outside the magical boundaries of Gloria. As sunset approached, both Caleb and Jericho lamented the loss of a great friend and their freedom.

King Efrin stepped forward to begin the ceremony. He was an eloquent speaker, and though he had not known Eve personally, he was able to evoke her soul beautifully. Queen Sophia was next to speak. At that moment, the island seemed to come alive with light. Tiny fireflies began to dance and weave around Eve in a beautiful ballet. To all watching, it looked like her soul was rising from her physical form - a beautiful, if somewhat sombre, comparison.

As each person who wished to speak stepped forward, the sunset cast its fiery glow over the gathering, bathing them in light on one of the darkest days they had experienced, though far worse was to come. Jericho had just given a rather brisk speech, though his unshed tears were clear for all to see in his black eyes. When the sun finally passed below the horizon, it was almost time to light the pyre and allow Eve to pass onto the realm of the dead. Caleb was the last to step forward. Still unsure as to what to say, he decided to keep it simple and speak from his heart.

"Eve was an amazing person. She saved my sister's life the very first night she stayed in Clear Water Valley. I knew then she was someone I wanted to know. Eve was beautiful, not just in appearance, but her very soul shone with light. She was brave and full of compassion for all creatures, even those that wished to do her harm. I loved her…and now she will never know." His voice catching in his throat on a sob, Caleb returned to his place and faced the lake.

"Archers prepare the royal flames," King Efrin called. The archers, a dozen in all, made themselves ready, their silver filigree dress uniforms flashing in the light of the flames. Each notched an arrow to their bow and awaited the order to let them loose across the lake.

Taking one last look at the island where Eve lay, Caleb turned back to towards the castle. It was over.

Chapter Fourteen

Nimayaorin held a ceremony to celebrate Grimmer's successful assassination. Holding his head high, the demon walked up to the grand throne and knelt at his master's feet.

"I welcome you all to my Fortress. You have come from the dark places in which you dwell. Be safe in the knowledge that no harm can now come to you. We can all move freely between the realms of Orea. The light has been snuffed out!" Nimayaorin exclaimed, raising his arms over his head. Looking around the room, he saw the creatures that nightmares are made of cheering and celebrating this most welcome news. Today was to be remembered for all eternity as the day the light was extinguished from the Orea…forever!

Gesturing for the gathering to quiet, Nimayaorin reached into his robe and removed a star ruby. Its polished surface was akin to a pool of fresh blood; it was hung on a thick rope of gold. Gliding down the steps of his throne, he stood before Grimmer's bowed form.

"Today we reward the one who was instrumental in the ascendance of the darkness. Grimmer, you have always been faithful and have served me well. I reward you with this star ruby," Nimayaorin said, placing the golden rope over the demon's head. The stone's deep red lustre flashed in the candlelight.

"Thank you, my Master. I live to serve," Grimmer replied, keeping his head bowed in respect. This was, indeed, the best day of his existence. To be rewarded so handsomely was a sign that he was rising through the ranks. Grimmer: the extinguisher of light. He liked the sound of that.

"Now, let us feast!" Nimayaorin ordered. No sooner had he uttered the command did the double doors at the far end of the room slid open to reveal a grand staircase. Taking the lead, Nimayaorin moved towards it with Grimmer at his right hand. The rest of the monsters followed at a respectful distance. The party was lead down to a lower level, at the end of a sconce lit corridor, and emerged into a large dungeon. The moment Nimayaorin entered, the screaming began. Chained to the walls and great iron rings in the floor, were men and women: witches, fae, and elves. Grimmer's yellow eyes flashed with glee when he spied a redheaded witch, who looked enough like the elf to make his mouth water. Knowing it was his master who was to pick first, he stood at attention and waited. Choosing a blond Fae girl for his first course, Nimayaorin opened the feasting, sinking his razor-sharp teeth into the girl's shoulder and tearing away a chunk of her flesh. Wasting no time, Grimmer leapt across the room and pinned the red-haired witch to the rough stone wall.

"Now I can take my time with you. Let me hear you scream," Grimmer whispered to the witch as he sliced open her arm. Soon the room was filled with the sound of screaming, and the walls were soon painted crimson. The darkness was coming - to consume and destroy all who dared to stand in its way.

EVE'S BODY LAY ON A bed of moss and wildflowers, her hair woven with silk ribbons. Even in death, she was beautiful. Across the lake, the archers were about to loose their flaming arrows that would consume her physical form. From out of the trees, the animals came to her. Gathering around her body, they rested paws, small heads, and cold noses against her. Lastly, a snow-white lamb approached. It looked at the other animals and laid its head over Eve's left hand. As the fireflies danced, casting a golden glow over the gathering, the order to loose the arrows reached their sensitive ears. The animals closed their eyes, in readiness for what needed to be done. The twang of bow strings acted as the signal. It was time the animals made their sacrifice. As if one being, the animals took a breath and gave a piece of their very souls to the maiden that they had come to save.

The energy transfer was intense; each animal gave a small part of their life force to Eve in the few seconds before the first flaming arrow struck. The wildflowers began to wrap their stems around her limbs, as they, too, offered energy from the earth.

The first arrow landed, but it did not hit its mark. Instead, each arrow veered off course and landed a few feet in front of Eve and the animals blocking the view to the mainland. Eve began to glow; her hair crackled with the energy coursing through her. The emerald shift that clothed her seemed to ripple in a phantom breeze. Deathly paleness was washed away by the warm peaches and cream complexion that had once been the envy of many elvish maidens. The glowing ebbed and finally dissipated into the night. The gift had been given, the sacrifice made. Behind the curtain of purple flames, Eve opened her eyes.

SOPHIA APPROACHED THE east wing with a heavy heart; it had been decided that she would break the news to their charge. Knocking on the door, she was surprised that it opened almost instantly. Before her stood a young man of eighteen, his indigo eyes flashing with excitement and joy. Sophia had no time to ask what had made him so happy. He smiled broadly at her, his blond hair shining like spun gold.

"I must get to the island, Sophia!" he exclaimed, almost bouncing on the spot, his need to leave tangible. Sighing, Queen Sophia took his hand and tried to explain that, going to the island simply was not possible. The island was partly ablaze and not safe. Unfazed, he just smiled and assured her that everything was as it should be and he must go to the island right this moment.

"There is someone there who I must meet; it cannot wait," he urged, turning and hurrying down the hall towards the main staircase. Sighing, Sophia hurried as gracefully as she could manage after him.

It was fully dark now. The archers had cleared away, and all that could be seen of the ceremony was the dying violet flames reflecting on the still water of the lake. Taking no time to collect a boat from the small boathouse, the young man waded into the cool water and began to swim with strong strokes towards the island.

EVE LAY ON THE MOSS. Her mind was clear; she was completely aware of what had happened to her. She should be dead, and, yet, here she was on her funeral bed surrounded by woodland creatures and being warmed by the violet blaze a few feet away. Sitting up slowly, Eve was conscious of everything around her: the sound of the animals breathing, the lapping of the lake against the shore, and the crackling of the fire. It didn't stop there. She could hear the trees growing! The world around her was teeming with life, and she was a part of it all. There was something else. Looking around, she stared in wonder. The world was alight with colour; Eve could see the aura of every living thing. This was going to take some getting used to.

Standing, she stroked the ears of a doe. As she made the connection, she heard a voice.

We are glad to have helped you, Light Carrier.

Eve was used to this kind of telepathic communication with Sapphire, but this was the first time she had heard another animal 'speak' to her. Looking deep into the doe's eyes, she leant forward and kissed it between the ears.

"Thank you, thank you all. I am so grateful for your help," Eve replied, stroking the doe and smiling at all the gathered animals. Suddenly, the peaceful gathering was disturbed by splashing and then hissing as water droplets hit the dying flames. The animals scattered, leaving Eve to face whatever had joined them on the island.

The first thing Eve saw was the person's aura glowing green against the night. Instinctively, she knew that whoever it was meant her no harm. As the person came into view, Eve gasped. Indigo eyes gazed out of a handsome face. Blonde hair hung in wet waves just past his shoulders. He was tall and muscular. Without knowing how she got there, Eve found herself in his arms. After so many weeks of searching, they had finally found each other.

Eli held Eve tight against his chest. He knew without a doubt that this girl was his sister. He had dreamed of her; the chubby hand that had reached for him was hers. The King and Queen had said that he was found alone, and that she must have vanished with his parents, but the dreams had continued. Now he knew why.

"Eli, my brother, I have found you," Eve sobbed into his sodden shirt. Making soothing sounds and rubbing her back, Eli held her in his arms. Realising that they could not stay on this island all night - the guards would be looking for him, soon enough - Eli decided it was best if he swam back and obtained a boat. Eve insisted that she was fine to swim. Smiling, Eli gently pointed out that she was very recently back from the dead, and maybe a swim in the cold lake was not the best idea after such an experience.

Once back on the mainland, the siblings went directly to the Queen. Sophia was at a loss for words when Eli and Eve walked in hand in hand. This should not be possible; Eve was supposed to be dead. Taking a moment to compose herself, Queen Sophia ordered a clean gown and robe be brought for Eve and asked that Eli leave to change himself. They would continue their conversation in the drawing room with the King present. Eve changed in the Queen's dressing room. The gown was cream silk, it felt cool against her pale skin. Shivering slightly, she reached for the navy-blue robe and tied it at her waist. Looking at herself, Eve smiled. She was alive, and she had found Eli.

King Efrin was speechless. His mouth opened and closed several times before he gave up and ordered ale from the larder. Along with the ale, Jericho and Caleb burst into the room, nearly knocking the servant to the floor. Caleb had no trouble articulating how he felt at seeing Eve standing before him. He ran to her. Scooping her up in his arms, he held her close.

"I never expected to see you again. You are a marvel, Eve - a gift from the Goddess," he whispered to her as he looked into her eyes. Eve smiled up at Caleb, glad to have this second chance with him. Turning back to face the Royals, Eve cleared her throat.

"It is true that the demon murdered me. The pain was beyond belief, and I am sorry you all witnessed that." Looking at the shocked faces, Eve raised her hand to halt any interruptions and continued. "Yes, I was aware some of the time during that experience. I do not want to dwell on it; there are more important things I must discuss with my friends and my brother," she concluded, smiling at Eli and reaching for Caleb's hand. Jericho huffed from the corner, not comfortable with the amount of love being handed out. He would much rather get down to business, though his black eyes were glassy with unshed tears at the sight of his friend once again standing amongst them.

"How is it even possible that you are alive, Evangeline?" asked King Efrin, finally finding his voice. Smiling at the king, Eve explained that she did not know how she was now alive, just that she was pleased to be. This wasn't wholly true; she did know how, but it felt wrong somehow to explain her rebirth. It had been a deeply powerful and emotional experience, one she was not yet ready to share with anyone. Asking for permission to leave so she might talk with her friends, she curtsied to the Royals and thanked them for their hospitality and kindness. Eli lead everyone to his chambers in the east wing. He wanted to be as far from the servants as possible during this discussion, and he knew they were less likely to be overheard there.

Jericho paced while Eve explained the best she could what had happened to her. She once again omitted her rebirth, for the time being. They did not need to know, and Eve was not ready for the questions that would follow such a revelation. Eve seemed to be in a state of transformation; every now and again her eyes would flash a spectrum of colours. This did not go unnoticed by Jericho, though for the time being he held his tongue. There were more pressing matters to discuss. Eli stood by his sister holding her hand, Caleb couldn't take his eyes off their joined hands. His jealousy was ridiculous, and he knew it.

"I would like to introduce myself; I am Eli. It is a pleasure to meet you all, and I thank you for accompanying Eve on this journey." Eli bowed to Caleb and Jericho. Caleb didn't like him, but he knew his judgment was clouded, so kept his council.

There was so much to tell them all, so much to learn about her brother. Eve was overwhelmed, and would rather like a rest, but there was no time for that now. The darkness was readying to battle. She had seen so many awful things while her soul had been held in limbo, though the place itself had been beautiful, with clouds for as far as the eye could see, their frothy whiteness bathed in rainbow light. Eve had marvelled at such vibrancy. Surely, she was on her way to another realm where souls travel to find everlasting peace. Then, the clouds had parted, and she had seen the monsters devouring the chained prisoners. It was a sight that was burned into her memory. Blood had coated the walls and floor. The creatures disembowelled their prey while they still lived, and then they devoured their organs.

The one who had injured Caleb and Bobby was there - the one who had taken her. He had picked a girl similar-looking to herself.

The torture that demon put the girl through was horrific. A single tear rolled down Eve's cheek at the memory. There were other things she had seen, like the copper doors - the ones in her nightmare. Behind the doors lay a great power that must never be unleashed. It had to be destroyed.

Caleb needed to tell Eve now what he knew about the prophecy. Gazing at her, he could see that she was remembering something painful. However much it pained him to have to do this now, no more time could be wasted. Clearing his throat, he knelt before Eve and took her hand.

"Eve, I have something I have to tell you about the prophecy, and it cannot wait." Stroking her knuckles, Caleb went on, "I know where the aurora stone is, and, more importantly, I know where it must go to restore the balance and banish Nimayaorin the Defiler, forever."

Jericho was livid; Caleb had known all along where the stone was and hadn't said anything! In one bound, he was on top of Caleb. Raising a meaty fist, he was about to knock some sense into the witch when Eve spoke.

"Jericho, stop! Telling me before would not have made a difference. I was not able to fulfil the prophecy until now," she explained. Looking put out that he was not going to get to hit anyone, Jericho dropped Caleb and returned to pacing.

"What do you mean, it wouldn't have mattered?" Caleb asked, rubbing his shoulder. Sighing, Eve looked at her hands, knowing this was going to shock them all.

"Something needed to happen for me to be able to complete this quest. I had to unlock my gift that was bestowed upon me on my eighteenth birthday, and there was only one way for that to happen... I had to die and be reborn."

Chapter Fifteen

Unaware of Eve's resurrection, Nimayaorin had gathered his generals. The legions of darkness had assembled in the great hall. These creatures were the most feared; they were the fiercest warriors Nimayaorin had at his disposal. Grimmer was now among them, his ruby proudly on display, glowing blood red in the flickering candlelight.

"Generals, now we have celebrated the destruction of the light!" Nimayaorin paused to allow the great cheer to quieten before continuing. "Now it is time to finalise our assault on all of Orea and cast them into the void." Taking an onyx pointer from his robes, Nimayaorin laid its diamond tip over their first target. "Lervirion, take your thousand legions of dark murmurs and ghouls through the portal to this location. Once there, I want every feeble mind infected by the ghouls. Let madness reign in the homeland of magic. Clear Water Valley will be the location of our first strike. The witches are the easiest to control, and, with some persuasion, I believe they may join the legions of darkness and assist in the destruction of Orea."

And sweet revenge against the council members will finally be mine, Nimayaorin concluded, smiling at his secret thought. He cast his scarlet gaze around the gathering. No one dared meet his eyes directly. However, a murmur of agreement rippled through the generals. Satisfied, Nimayaorin continued to dictate the battle plan.

Grimmer stood and listened. This was his first time in such a meeting, and the sheer scale of the gathering was quite impressive. He watched as his master organised his legions with such cunning and ruthlessness that it was like a macabre dance of death, which Grimmer realised was quite an apt description. The Ruby on his chest glowed with scarlet fire, its presence a constant reminder that the light was destroyed, and by his own hand no less. his chest swelled with pride once more. The red head he had tortured at the feasting had been most enjoyable, no latent magic running through her sweet blood to taint his enjoyment, just the weak magic of a common witch, which had no effect. Saliva pooled in his mouth as hunger began to claw its way into his thoughts. Glancing around the room, Grimmer realised that sustenance was not going to be offered anytime soon. He forced the memories of the witch's organs, melting in his mouth, still warm with her blood, from his mind and tried to concentrate on what Nimayaorin was saying.

It was long after the moans and screams from the pits had quietened that the meeting finally concluded. The plan for conquering Orea was now complete. Nimayaorin stalked the halls leading back to his chambers. *My plan is guaranteed to succeed; now that the light is destroyed, there is nothing to stand in my way*, he thought while gliding, silent as a shadow along the arched corridors of his fortress. Without realising it, Nimayaorin found himself outside a chamber he never, ever entered. Tonight, however, there was no longer anything to fear from this room. His control over Orea was all but complete. The darkness had won; the contents of this room was no longer a weight hanging around his neck. Raising a clawed hand, he chanted the incantation to unlock the ivory door.

The chamber's black tapers were lit. The blue flames cast eerie shadows off the objects, throwing grotesque shapes onto the blood red walls. Gliding further into the room, Nimayaorin considered the contents. For many years, this room had been a form of torment for the great Nimayaorin, laying bare his true identity and how far he had truly fallen. Casting his scarlet gaze over the boxes of books and frames which held faces he was still not able to look at, he made his way to the larger traveling chest, its brass stud-work glinting in the candlelight. This one item was by far the most personal he owned, one he shied away from. Too many memories, and memories were dangerous. They led to feelings, and feelings were not something Nimayaorin wanted to ever experience again. So far into the darkness had he fallen, his depravity so completely absolute, that Nimayaorin no longer saw in colour. His sense of smell was dulled, and he felt no pain. Any sense of touch he had, had been lost long ago. This suited him just fine; feelings were for the weak.

Running a claw over the elvish-carved lid, Nimayaorin considered opening the chest and casting light on the contents that he had locked away so many years ago. Minutes passed. Nimayaorin didn't move, indecision flickering in his eyes. Letting out a screech of rage, the great dark tyrant snatched his claw back as though burned and fled the chamber, making sure to relock the cursed room and all its memories. Storming back to his chambers, Nimayaorin ordered for three slaves to be brought to his chamber. He paced while he waited. Surely a spot of torture, followed by glutting on the blood and warm entrails of his victims, would better his mood.

The screams that emanated from the grand chamber were those from nightmares; they continued for hours. Nimayaorin took his time with each victim. The first, a woman of vampire descent, fought back, which added an extra element to the proceedings and allowed the tyrant to exert himself more than usual. All traces of vulnerability he had felt earlier vanished once the vampire's heart was cupped in his hand. *I am invincible; nothing can stand against me now!* Nimayaorin thought, licking his claws clean of blood. The feasting had been enjoyable. Now fully sated and feeling more in control, he left the pile of skin and broken bones for his attendant to clean away. Stopping to pick up the three sets of eyeballs he had carefully removed from his victim's skulls, he took his gruesome trophies to his study. Nimayaorin placed the fleshy orbs into a crystal jar. Placing it along with the other jars he kept as a macabre record of his murders, he turned to his Book of Shadows and pored over the dark spells while awaiting news from General Lervirion.

LERVIRION AND HIS DARK legions entered Clear Water Valley. The ghouls were under orders to only infect the minds of the witches; there was to be no partaking of the flesh here. Hissing their displeasure, they turned to mist and targeted high-ranking witches throughout the Valley. The plan was to possess the leaders. The rest would follow them, just like sheep. Ghouls would never be suspected, as they were believed by all to have been eradicated in the last magical war.

Ghouls were known for their mind control, so it was imperative that not one of the foul creatures were discovered. It was hard to kill a ghoul but not impossible. Gliding like ghosts through the houses, the ghouls hunted for the most influential of the witches. They were able to do this using their ability to 'taste' someone's will. The stronger the 'taste', the more influence the creature had over its peers. For the ghouls, this was child's play. Within an hour, they had possessed every witch of influence in the realm.

Phase one was complete. Now the dark murmurs were on stand-by to help stir up the population and guide their thoughts towards the darkness. Chaos was about to have rein throughout Clear Water Valley.

SAPPHIRE WAS BECOMING concerned; she had not yet found a portal into Gloria. As she swooped down to catch a tree cat for her supper, she pondered once again over the intense pain she had felt not long ago. This had been followed by...nothing. This disturbed the great owl. A mental numbness was never a good sign when one mind was connected to another. It usually meant the connection had been permanently severed. Making the kill swift and clean, Sapphire delicately ate her meal. *Evangeline cannot be dead; the prophecy is tied to her life force. If she has indeed passed to the realm of the dead, then all of Orea shall perish in the void.*

After cleaning her beak and talons in a nearby brook, Sapphire once again took to the skies. The Olia landscape was indeed beautiful, though she hardly saw the russet treetops or the golden grass fields. *I must find another gate into Gloria, if only to have my darkest suspicions confirmed.*

Chapter Sixteen

The coven was restless. It had been weeks since the scouts had been sent to fetch fresh blood. Fights were beginning to break out over nothing; the atmosphere was heavy with tension. Winter was becoming bored. She wanted to go to the feeding grounds and have a dalliance with a handsome man and then sup his rich blood. Just thinking about it made heat pool low in her belly and made her gums itch. Though she only appeared to be a young woman of no more than twenty-one summers, Winter was, in fact, hundreds of years old. Rising from her four-poster bed, she moved languidly to her vanity. Her father would return shortly from his meeting with a small fraction of rebellious subjects, and on his return, he would no doubt expect an audience with her.

More suitors to parade in front of, I shouldn't wonder, she thought while picking a lipstick from her new makeup box. Such treasures she had gathered since her people discovered the other world. Settling on a shimmery pink, Winter carefully applied it to her full lips. The colour worked perfectly with her chestnut waves and ice blue eyes; Ariana was going to be so envious of her new look. Getting up, Winter picked up the gift she had for her best friend and headed out of her room.

"Where are you going, Your Highness?" inquired a silky voice that set Winter's teeth on edge.

"Nowhere that concerns you, Archie," she spat back, hoping it would deter him from following her. Sadly, it seemed to amuse him.

"Come now, Your Highness, I am only concerned for your well-being, as any man who cares for you should be," Archie crooned. Winter resisted the urge to bare her fangs. She had learned that this seemed to excite him, which was the very last thing she wanted. Winter scowled at him. Archie Van Grüber was becoming a problem, one she hoped her father would deal with on his return. Picking up her pace, she rushed along the corridor with a love-sick Archie hot on her heels.

"How did you manage to get into my wing of the castle, Archie? You know full well, no would-be suitor's - or in your case, stalkers - are allowed down here."

Looking very pleased with himself, Archie explained how he had convinced the guards they were now an item. Well, that was the last straw! Stopping abruptly, Winter spun to face the smirking vampire. Everything about him screamed narcissistic. All vampires were beautiful, it was how they lured in their prey. However, Archie was overkill: slicked back black hair that shone with oil, a dinner suit, spats, and a very thin, perfectly oiled goatee.

Who dresses like that?! Winter thought to herself as she took in his appearance. Looking directly into his eyes, she suddenly had an idea. Stepping closer to him, Winter gave her thick eyelashes a flutter.

"Well, seeing as you are so resourceful, maybe I should give you another chance, hmm?" Winter almost gagged on the words as she stared, in what she hoped was an adoring fashion, into his eyes. Clearly, he was as gullible as he was irritating. Archie went into full on smoulder. The over-confident fool reached out and stroked her face. It took all of her willpower not to break his arm clean off.

"I knew you were attracted to me. You play hard to get, but I knew you burned for me," he boasted, still stroking her jaw. Taking his hand gently in hers, which neatly stopped the creep from touching her face, Winter arranged to meet him later that night in the courtyard for a romantic stroll. Archie readily agreed. Lifting her hand to his lips, he kissed it.

"Until later, Princess," he smouldered.

"Yes, until later. I must get on now, Archie; I am meeting Ariana, and I am already late." Winter smiled, reclaiming her hand, and discreetly wiped the wetness from his kiss onto her leather pants. Taking this break in physical contact as her chance to leave, Winter turned and headed along the corridor. She didn't look back. *When I find out which of the guards believed that oily creep, they will regret the day they were turned!* she thought.

Ariana's face was a picture. She was practically drooling over the lip gloss and compact mirror Winter had gifted her. Winter hoped it made up for her not being able to cross into the other world. It was hard for Winter knowing what had really happened that night in the human world. What she did know was that Ariana was innocent. They had only spoken of it once, just after it had happened, and that was when Ariana begged her best friend to never disclose what truly happened. It would bring shame to the whole coven, rather than just the House of Dai. Reluctantly, Winter had agreed.

Ariana Dai had been taken before the high council and the King, found guilty, and branded across her back. To this day, Winter could still smell the burning flesh and hear her best friend's screams. She had stood with the rest of the coven and watched the punishment. Thanks to Vampire healing abilities, Ariana had healed well, though with the brand being bewitched, she still bore the scar of the bewitched branding. The image of the rising sun covered the top half of her back for all eternity.

"So, why were you so late? Surely it didn't take that long to put on your makeup," Ariana teased, poking her friend in the ribs. Winter explained with much eye rolling about Archie and his antics. "Seriously, the guy has some serious guts to pull a stunt like that."

"No, Ariana, he is seriously stupid to pull a stunt like that; my father will not be pleased," Winter fumed while her oldest friend merely laughed. "And did you just refer to a vampire as a guy?" Winter teased her friend. She was amazed at how easily the coven had picked up the casual way in which the human creatures spoke. It was so much more fluid than the way they had all been taught.

The girls chatted for hours, comfortable in the plush recliners, glasses of red wine in hand.

The atmosphere changed rapidly when one of the royal scouts appeared on the threshold.

"The King has returned! All of you make haste to your posts! Has anyone seen the Princess?" he shouted into the crowd, though there was no need, as everyone was silent. Suddenly the room was a hubbub of activity, as vampires scrambled to return to their duties. Winter sighed. It was now her duty to go and greet her father at the gate and offer him a goblet of blood. The custom was so outdated. She had asked on many occasions why they must continue it. Her father had looked aghast and explained that to her while it may be outdated, to a two-thousand-year-old vampire, it was practically modern!

King Fredrick was tired. It had been a very tiring few weeks. The civil war had broken out over Coven supremacy, of all things, and it was a bloody mess. Many lives had been permanently ended. He stroked his trimmed beard, a relic from his human life. If he chose to shave it, it would, in a matter of hours, grow back to the exact length and style it had been when he was turned. Fredrick often counted his lucky stars that he had trimmed it the day he had become a vampire. His horse snorted with impatience. The beast was no doubt as road-weary as he was.

"Soon, Ulysses. We must uphold tradition, much to my daughter's disgust," he chuckled while patting his grey stallion's neck. After another few minutes, Winter appeared from the grand front door and met him and his warriors. Just to rile her, he often referred to his warriors as 'knights.' She looked just as beautiful as she had the day he left, though this should come as no great surprise to a vampire. Fredrick was always amazed by his daughter's beauty. It was her smart mouth that hindered her marriage prospects. The thought pained him. He wanted her to be settled, and he needed her to ready herself to undertake Royal duties.

"Father, how glad I am to see you home and well. Here is the blood, the elixir which sustains us," Winter said. She had been saying the same line for a hundred and forty-two years since her mother died. Winter quickly shook the image of her mother's beautiful face from her mind.

Smiling down at his daughter, Fredrick took the goblet and drank deeply. The rich, velvety blood was welcome after so many hours with only wine to sustain him. Many of the myths surrounding Vampires in the other world were simply fabrications, though drinking blood and not being able to consume food were two that held true. Reaching for his kerchief, he dabbed at his lips and returned the cup to his daughter.

"How wonderful it is to be home and to see you well, my daughter," he replied in a formal greeting. Fredrick dismounted Ulysses in one fluid movement and casually handed the reins to a stable hand, instructing that he was to have an apple and a bucket of oats after his rub down. Turning back to his daughter, Fredrick offered his arm. Smiling up at her father's kind face, Winter slipped her arm through his, and they made their way back into the castle.

"How was your trip, Father? I hope all is well and the fighting will now stop."

Looking at Winter, his heart swelled with pride. *So, she is interested in the governing of the realm*, he thought as they walked towards his chambers. *Maybe she shall surprise me and pick a husband.* Feeling foolish for getting ahead of himself and zoning out of the conversation, Fredrick returned his wandering mind to his daughter.

"I am sorry, Sweetheart; I missed what you were saying. Too many conflicting thoughts are taking up room in this old head of mine," he said, smiling down at her. Winter smiled. She knew her father had much on his mind, and so she would not be unreasonable about his lapse in concentration.

"It's fine, Father. It wasn't anything that can't wait. Once you have had supper - or even tomorrow - once you have rested, I can tell you then." Kissing his dusty cheek, Winter let go of his arm and headed toward the corridor that lead to her wing. When she reached the door, she called to her father, "I will see you at dinner. Ariana needs my help with a project, and I know how much you need a rest."

Nodding to her, Fredrick waited for her to go before he continued at a slower pace towards his chambers. Though he was well enough, he was tired after such a long ride and felt the need for a long bath and maybe a nap before supper. Upon reaching his chambers, Fredrick walked to his desk, and, as was his ritual, he picked up the ornate gold frame and gazed at the image of his beloved late wife, Helen. How beautiful she had been. He missed her so much. Just as he had when Helen had graced these chambers, he repeated the words he had said to her a hundred times: "Hello my love, I have returned to you unscathed, and, well, I have missed you every second since we parted. Now that I am home, I feel whole once more." Raising the image of Helen to his lips, Fredrick kissed the cold glass and sighed. The last part of his homecoming always felt hollow these days; he did not feel complete returning when his beloved wife was no longer here to greet him. Every homecoming was the same. How happy he was to see his daughter - who had her mother's face, apart from her eyes. No one knew why her eyes were ice blue. All vampires had the same colour eyes, a rich burgundy. When viewed up close, any beholder could clearly see the flecks of bright red within the irises.

Replacing the photo frame, Fredrick picked up the pile of missives, which were neatly bound with a golden ribbon, and dropped down into his comfortable armchair. Kicking off his riding boots, he untiled the ribbon and flicked through the notes, party invites, a petition for marriage, and a dispute over payment for goods. Content that he was not going to find anything that could not wait until tomorrow, he put the pile on the coffee table and headed to his wet room for a long soak in his rather large bath.

Winter found Ariana waiting outside the entrance to her wing of the castle. Smiling at her friend, she quickened her pace. Ariana didn't return her smile as expected. In fact, she was crying. Concern suddenly filled Winter's heart. She hurried the last few feet between them.

"What's wrong, Ana?" she asked, reaching for her hand.

"Nothing. It's nothing," Ariana mumbled, wiping her eyes and smudging her mascara. It didn't look like 'nothing' to Winter. However, there was no point in trying to find out what had happened; Ana would tell her when she was ready.

"Well, I am ready when you feel like talking. In the meantime, we need to sort your face. You have mascara all over the place," she said, smiling and pulling Ariana along with her. They half ran to her bedroom where they spent the next hour giving each other makeovers and doing impersonations of Dame Higshot, their old-school mistress.

"The others are blaming me for the lack of raids," Ariana suddenly blurted out. Winter was horrified. That was in no way true, and every vampire in the castle - indeed, within the city walls - knew that the reason the raids had stopped was due to her father being away dealing with the civil unrest. *How dare they blame Ariana*!

"Nonsense! They know full well why, and they should not be blaming you for anything!" Winter replied as anger flashed in her eyes. Feeling worried her friend would make things worse, Ariana begged her not to tell her father.

"We both know why they do it, and they shall continue to do so. It was silly of me to get upset. I have made my bed, and now I must lie in it," Ariana replied.

Sighing, Winter promised. This whole situation had to end, and one way or another she was going to make it happen. Her father needed to know that his subjects did not always behave in the way he expected. Indeed, under her rule - in his absence - they seemed to do exactly as they damn well pleased.

"I will speak to my father, but I will not mention the incident you have confessed to me. There is more than one way to get the right result for this," Winter assured her friend, determination radiating from every pore. Right then, Ariana could see the great Queen Winter would one day become.

Chapter Seventeen

Eve and her companions travelled as far and as fast as their mounts could accommodate. Being from the Royal stable, the horses were incredibly quick. They were almost at the portal that would allow them to exit Gloria when, finally, they began to slow down.

"I think it's time for a break. The horses are beginning to tire, and we have been in the saddle all day. We should stretch our legs and have a moment to gather our thoughts before we head through the portal," Jericho said as the group slowed and finally stopped. Eve slid from Bobby's back and promptly landed on her backside.

"Ooof!" she huffed, glad it was only her pride that was bruised, though by the feel of her bottom, she could be wrong. Deciding she would wait until feeling returned to her legs before trying to move, Eve lay back on the clover and stared up at the late afternoon sky. It had been such an eventful few days; she could still hardly believe that they had found Eli. Turning her head, she saw her twin talking with Caleb. They seemed to be getting along fine.

"Are you alright, Eve? Would you like some help moving further into the field?" asked Jericho, his shadow shielding her eyes from the sun. Smiling at him, Eve explained that helping her would require her being carried, as her legs felt like they were made of custard root pulp.

"Well, allow me to assist you," he said, laughing as he bent down and gently scooped her up in his arms. After walking a few meters into the lush clover covered field, Jericho deposited a grateful Eve with their companions on a blanket.

"Here, you must be hungry and thirsty. I know I am!" Caleb said cheerfully as he handed her a lump of fruitcake and a flask of water. Laughing, Eve took the offering; she was, indeed, extremely hungry. Bobby was keeping the palace horses in check a little further into the field. How idyllic this would have all been if the fate of Orea didn't weigh so heavily on her shoulders.

"What are you thinking about, dear sister? I can feel your worry," Eli said as he moved to her side. Taking her hand, he rubbed the skin on her knuckles in a soothing manner. Eve sighed. She really didn't know where to begin; it was all too difficult to explain. Looking at her twin, she saw the concern on his handsome face, and it pained her that she should be the cause of such a look.

"Do not worry yourself, dear brother. I am just road weary. I shall feel more like myself once I have finished my snack and regained feeling in my legs," she replied. Knowing there was far more to the pensive look and the deepening colour of her chameleon irises, Eli gave a nod and the twins sat in a comfortable silence.

"Sorry everyone, but we should be moving on now," Jericho announced as he walked towards the group leading the horses. Bobby, of course, made his own way. Eve stirred; she hadn't meant to fall asleep. Shortly after Eli had joined her, Caleb had offered to help her with the aches she had from the hard ride. He had cast a healing spell over her. It had been exactly what she needed. She hadn't been aware of how sore she truly was until the pain was completely gone. Jumping to her feet, pleased that she was able to do so, she headed for Bobby, and, with a boost from Caleb, made herself comfortable on his back.

"We need to follow this road until we reach the black hills," Caleb explained while pointing to the charcoal-coloured mounds on the horizon. "We will make it within four hours if we ride like the wind," Jericho added, looking at each member of the group in turn.

"Caleb, you stay with Eve. I shall ride at the rear with Eli." They set off at a rolling canter, their eyes fixed on the black hills.

TWILIGHT HAD ARRIVED as the group approached the foot of the black hills. Not wanting to rest for a second, Caleb cast another healing spell, only this time over everyone - including the horses. Passing around a flask of water, they walked their horses to a cluster of apple trees and tied them loosely. They would not be able to accompany them on the next leg of the journey. Bobby followed them as they made their way around the foot of the hill. After about half a mile, Caleb stopped, pointing ahead of them to the top of a large boulder of black rock.

"Up there; that is where the gate is," he said

"Wonderful. How are we going to get up there? I really don't feel like scaling a boulder. Even though I feel just fine, my memory is very aware of the hardship my body has been through today," groaned Eli. Everyone turned in shock. It was Jericho that reminded everyone that Eli, though clearly a strong young man, had grown up in a palace and was not as hardened to the road as the rest of them.

"We have to, so I suggest that Jericho climbs up first, as he is the most agile and the strongest. He can help pull the others up with the help of Bobby... if he is willing?" Suggested Eve. Turning to look at the beautiful unicorn, she felt a connection flare between them. *Yes, I will help you, Light Carrier, in any way I can.* His voice was pure and his aura glowed a brilliant white. "Thank you, dear Bobby. You are, indeed, a most noble being," Eve replied aloud.

One by one, they followed Jericho up onto the boulder. Eve requested to go last so she could say goodbye to Bobby. Opening the connection between them, she thanked him for his help and his bravery.

You are most welcome, Light Carrier. If you should need me, call my true name within your mind, and I shall find you. Honoured that such a pure creature should offer yet more help, Eve reached out and stroked his soft nose.

Thank you. I shall be forever in your debt, but, Bobby, I do not know your true name, she replied.

My true name is Shakti; it means 'divine' in the language of my race, Bobby answered, his eyes gleaming. Eve thought it one of the most beautiful names she had ever heard, also the most befitting. Leaning forward, Eve placed a kiss on his nose in farewell and then vaulted onto his silky back, ready to be lifted onto the boulder by Jericho.

Bobby looked up at the group and dropped into a bow. Once he had risen, they each bowed in return and called out farewell. Turning to the portal, each member of the party wondered what was waiting for them on the other side.

"I shall go first this time," Jericho said, eyeballing Eve. "Eli, you shall follow, then Eve and Caleb, you bring up the rear." Everyone agreed to this, and one by one they crossed the celestial border to land feet first in another place that was certain to hold another set of challenges.

Thankfully, nothing was lying in wait for them immediately on the other side of the gate. Where they were, no one was sure. Eve consulted the map she had, but, according to it, they were still in Gloria, because the black hills were now just behind them. She was just about to suggest taking a look around when she heard the most welcome voice enter her mind.

Thank the Goddess you are alive, Dear one. Though, you are much changed. Sapphire's soothing voice sounded full of joy and relief. Eve was so pleased to hear from her that she started to rush. Her relief was evident as she lost herself in overflowing emotions. Thankfully, Sapphire managed to glean from the muddled message that they were standing at the foot of some black hills. Asking Eve to wait, Sapphire circled until she saw, far off in the distance, the low black mounds that must be the hills. Flying higher, she caught herself in the air currents and sped towards her friend.

Soon enough, Jericho was pointing at an ever-growing speck in the sky. Sapphire landed a few metres away from the group, doing her best not to stir up too much of the black dust that covered the ground. Eve raced over to her friend. Throwing her arms around the great owl's neck, she held on and finally relaxed. After introducing Eli, she explained what had happened during their enforced separation. Sapphire listened, and although she knew Eve was not telling her the full story, she was aware that Eve had activated her powers, and only now was she truly ready to complete her quest.

"We need to enter the realm of Vampires. Do you know how far we are from the border, Sapphire?" asked Jericho, bowing in respect. He, too, was grateful for her safe reappearance. Sapphire turned to Eve to indicate that she was relaying the answer. After a few moments, Eve turned to the group looking slightly stunned.

"We are very near the border;" Eve replied, relaying Sapphire's words.

"How close is close?" asked Caleb while keeping a wary eye on the Protector. He still did not like flying and was hoping he would not have to ride again anytime soon.

"We have to enter a cave that is a mile from here. From there, we must travel by river to Mieron." Eve clarified, trying not to smirk at the fearful expression Caleb kept throwing Sapphire.

"Then there is no time to lose. Come on, we should get moving," Jericho announced while picking up his pack. Sapphire gently plucked the pack from his hands and let out a low hoot. Understanding, he collected the group's packs except Eve's and handed them to the protector. "Sapphire will fly alongside us, as she is now able to accompany us once more," Eve relayed as they began the mile walk to the mouth of the cave.

Eli had remained quiet through the whole exchange. He had never been outside the border of Gloria, and now he had passed through a portal and was in the company of a giant owl. It was an awful lot to take in; his senses were reeling. Catching up with his sister, he asked her about Sapphire and how trustworthy she was. Understanding his concern, though hurt that he felt the need to question her, Eve explained that Sapphire was a dear friend, and that he would have to trust her. Accepting what he was told, Eli then continued to ponder his next dilemma: when to explain his extra ability to the group. The opportunity came sooner than he had anticipated.

Their group arrived at the mouth of the cave. It reminded Jericho of a fanged mountain cat with its mighty jaws open, ready to devour its prey. Caleb created an orb of blue fire that bobbed in the air ahead of them, lighting the way. Eli was horrified; the cave was dank, dark, and full of dirt and puddles. His shoes and the bottoms of his trousers were soon splattered with mud and Goddess knew what else. Glancing at his two male companions, he was shocked to see that they didn't bat an eyelid at the mucky conditions. Indeed, even his sister was unfazed by it. Feeling foolish, Eli continued to walk while trying hard to be more manly and world-wise than he was. Adventures, it turned out, were not as glamorous as the books that he had whiled away his afternoons reading had led him to believe.

The cave was massive, so Sapphire had no trouble flying through, and due to her excellent sight, she flew ahead of the group and the fire to check for hidden dangers. Sometime later, they all emerged unscathed a few metres from the banks of a great river. Taking time to look for some sort of jetty that might hold simple boats for them to use, it soon became clear that whatever method had once been used to travel the waters was long gone. This was confirmed when Sapphire performed an aerial scout and came back with a large part of a broken hull.

"Well, I guess we can either swim or fly," Jericho concluded. Looking at Eve, he asked her if Sapphire would mind very much making a couple of trips to the border, given she was only able to carry two people at a time.

Eve was in silent conversation with Sapphire when Caleb stepped forward, and with a sigh of resignation blurted out, "I can fly, so there is no need for her to come back for me."

The silence that followed that statement was deafening. Four sets of shocked eyes were trained on his red face. He had not kept it a secret to save from doing it. In fact, it wasn't until he was about to leave the Royal household after Eve's death that he realised that the ability to connect with the ley lines was active once more.

"I'm sorry, Mr. Aerophobia. I swear you just said you could fly, which of course can't be correct. I have seen the impressive shade of green you turn at the very thought of sitting astride a Protector!" Jericho scoffed. Right on cue, Caleb's face turned a sickly green tinge.

"I know, and until very recently I had lost the ability. Now, however, I am confident that I am able to once again travel by ley lines, so that is one less body for Sapphire to carry. I am able to travel extremely fast and, if need be, carry another," he explained, all the time looking at Eve. Would she think he was lying? The look on her face told him that she was shocked but nothing more.

Just as Eve was about to make a move to climb onto Sapphire so they could begin the journey to Mieron, Eli piped up.

"There is no need to come back for me, either."

"What? But you need to come! And Caleb hasn't flown for a long time going by what he is saying, so I think it unfair to expect him to carry you," Eve said doubtfully.

"No, I meant I can make my own way," Eli continued, looking anywhere but into his sister's eyes.

"Time is getting away from us, Eli. Spit it out or climb aboard Sapphire. We need to get moving," Jericho growled. He had no time for dramatics. He had had his fill of such things of late.

"What do you mean, brother?" Eve encouraged, seeing how pale Eli had turned at the sound of Jericho growling.

"I mean; I can alter my shape at will."

"I don't fully under..." Eve never finished that sentence, as before her eyes her blond twin slowly morphed into a blue jay.

You see, Sister, I am able to change my body into any living creature with a beating heart.

Eve was completely lost for words, the mental connection with her brother was the strongest she had ever felt, which, had she thought about it, would have made sense. They were twins after all.

"Right...Jericho, you and I shall ride with Sapphire, and the others shall make their own way."

"As you say, Eve, though how will we contact Eli should we be separated?" Jericho asked, eyeing the slightly larger than normal blue jay.

"I can hear him the same way I can hear Sapphire, so we shall be in contact. Caleb can use his magic to find us if we are separated. We should get moving; I have a feeling we are not alone," she answered while scanning their surroundings for watchful eyes.

Casting his sharp eyes into the mouth of the cave, Jericho caught site of a small leathery creature carrying a crossbow. Quick as a flash, he threw one of his poison-tipped knives at the creature. Eve followed the knife and saw the aura of whatever lay in wait; it was a dirty-brown colour that was shot through with red and black streaks. The enemy must be watching the portals; her survival would soon be known.

Chapter Eighteen

Jericho hit his mark. The creature cried out in pain. Eli was about to congratulate the Miscurt on his excellent shot when an orange light appeared next to the creature, illuminating its leathery body. Jericho's knife was embedded deep in its chest. Realising that the creature was about to escape, Caleb threw a paralysis hex at it, but it was too late. The creature pitched forward through the orange portal and vanished.

"Damn!" exclaimed Caleb, running his hands through his hair.

"We need to move; the creature may already be dead, but it has one of my knives in its chest, which means our location will soon be known," Jericho added pulling his ears.

"What's more, if the creature isn't dead, then the darkness will know that Eve is still alive!" Caleb concluded, casting a worried glance at Eve. Not wanting to wait around for the creatures Eve knew would come, she ran up Sapphire's wing and beckoned for Jericho. Within moments, Sapphire was airborne along with Eli in his bird form, and there was a whoosh as Caleb shot skywards. Eve watched him vanish into a bright yellow ley line.

"Let's go. Caleb will meet us there," Eve said as she gripped handfuls of snow white feathers.

MOROAK STAGGERED FROM the portal room. The filthy Miscurts knife was stuck through his heart. He needed to reach his master or, failing that, another high-ranking Demon. The news he carried was not going to be well received. However, he must pass it on before the poison killed him. Leaning against the wall, Moroak made his slow painful way along the corridor. His joints were beginning to seize and his tongue was burning. Soon it would be too painful to speak. Falling to the floor, he let out a cry of pain, hoping someone would find him so he could unload his burden and beg them to snap his neck and end the pain.

Grimmer's apprentice, Tor, found Moroak moments from death. He listened, horrified at the news and had him repeat it twice just to be sure. Once sure he had heard correctly, he killed Moroak and carried his body to his Master.

Nimayaorin roared at the news. Reaching out, he pulled the knife from Moroak's chest. Black tar-like blood oozed from the wound. He paced, holding the knife aloft. His manic crimson eyes flashed in the candlelight.

"So, the girl lives. How is this possible? I saw her die!" Nimayaorin screamed. Pacing to his Orb of revelation, he demanded it show him the elf girl. He wished to see her in the flesh before he accepted this news. The orb did not show what he commanded. This had never happened before. Nimayaorin considered the possibility that Moroak was, indeed, mistaken. *Unless...no...* He stopped the thought in its tracks. If Eve still lived, it meant she had returned from the dead, and that would be catastrophic. "Tor, I want you to go to the border of Merion. Take the remaining ghouls, and have them infect the Vampires. I shall create discord within the Kings household. This shall keep our adversaries occupied until the legions arrive and finish her once and for all!"

Nodding, Tor took the body and hurried from the room. After disposing of Moroak, he gathered the ghouls. There were only two dozen in total, but that would be enough to cause trouble in the Coven of the Blood Moon. Feeling proud that he had been given such an important task, Tor put on his armour and led the ghouls to the portal room. He coveted Grimmer's ruby, and hoped that, with success, he too would be as richly rewarded.

They arrived a mile from the castle. Tor was not able to go any closer, so he ordered the ghouls to go forth and create havoc; no one was to be eaten. Once the deed was done, they were to get a possessed Vampire to lower the flag as a signal.

Winter was making the final touches to her hair. Her fake date was in an hour, and she still had to tell her father and report the guards. It was easy enough to discover their identities. The idiots had been heard taking bets on whether or not Archie would make it into her bed. She wondered how amusing their bet would be when they found themselves in the dungeons for endangering the Princess of the Coven and, not to mention, for taking a bribe.

Walking to her father's chambers, Winter cast her gaze to the gardens beyond the large windows. It was getting darker, the twilight giving way to the inky blue of night. Soon the stars would be out, and then Winter would climb onto the roof and use her new telescope to view the stars. It was one of her favourite places. Smiling at the thought of star gazing later, she quickened her pace, wanting to get this business with Archie sorted, once and for all.

The ghouls ghosted through the corridors, picking those of rank or those who looked ready to rip someone's head off. How fortuitous that the vampires were already wound up due to a lack of fresh blood. This was going to be even more enjoyable than they first thought. Once each one had picked a host, all hell broke loose. Jörg, the ghoul who had been picked to signal Tor, glided through the upper floors. Finally, she found the flagpole cables, and slowly she lowered the flag. Satisfied that her task was complete, Jörg set off in search of a Vampire to possess, and she knew exactly who she wanted.

Winter was correct in her assumptions that her father would be extremely angry. The two guards were stripped of rank and thrown into the dungeon. He also agreed to meet with Archie in her place and make it very clear that any chance he may have had with his only daughter was now ashes, which is what he would become if he ever touched her again. Pleased that her problem was about to be solved, Winter kissed her father and hurried off to the tower. It was time for some star gazing.

The tower was Winter's special place. It contained all her treasures. Opening the door, she lit the candles. She had requested that this place was not modernised. The human's technology was wonderful, but the tower was her place and the candlelight, in her opinion, made it all the more romantic. Walking to her mother's old dressing table, Winter opened the drawer and withdrew a velvet box; inside was a stone about the size of a duck egg. Its many facets threw colours around its interior whenever light touched it. It was so very beautiful. Her father had given it to her mother many years ago, and now it was hers. For her last birthday, she had commissioned the Royal jeweller to make a chain and cage for it so she could wear it at the grand balls. Winter opened the cage and placed the stone inside. The thick rope of silver felt cool against her throat. Making her way to the trap door in the ceiling that would take her to the roof and her beloved telescope, she glanced at herself in the mirror. The stone shone with otherworldly light. Pleased to have something of her mother's so close to her heart, Winter climbed up and out into the clear black night.

Jörg found her target. He was in the ornamental gardens, giving a younger vampire a piece of his mind. This amused the ghoul. She could have a lot of fun with this, and as luck would have it, the young Vampire had his head bowed, so he did not witness when Jörg took possession of the coven's King.

FIGHTS WERE BREAKING out all over the castle when Winter returned around dawn. She had been so far away from the main building that she hadn't heard anything. It was only once she entered the lower corridor that she heard the sounds of fighting vampires and smashing china. She grabbed her grey hoodie and zipped it over her necklace; she had forgotten to remove it in her haste to find Ariana and tell her all about the shooting stars she had seen. All of that was forgotten as she rushed along her wing and out into the grand entrance hall. Immediately, she had to duck as one of the large copper urns that stood on either side of the front doors was launched across the hall. Its intended target sprang up onto the banister of the grand staircase and was busy reaching for the claymore that was mounted on the wall just above his head.

She was not interested in hanging around to find out the cause of the disagreement – heck, the guy had a claymore! Winter ran down the main hallway, dodging fights and projectiles as she went. She reached the great hall and was shocked by what she found there. It had turned into an arena. However, what was even more disturbing was that her father was in the middle of a fight with two other Vampires!

This is not happening. I am asleep... this is a nightmare, Winter thought as she pinched her arm and opened and closed her eyes, hoping that the reality would change back to how things should be. Even without opening her eyes, after the second try, she knew she wasn't asleep. It had been worth a try. Sighing, Winter decided to find a sane vampire and find out what had caused the sudden madness within the coven.

Thankfully it didn't take long. Winter found Ariana and Grace, one of her many cousins, hiding in the laundry. Grace had a cut cheek that was half way to being healed, and Ariana was repositioning her dislocated shoulder. Winter grimaced at the sickening crunch of the joint returning to its natural position.

"What is going on up there? It was like a madness suddenly overcame some of the nobles and guards!" cried Ariana as she stroked Grace's hair.

"I have no idea. I went to see my father, but he was...not himself," Winter finished in a mumble, not wanting to remember the snarling face and bared fangs. *How upset he will be when he comes to his senses,* she lamented. Deciding it was, at this time, too dangerous for them to wander the castle, they moved into one of the storerooms and made themselves comfortable.

"At least from here, we can see the Jetty. Maybe if someone visits we can ask for help?" Mumbled Grace, ashen-faced. Trying to swallow down her ire at the young girl, Winter didn't comment. She was a princess, and there was no way she was asking any outsider for help. Her father could not be seen as he was right now. The shame it would bring him and his house, once he returned to himself, would be too great. *No, we shall sit and wait for this storm to pass us over,* she thought, though, in her heart, she knew it wasn't going to be that simple.

THE FLIGHT TO THE BORDER took all night. Dawn was just breaking as they landed at the edge of a great lake. This was not by choice; they seemed unable to fly across it.

"More witchcraft," grumbled Jericho as Sapphire glided to a perfect landing. Caleb and Eli were already on the ground.

"It seems like we have to cross the traditional way," said Caleb as he looked at the jetty.

"Trouble is, I don't see any boats," piped up Eli, who had returned to his natural state and was, thankfully, fully clothed, much to Eve's relief.

"When I said the 'old-fashioned' way, I meant ancient," Caleb explained while walking purposefully along the jetty. Not sure what he meant, but having no other option, they followed him as far as where the jetty met then bank.

"Jericho, could I borrow a knife, please?" he called while digging about in his pockets. Looking at the others, Jericho shrugged and walked along the old planks to where Caleb stood and handed him his gutting knife. To Eve's utter horror, Caleb then quickly slashed his palm with the razor-sharp blade and placed four silver coins into his bloody grip.

"Ferryman, Ferryman, we wish to cross the Lake.
We have our payment; blood money is all you will take.
Ferryman, Ferryman, four await your vessel.
We are aware we cross at our peril,
To sail on the lake of the dead."

The silence that followed was absolute; not even the water moved. Then, before them materialised a great vessel. Its mast was high, its sails grey and ripped. It was impossible for them to have caught a breeze, yet the boat moved through the oily water at speed. Once at the jetty, Eve was aghast by what she saw: a sailboat made entirely of creature's bones. She could hear their screams. Moaning, she covered her ears and turned to bury her face in Sapphire's breast.

You can hear the souls of the ones who did not pay the Ferryman, dear one, Sapphire explained, their connection flaring.

But they did pay, Sapphire. They paid with their lives! I don't want to get on the boat. There has to be another way, Eve replied as silent tears coursed down her cheeks.

Have courage dear one, you will not be alone, and though I once again cannot join you, this time our connection shall not falter, crooned the protector. Taking comfort and strength from her words, Eve wiped away her tears, picked up her bag, and walked towards the nightmare that was the ferry.

"You have summoned me, Boy. Payment I require, and payment I shall have, be it blood, money or your bones. I shall have payment before you step aboard this vessel." The Ferryman's voice reached them on the jetty, but they could not see him.

"We are a company of four, Ferryman, so four bloodied silver yits we have brought for payment," Caleb replied to the sinister bodiless voice. He opened his hand to display the blood-soaked coins.

Eve covered her mouth to stop the scream that almost escaped her. Out of thin air, a skeletal hand appeared; tattered ribbons of grey flesh hung loosely from the appendage. Following the hand up the owner's arm, she was relieved to see that a dark cowl covered the creature's body and face, if indeed it had a face. Eve could not detect an aura at all. The gaping black opening of the cowl seemed to be just that, pitch black and empty. This sent chills down her spine. The ferryman was not of this world.

Taking the coins, the ferryman waved his arm, and a gangplank appeared.

"Climb aboard, though remember, it is at your own risk that you sail these waters. If you wish to live, do not be led," the creature said as he proceeded the group on board. Looking at Caleb, Eve reached for his hand, only to remember that he had hurt himself to make the payment.

"It's fine, Eve. I have already healed the wound," he assured her, showing his palm as proof. Taking his hand, she boarded the ship along with the others. Looking about, she saw that there were no seats of any kind, and the floor was filthy.

"How long will it take to make the crossing?" she asked Caleb just to fill the eerie silence.

"It takes as long as it takes, Light Carrier. It really depends on each of you," came the Ferryman's reply from directly behind her. Yelping, Eve scrambled away and turned to face him. "Yes, I know who and what you are, Evangeline. Though you need not fear me, I take no sides but my own," he said before heading for the wheel.

"What does he mean, Caleb, *it depends on us*?" Eve squeaked. She clutched his arm in a vice grip, which made Caleb wince.

"He means that the lake can play tricks on the mind. If we are distracted by its trickery, time becomes warped for us here, like a kind of limbo, but in actual fact, it carries on as normal everywhere else. I have heard tales of people being lost on this lake for years." Seeing the look of complete horror on her beautiful face, Caleb realised far too late that this could possibly have been the most stupid thing he could have said. *I am a moron! Goddess forgive me*, he thought while mentally kicking himself. Taking her in his arms, he held his love while humming a song, hoping to soothe her anxiety and help her forget his stupid comment.

Chapter Nineteen

The boat barely stirred the waters as it carried the foursome across the lake. Eve tested her connection with Sapphire and was pleased to find that it was still active. Caleb held on to her, humming a sweet song, which helped to calm her. He also kept her away from the sides, though she didn't know why. Eve didn't care. The last thing she wanted to see was the murky waters of this lake, and she definitely didn't want to be close enough to see the grain in the bones that made up the ship.

Eli and Jericho were standing together by the mast. Neither had anything to say. Eli glanced at the Miscurt every so often, only to find that his stance and expression had not changed. Sighing, he moved to the port side and looked out at the mist that hung like cobwebs over the grey waters. After a few moments, Eli noticed a person swimming in the lake beside the boat, then another. Leaning over to get a better view, he was shocked to see his parents. Though he had been just a babe in her arms when he was abandoned, his heart would know his mother anywhere. How beautiful she was, with her long hair flowing out behind her.

"Mother, Mother! It's me, Eli! Let me help you aboard," he called, leaning further over the side to reach out to his mother. Caleb looked up and, more roughly than he intended, pushed Eve from him and ran to Eli, all the while calling for Jericho. Startled, the Miscurt reached Eli at the same time Caleb did.

"Mother! It's me, Eli, reach for my hand," he called out again. Now only the tip of one boot was touching the deck.

"Grab him, Jericho, but do not look into the water!" Caleb yelled, having to compete with Eli's calls to his mother. Nodding, Jericho grabbed the distressed elf just as he pitched forward over the side. It was at this point that Eve rushed over. Shouting to her to keep back and not to look into the water, Caleb reached over Jericho, which was no mean feat, and placed his hands over Eli's glazed eyes.

"But...what's happening? Eli says our mother is down there. How can he know that? He has never seen her." Eve remarked as she moved closer to the rail.

"NO!" shouted Caleb, his eyes flashing with fear. "There is no one in the water. It is the curse of the lake. Those who gaze into its waters will see what their heart yearns for. This is what kills people. They think they see someone they love or something they covert, and over they go to get it. Once in the water, there is no getting back on this vessel," he explained.

Ashen-faced, Eve moved back to the middle of the deck and covered her face with her hands and wept.

Thankfully, Eli, who was exhausted by his ensnarement of the lake, fell asleep. Jericho carried him back to the mast and sat with him, all the while keeping a vice-like grip on his right ankle should he awaken and feel the need to return to rescue his mother. For the next hour - or it could have been a week, nothing changed on the lake of the dead - there was nothing but the silence. Caleb held Eve until her tears stopped and then resumed his humming.

Suddenly, there was a grinding sound, and the ferry slowed, then stopped.

"We have arrived," came the voice of the ferryman. Eve did not need telling twice. As soon as the gangplank appeared, she was across it and back on solid ground. Eli came to the moment he was placed on the bank. He was groggy for a few minutes, but soon he was fully himself and horrified at his behaviour. However, he was saddened that the vision had not been real.

"There will be time for lamenting lost loved ones later; now we must move. We still do not know if that creature made it back alive. It is better we find the Princess and retrieve the Stone as soon as we can." Jericho stated, his tone clearly implying that negotiation was not an option. Getting their packs together, they turned to face inland, and, - joy of joys - only a few miles away they could see the brown walls of a castle.

"Come on, we can be at the castle in an hour or so." Caleb encouraged, picking up a long branch from the tree line just on their right to use as a staff. The ground was covered in long grass for about a third of a mile and was boggy. However, after stopping for the fourth time to pull Eli out of the boggy ground, Caleb instructed everyone to fall in line behind him, and he would use his staff to test the ground and map out a clear path for them. The rest of their journey went a lot more smoothly after that, and soon they had passed through the bog and were greeted with a gravel road that meandered its way to the castle.

GRACE HAD FALLEN ASLEEP in Ariana's arms. The three girls had been in the laundry room for a while, Winter had marked off six sun rises on the wall with a piece of chalk she had found. With no sign of the noise - that filtered to them through the vents in the door - stopping, they were resigned to the fact that they were in here for the foreseeable future. Winter was gazing out at the moor that surrounded her castle. It was so peaceful out there. How she wished they could all climb through this barred window and escape this nightmare. Reaching inside her hoodie, Winter clutched her mother's stone and sent up a silent prayer that help would come.

"I DON'T BELIEVE IT!" Winter exclaimed a while later. Time seemed to drag in the confines of the room. There, walking along the road right towards the castle was a group of travellers. Using her exceptional sight, Winter was able to see that the company was made up of three males and a female. One of the males was a Miscurt. Wondering what the strange troop was doing on the moor, Winter turned and beckoned Ariana to wake Grace, because help was on its way.

"How are they going to help us, Winter? They do not know to look through this window. They will head for the grand entrance and get caught up in a brawl for their trouble," Ariana said, despair seeping into every word. Winter was not going to allow these creatures to miss them. Looking around the room, she was pleased to find several heavy stones that were used to wash the linen. The scullery maids held true to the traditional methods.

"Right, as soon as they are close enough, I am going to smash the glass in the window and call for help. We will just have to hope that the noise going on in the rest of the castle is loud enough to mask the sound," she rushed, as excitement and fear coursed through her in equal measure. Ariana didn't look convinced, but, admitting they had very little choice, she gently woke Grace and explained the plan to her.

"Finally!" Winter said. She had been sitting, watching the travellers progress, and now they were close enough for her to put her plan into action. "You two, cover yourselves with a sheet in case any shards fly back into the room," she instructed as she positioned herself ready to smash the glass and call out.

"Did you hear that?" Jericho said, stopping suddenly. Everyone shook their heads. "Listen...there!" he said, pointing off down the left side of the castle. "Breaking glass." Everyone stood perfectly still.

"Over here...Please.... Help!" came the muted plea on the breeze. Jericho turned to the group.

Looking each in the eye, he said, "Now, we have two options. We could believe the that girl calling is in need and go and assist. Seeing as this is the Coven that houses the Royals, it could well be a trap. So, should we walk into a possible trap or knock on the front door?"

"What if the girl is calling us over because she knows there is a trap waiting for us on the other side of the main door?" Eve asked, completely calm, her eyes switching between gold and deep fern. "Once close enough, I will be able to tell if this is a ruse, and then we can make a new plan," she finished. Not able to find a solid counter argument, the men agreed to go and see what the mystery girl needed help with.

"Oh, thank goodness! My name is Winter. My friends and I have been forced into hiding. There is a strange madness that has descended on the Coven; fights haven broken out all over the castle. Even my father is brawling," Winter rushed once the group had reached the window.

"How can we help you?" asked Eve, kneeling a short distance away so she could get a good look at the striking Vampire. Eve was sure that the girl was being honest; her pale aura was a soft violet. Had she been fully alive, it would have lost its sickly greyness and pulsed with vibrancy.

"We need to stop the fighting somehow. I don't know if you can help us , but I didn't want you walking into a vampire war zone, especially as we haven't had fresh blood in a while," Winter explained with a gulp. She was trying to look anywhere but at the sweet pulsing vein in the redhead's neck.

Turning to Caleb, Eve asked if he would be able to create a diversion so that they could help these girls escape. Frowning, he said that, yes, that was possible, but surely freeing three hungry Vampires was a very bad idea. Eve just smiled at him, knowing he wouldn't refuse her. Sighing, he headed back to the corner of the building and began to chant. Once satisfied, he returned to the group.

THE AURORA STONE

"That should do it. I cast a nullifying charm. If this is just blood lust and contagious rage, they should stop. If it is something more, then the ones who remain enraged will need to be contained," he said. Then he added, "Could you let me know if the fighting stops, please, Miss Winter, so I know if further intervention is needed?"

"It's just Winter, and sure," she replied.

Minutes passed, and Winter could still hear sounds of angry vampires, though it was greatly reduced. She relayed this to Caleb, who sighed and explained that it was possible that there was a possession taking place - most likely Ghouls - which would mean that the creature Jericho had wounded had survived long enough to pass on his knowledge.

"What's the plan then?" Eli asked. He was bored with the looks the vampires were throwing him, they were making the hairs on his neck stand on end.

"What happens next is we go in there and kick the Ghouls out of the Vampires. If you are not up for that, you can stay here and keep the girls company," Jericho bit out, flexing his biceps. He might be Eve's twin, but Eli was really starting to get on his nerves. She was so much *more* than he... in every way.

Jericho and Caleb made their way to the main doors. Hearing footsteps behind them, they turned to find Eve chasing after them. Caleb tried to send her back, but Eve was having none of it. Time was of the essence, so he gave up, and the three approached the main doors, keeping as close to the wall as possible.

"Okay, once the doors are opened, I am going to hope and pray that there is only one active vampire in there, two at most," Caleb muttered. "If there are more, Jericho, I am going to need you to keep the others busy."

"Wonderful, I haven't had a good fight in ages! I could do with the exercise," he replied, cracking his knuckles and neck. On the count of three, Jericho kicked the doors open and burst into the grand entrance hall. It was a mess; dismembered bodies were scattered on the marble floor. There were no active vampires in sight, so, slowly, the three entered. They made it as far as the ballroom, four doors down the main hall, when a vampire burst from the room, Jericho punched it, connecting with its jaw and sending him reeling back into the room. Caleb acted quickly. He exorcized the ghoul and banished it to the land of its forbearers, and so they continued for the next hour. However, by the time the last vampire had been exorcized, Caleb was pale and sweating.

"Eve!" Jericho yelled, as suddenly a vampire grabbed her from behind and held her up by the throat.

"You have banished my brothers and sisters, but where did it get you? I have the Light Carrier by the throat. One quick twist and your salvation is dead - permanently this time," the vampire spat. Reaching to her hip, Eve grabbed for her dagger. Finding it just as her vision became spotty due to lack of oxygen, she thrust the blade backward, stabbing the vampire in the midriff. It was enough; it bellowed and released her, sending her crashing to the ground, gasping for air. Using the last of his reserves, Caleb banished the last ghoul and slumped to the ground.

Chapter Twenty

"Cal!" Eve yelled, forgetting her sore throat. She crawled to her fallen friend. Caleb was pale, and beads of perspiration appeared on his forehead. Eve was worried. His aura was shot with grey and brown. Not knowing if it would work, but not willing to sit by and watch him die, Eve lay her hands over Caleb's heart and imagined passing some of her energy into him. Moments passed, and nothing happened. Jericho had tended to the wound in the Kings' side and was standing over his friends.

"Eve, I don't think that will work," Jericho said softly, bending down next to her. Tears that had pooled in her eyes now slid silently down her cheeks, falling onto Caleb's face and hair.

"But he cannot die, I...he just can't!" Her anguish was painful to see; Jericho was at a loss. He couldn't make this better.

"I can help him, if you will let me," came a voice from behind the trio. Turning, Jericho saw Winter and her two companions standing in the hall. "It would change him, but he would remain alive," Winter concluded, looking at the young man in the elf's arms.

"How changed?" Eve's voice was a whisper. If it hadn't been for Winter's exceptional hearing, she would not have heard her.

"He will be a halfling, sort of. Halflings are usually born; however, I can make him half vampire and half witch. He will be able to consume his usual diet and have children, rather than create them as we do." Winter stopped to allow Eve to process what she was telling her. "He will become very strong, and his eyes may change. He may also grow fangs. Although, all of this is dependent on how the venom reacts with his witch blood."

"Do it; I will give you anything if you save his life," Eve replied, her eyes never leaving Caleb's pale face. Moving towards the couple, Winter bent down next to Caleb and took his hand. Raising it up, she placed her other hand half way along his forearm, and, looking at Eve, she explained that this would cause him little pain, but he might stop breathing, which was normal, and not to worry. Looking determined, Eve nodded and looked away as Winter exposed her fangs and lowered her head to Caleb's wrist, ready to bite and inject her venom.

"Wait, just so we are clear, vampire; if you decide to feed instead of heal, I shall remove you head from your shoulders, so think carefully before you act," Jericho warned, drawing his short sword. Meeting his black gaze with her ice blue one, Winter nodded and once again lowered her head. This time, she bit down. Caleb didn't respond like Eve had expected him to. Being bitten by anything, especially a vampire, must be quite a painful experience. His lack of response just served to cement in her mind that this was the right thing to do.

Lifting her head, Winter reached into her hoodie pocket and retrieved a kerchief and delicately wiped the smear of blood from her lips.

"Now we wait. Though, moving him to one of the guest chambers would be better. It will be more comfortable for him, and the rest of you can clean up," Winter offered. Standing, she brushed plaster dust from her jeans. Thanking her, Eve asked Jericho and Eli, who had just appeared, to carry Caleb to the room Winter had offered. She wanted to have a talk with the vampire. Not happy about leaving her with Winter and the one called Grace, but seeing the determination in her turbulent eyes, Jericho didn't dare try to discourage her.

As soon as the vampire called Ariana and the men disappeared from sight, Eve asked Winter if she would like help sorting the mess out. Smiling at the elf, Winter said that was kind, but the others would sort the mess once they regained their senses. After all, they made the mess, so they could clean it up. What Winter really wanted to know was what brought such a motley crew of creatures to her home. Knowing time was clearly running out much faster than she would have liked, Eve decided to just tell the truth and hope it didn't get her killed.

"My friends and I are seeking the princess of this coven. She has something that will save us all, and I need to speak with her about it urgently," Eve answered. Completely calm, she carefully watched Winter's aura for a reaction.

"What is it you seek from her? And how do you know she will want to part with whatever it is you are seeking? What if she refuses?" Winter countered. She had a sinking feeling in the pit of her stomach; she had a pretty good guess as to what they wanted. She didn't know how she knew. However, she also knew that she didn't want to part with it, not even to save herself.

"It is an item that can stop the darkness from consuming all of Orea and casting each of us into the void. Death is on the hunt, and it will capture and kill every living being if I do not stop it," said Eve, trying to get Winter to understand just what was at stake and how much she had to see the princess. Winter was in turmoil. Her mother's stone felt leaden hanging from its chain.

I don't know what to do. She could be lying, but then, how would she know there was something here...? Don't be silly. You don't know it's the Stone she wants. Winter fought with herself, though, deep down, there was a flicker of a memory, a lecture she had once heard in the school room many, many years ago. About a great Evil that had been weakened and banished to a realm without light and something about the use of an ancient power called Aurora's light. She could picture the image in the textbook of a figure holding aloft an item the same size and shape as her stone. The memories caused her to despair, and it resonated deep within her soul.

"I...I will take you to her quarters." Getting up, Winter waited for Eve to do the same, then, casting one look at her father, who was already looking a lot better, she escorted Eve through the debris to the other side of the grand staircase and towards her wing of the castle, hoping that she wouldn't be too angry when she discovered she had been talking with the one she wished to meet the whole time.

THE NEWS OF EVE'S SURVIVAL had sent Nimayaorin into a rage so terrifying that even the generals had taken refuge in their quarters. His manic screams and the sounds of objects being thrown could be heard all over the fortress. Grimmer was especially worried. It was he who had killed the Light Carrier, he, who had been so greatly rewarded and risen in rank. It was not his fault; the poison must not have been strong enough, though there was no way he was going to suggest such a thing to his master. The fact that Nimayaorin had not called for him as yet was promising, or so he hoped.

In his study, Nimayaorin was furious. His plan was unravelling like the old tapestries in his secret room. He knew it was not Grimmer's fault that the cursed girl still lived; something had happened to her. He was sure of that. He was unable to see her now, and that suggested magical intervention and not from the witch. No, this was ancient magic. The only thing to do was to do nothing at all, he realised with a wicked grin. The vampires loyal to him from the lesser covens were already making their way to the King's residence. They would cause a distraction, maybe even kill some of her companions. That would give him time to prepare for her arrival. He would let her come and die by his own hand.

WINTER AND EVE ARRIVED at her quarters. Winter took a deep breath and retrieved her key from her pocket. Holding the small brass key in her hand, she turned to Eve. Giving her a small smile, she opened the door to her private rooms. Eve took in the beautiful entrance; the marble floor polished to perfection stretched before her, with heavy wooden doors along both sides. In the centre of the hall was a large octagonal table that held an overflowing display of lilies, their heady perfume scented the air.

"Come with me, I will take you to the princess," Winter said, still stalling for time. Why, she didn't know, but there was something about Eve that made her want to spend time with her. She realised that she wanted the elf to like her. *Well, that's all about to change once she realises I have not been completely honest with her*, she thought sadly. On entering the main sitting room, Winter turned to face Eve.

"What is it you seek?" she asked again, looking at Eve's amazing eyes and glorious mane of hair.

"I wish to tell the princess myself that I mean her no harm, so please do not fear for her safety," Eve replied, removing her dagger and laying it on the floor. Then with the tip of her boot, she nudged the dagger out of her reach. Realising that she couldn't stall any longer, Winter squared her shoulders.

"I am the princess you are looking for. The vampire you stabbed is my father; I am sorry for not telling you sooner. However, you must understand that the situation called for caution," she rushed, keeping her body language open and non-threatening. This was a relief to Eve who had been starting to wonder if the princess was even here. Smiling at Winter, she dropped a curtsy.

"I completely understand, Your Majesty. I am Evangeline of Hermoria, and I have travelled a very long way to meet you."

Winter knew she was going to have to reveal the stone to the girl. She was already absent-mindedly playing with the zip on her hoodie.

"I believe I have what you seek. However, if it is what I think, it will be hard to part with, as it was my mother's, and she is no longer with us. She passed to the realm of the dead many years ago." Winter paused to compose herself. Speaking of her mother always made her misty-eyed and melancholy. "If I do not give you what you request, will the world truly end? I mean, I have heard nothing of this great evil."

Eve was surprised that the princess was not aware of the danger, but then again, why would she be? She was protected at all times by warriors, and her father no doubt shielded her from anything that might upset her, as any good father should. Maybe she could bargain with her? The fate of Orea was clearly not something that bothered her, which Eve could understand, given her cosseted upbringing. Not sure what she could offer, Eve decided to ask what it was Winter might want in exchange for the item.

Sighing, Winter unzipped her hoodie and removed the stone from the cage. She held it in her cupped hands for a moment, and then, walking to Eve, she opened her hands to reveal the treasure nestled there. Eve had never seen the Aurora Stone, so she had no idea if this was the right stone. It was so beautiful and seemed to be more fluid than solid. Like fresh spring water shaped to resemble a glittering jewel, though she could clearly see that it was as solid as she was. Eve glanced at Winter. The princess looked both proud of the treasure she held and sad that she might be parting with it. It broke Eve's heart to cause anyone pain.

"I promise you. If this is the stone I seek, I will do all within my power to return it to you. To truly know, I need to hold the stone, just for a moment." Eve requested, not wanting to rush the princess. However, she was extremely aware of time and its eagerness to gallop on regardless of the outcome.

Winter hesitated. She believed what Eve was telling her. Her mother often spoke of the 'ring of truth.' When you hear the truth, it resonates in your very soul. Winter was experiencing that now. Hoping her mother would have approved of her decision, she nodded and offered the stone to Eve.

Flashes of colour assaulted Eve as she held the stone. It was unusually hot, hotter than one would expect. The colours slowed in their kaleidoscopic frenzy, and Eve saw a young halfling. He was half elf, the slight point to his ears, as well as his height, indicated that he was also half witch judging by the orbs he was manifesting and making dance on the wind for the two younger children with him. He was a handsome young man with amber eyes and hair the colour of chestnuts. The two children with him were clearly related, as they, too, bore the same chestnut hair, though the girl's eyes were golden rather than amber. It was such an idyllic scene.

Then it changed. There was blood everywhere. The young man was kneeling in a sticky black pool of it, holding the girl's body. She had been very badly beaten. It was only her hair and her large vacant golden eyes that revealed her identity to Eve. Then the young man was in a room. He had a wooden box; elf carvings adorned its sides. The box was open, and, inside, there was a picture of himself with the two children, a dried flower, and a broken shoelace. As Eve watched, he added a lock of hair. With her heart breaking, Eve realised it must belong to the dead girl. There were other things in the box: two bands of gold, wedding rings maybe? Before Eve could get a good look, the scene vanished, and another took its place. This one was before the elders of Hermoria. Eve recognised a couple of them, though they no longer held seats. Even though she could not hear what was being said, it was clear that they believed the young man was responsible for the death of the young girl. On trying to protest, he was subdued and then shackled like a criminal. The council droned on, but the young man was so enraged that he used his magic to break his bonds. He then fought with the guards, ultimately killing them with fire that shot from his palms, a physical manifestation of his pain and rage.

As he continued to burn and kill any who tried to get near, the elders sent an errand boy to the back chambers. When he returned, he had seven witch elders with him. On seeing the 'out of control halfling,' they began to chant. A vortex opened slowly in the floor, just behind the young man. As he stepped back to get a better aim on another guard, who had tried to sneak up on his left, he fell. For a moment, he was suspended; then he felt the vortex stop sucking him down. He was trapped from the knees down, his pyrotechnics ceasing. He forced himself around to see who had captured him. Spying the witches, he once again raised his palms to blast them all to the realm of the dead.

Realising what he was about to do, one of the seven, a woman with long white curls, stepped in front of the vortex, and as the fire shot from the young man's palms, she cast a charm that reflected the inferno back three-fold. Her robes caught fire, but even as she burned alive, she held the charm. The young man's dark magic ravaged his body. His skin bubbled, and his once beautiful hair fell out in clumps, leaving a blistered scalp with only sparse patches remaining. His hands became claws, the nails thickening and turning yellow in the inferno. His once handsome face was ruined, lips burnt away and cheeks blistered, but it was his eyes that took Eve's breath away.

The once warm amber irises were now a sinister crimson. They glared at the burning witch. Too late to save himself, he hunched over, and the fire raged on, consuming more of his battered body and broken soul. The witch fell to the floor, turning to ashes as she made contact with the ground. The rest of the witches gathered around their fallen comrade and began to chant. Within moments, the ashes had swirled and had then been made into a jewel: the stone! It was the very stone Eve now held in her hand. The stone was taken to the elf high councillor, and he put it to his lips and gave it a part of his life force.

The creature that had been the handsome young man watched in horror as the witch then brought the stone closer to him. The closer she got, the more discomfort it seemed to cause. Once the witch was within arm's reach of the creature, who now seemed to be screaming, she touched the stone to his forehead and murmured something. A blinding light erupted from the stone so pure that, even witnessing it as a memory, Eve's eyes teared. The creature screamed in rage and tried to lash out, but found he couldn't. Then suddenly, he was sucked down into the vortex, and both him, and the stone, vanished.

"Oh. My!" Eve whispered.

Chapter Twenty-One

"I don't know what just happened, but you need to sit down," Winter squeaked as she stood staring at Eve. The strange glow that had encompassed the elf while she held her mother's stone had been beautiful, if not a little unsettling. Winter guided Eve to the chaise and lowered her onto the cream leather. The Stone was still cupped in Eve's hands. As much as Winter didn't want to believe it, she was in no doubt that this, indeed, was the stone that could save them all.

Eve was lost in a torrent of information. The anger and pain she had witnessed had been immense. Now that she knew the origins of the Evil, she felt winded. How quickly circumstances could change, and what a profound effect those changes could have. She knew she should be elated. She knew how to use the Stone to defeat Nimayaorin - that was the name Cal had given the creature after her rebirth in Gloria - but all Eve could think about was: who had murdered his family to make him into the monster he had become? Were the two councils right to banish him after accusing him of such wickedness? She didn't think so, no. The scenes that had played out before her were not of a cold mindless killer. Something more had happened. *Who else had been involved*? Eve wondered, her hands shaking. She could feel tears pricking the corners of her eyes.

"I'm sorry, I just needed a moment to organise my thoughts." Eve smiled apologetically up at Winter, who was watching her from a few feet away, her icy blue eyes regarding her with a mixture of awe and caution. Looking down at the Aurora Stone, Eve knew there was no way she could leave without it. But how was she going to convince the princess to allow her to take it, her most prized possession and a memory of her mother?

You will know them by their stones.

Reena's words floated through her mind. That was the answer! Winter must *come with them*; she was the third companion! But what if she was wrong? This wasn't Winters stone to give and endangering a princess seemed reckless. Feeling conflicted, Eve turned to Winter.

"Your Highness, this is, indeed, the stone we have been searching for. I know how much it means to you. However, I simply must take it with me to save us all."

Winter knew this was the case. Part of her was honoured to be able to help in such a momentous way, but the child that had lost her beloved mother was stamping her feet and screaming in her head that this was *her* stone, and that no one but her should have it. The two young women regarded each other. After what felt like an age, Winter sighed and agreed that Eve could take the Stone.

"However, I would like something in return. This is a rare and precious item to me. It cannot be replaced, and, should you perish in your attempt to save Orea, I shall never see it again," Winter stated in a small voice, unsure for the first time in many years that her choice was indeed the right one. Her inner broken child was still kicking and screaming in protest. Forcing that part of her to be quiet, Winter stood and waited for Eve's answer.

"What is it you would like? You could come with us if you wish." Eve wasn't sure what else she could offer. There was no possibility that any of them could stay. Eli could, she supposed, but then he would once again be somewhere she was not, and that thought was too simply painful.

"I have no wish to leave my home and fight a great evil; I am needed here. You have a witch amongst your group, well a halfling in a few hours. He could grant my request?"

Feeling bolder, Winter knew exactly what to ask for and how pleased her father would be if she managed to pull this off. Thinking of her father, Winter suddenly wanted to be with him.

Relief flooded Eve as she confirmed that yes, they had a witch with them, though he was not able to stay with the vampires, since he was needed to assist her in fulfilling her task. Winter nodded and assured Eve that she did not wish to keep the witch here.

"I would ask that he perform a spell that will aid my people in our own endeavours. Surely this is an acceptable trade for something so precious?"

"I am sure Caleb would be willing to help. As long as he is not asked to kill or enslave anybody, I am confident he will do his best to fulfil your request." Eve hoped she was saying the right thing here. There was just no way that she could leave without the stone in her hands.

Content with the response, Winter suggested that they go in search of Eve's companions to make the trade, and then they could be on their way. Eve agreed. She also reminded Winter that Caleb was now part vampire – if he survived. Seeming unfazed by this, Winter led them back through the maze of opulent corridors to the main hall. On reaching the bottom of the grand staircase, Eve was amazed to find dozens of vampires busy cleaning up the mess.

"Jason, have you seen Ariana at all? I need to know where she has taken a guest who was injured in the skirmish earlier," Winter asked a tall vampire, his black hair falling into his eyes.

"I am pretty sure your guest is in the yellow room. I saw Grace enter not long ago with clean sheets and leave with blooded ones, Your Majesty," Jason answered. His voice was silky smooth, and his eyes held Winters for a moment too long.

They are interested in each other, Eve thought as she watched the exchange, observing the gentle blush that coloured Winter's cheeks and the sparkle in her eyes.

Thanking Jason, Winter led Eve down the corridor she had watched the others carry Caleb down earlier. Eve found her pace quickening; she wanted to see Caleb, to see with her own eyes that he was alive. Winter led her to the only closed door along the hall and knocked. Ariana opened it almost instantly.

"He has survived," she informed them before stepping aside to allow them admittance. The smell of blood was nauseating even though the girls had made every effort to keep the room as clean and sweet smelling as possible. The windows were open, and scented candles burned in holders on the fireplace. Eve noticed Jericho and Eli sitting by the fireside. They both rose when she entered. Giving them a quick smile, Eve stared at the figure in the large bed on the other side of the room, hardly believing it were possible. Caleb was resting against a mountain of cushions and pillows.

"Caleb..." Eve breathed, moving swiftly to be at his side. Within seconds, she found herself in a vice grip from behind. Ariana had grabbed her when she was a foot from the bed.

"NO! Do not move so fast! He is not long awake, and we do not know how he will react to your scent. Please, move slowly." Ariana cautioned, letting go of Eve, and giving Winter an apologetic smile for manhandling her guest.

"I'm okay. I won't hurt her," Caleb assured them. He felt strange. He could hear everything, even the sound of a bird pecking the ground for its dinner down by the lake and the hum of someone's voice on the other side of the castle. He could hear the heartbeats of everyone in the room and smell their scents. Caleb was amazed that his skin felt firmer and was a shade paler than it had been. He knew this must be his new vampire nature. It had all been explained to him once he had stopped vomiting fountains of blood and the pain that tortured every fibre of his being had ended. He was relieved to discover that the smell of the non-vampires in the room did not affect him at all. Smiling at Eve, he held out his hand to her, and moments later she was at his side, her small hand in his larger one.

"How are you feeling?"

"Not too bad, considering I have quite literally been through a life-changing experience!" Caleb chuckled as he reached with his free hand to tuck a stray piece of hair behind Eve's ear, following the curve of her cheek down to her chin. Her cheeks flushed an enchanting pink. Eve removed Caleb's hand from her face and braced herself for what could be a difficult conversation.

Looking about the room, Eve noticed that everyone was watching the two of them. Blushing once more, she gave Caleb's hand a squeeze and left the bed. Walking over to Winter, she asked if it would be possible to discuss the proposal with Caleb and her friends alone. Winter was not happy about leaving the stone so soon, so she agreed - on the condition that she be allowed to stay, as she was indeed part of this now.

Asking her friends to return to the great hall and see how the clean-up was going, Winter closed the door behind them and turned the key, affording them privacy while they discussed the trade. Eve motioned for everyone to gather around the bed, so that they could all hear what was being proposed. From within her pocket, Eve withdrew the Aurora Stone for them all to see. There was a gasp, and the atmosphere became charged with joy and hope.

"It's beautiful. To think, after all we have been through together, that you now hold the Stone in your hands," Jericho whispered, his eyes wide with wonder. Caleb, too, was captivated by the stone. His eyes were glazed from unshed tears. He, second only to Eve, had endured the most on this quest, and to see the fruits of their labour was a truly emotional experience.

"Princess Winter has agreed that we may have the stone, though there must be a trade. The stone is of great importance to her on a very personal level, so I feel that it is fitting that we honour her request," Eve explained while gesturing to Winter. Immediately, the men bowed. Even Caleb respectfully dipped his head from his seated position.

"Thank you for your respect, gentlemen. I am pleased you are so well recovered, Caleb, as it is you that I wish to speak with about the trade. My people, as you all know, are blood drinkers - we can't eat normal food. We need fresh blood to replenish our own, and that is where the problem arises. We have found creatures, humans to be exact, whose blood sustains us like no other, and they are, for the most part, happy to let us partake. However, there have been cases where we have been spotted feeding. As you can imagine, secrecy is of the utmost importance; we don't want to cause affray in the human world.

What I ask is for a spell to be cast over every vampire in my Coven so that we may alter the human's memories, so they may only remember a pleasant interaction, or in some cases that they not remember us at all if that is their wish." Winter concluded her request with a small smile, hoping she had explained herself adequately.

The silence was deafening. Four pairs of eyes stared at Winter. It was Eli that broke the silence, which was a surprise, since, so far, he had kept quiet and followed the others without question.

"So, you want Caleb to enable you to feed on the same creatures - these 'humans' as you called them - over and over, and they will have a false memory of you? Do you not think that that is dishonest and morally wrong?" Eli asked incredulously, staring directly into the ice blue gaze of the Princess. Winter was worried that this was not going the way it should. How could she make them understand that they never killed the creatures they fed on? She had even made friends with some of the humans. This enchantment would not only protect the vampires and their human donors, it would protect all of Orea. The humans could never learn of their homeland. Their blood might be sweet, but Winter had seen how wicked they were to those they feared or wished to conquer. This charm would eliminate the risk of them finding their way back to Orea and discovering the existence of every creature in their world. She relayed this to the group and was relieved to see their expressions change from ones of shock to ones of pensive contemplation.

"I will try and perform the enchantment you wish, Princess. Although, since my change, I am not sure that I even still possess my magic," Caleb answered. Winter looked horrified at his reply.

"What I mean is," he continued. "My magic is born in my connection to nature and the Goddess. Now that I am part vampire, I do not know if my magic will be as potent or, indeed, there at all. But do not worry. I am a halfling now, so I should have retained something," Caleb reassured the group, his eyes never leaving Winter's. Nodding, Winter waited while Caleb climbed from the bed and moved to the middle of the room.

Caleb began to ground himself, and to his complete amazement, he felt a deeper connection to nature than ever before. Not having the time to ponder this, he completed this foundation stage to any enchantment and then turned to Winter.

"Please, I need to have contact with you in order to channel the magic into your kind." Reaching out his hand, Caleb smiled at the princess. Hesitating only a moment, Winter walked to where Caleb was standing and took his hand. The difference in their temperature was not as great now that he was half vampire.

"Camouflage and misty sight,
Change perceptions and insights.
Vampire glamour, but do no harm.
Leave pleasant memories as a legacy,
Or disappear completely.
Goddess, hear me.
So mote it be."

On completing the enchantment, Caleb knew it had worked. Even as a halfling he, too, had been affected by it. Winter could also feel a change within herself. Looking at her pale skin, she wondered how this new gift would manifest.

"You are now able to perform a simple glamour on the human donors and anyone else you need to. It will not hurt them. Just maintain eye contact and mean what you are telling them. This will enable the Coven to stay hidden. Though, know this, if you use what I have given to harm, the enchantment will backfire threefold, and that is not an experience you want to inflict on your people," Caleb warned.

"Now that you have upheld your half of the trade, I shall uphold mine. You may have the Stone," Winter said with tears in her eyes. She knew her mother would be proud of her negotiating skills.

"Thank you, Princess. We really must leave now if Caleb is up to it. Time is of the essence." Eve thanked her and hoped that Winter would allow them to leave. The stakes had risen, and she was sure that the final battle was not far into the future.

"Yes, of course. Come, I will escort you out myself."

Leading them back along the corridor, Winter thought of her father and how he would react to her news. Smiling, she opened the huge front doors and proceeded the group onto the front steps.

"Thank you for all you have done and all you are about to do," Winter murmured as she hugged Eve close to her. The two girls smiled at each other, and then it was time to go. Heading down the winding drive, Eve felt her connection with Sapphire flare. Something was wrong, very wrong.

"We must hurry, Sapphire needs us." Eve urged as she broke into a run back towards the lake of the dead.

Chapter Twenty-Two

The return crossing was painfully slow, and the Ferryman was not happy about taking them at all. After paying yet more blood money, they boarded the ferry and made sure they all stayed in the centre of the deck, looking only at each other. Once the ferry reached the jetty, Eve was off like a rocket. She knew that Sapphire was worried, and that concerned her greatly. The others caught up with her, and they ran in the direction Eve led. It was not the one in which they had parted ways with Sapphire. She should have been on the bank waiting.

"Where is she?" Jericho asked Eve. His breathing was steady, but there was an edge to his voice.

"Not far ahead. We should see her soon. I can sense her," Eve answered. What she didn't say was how worried she was about her friend, Sapphire was always so calm.

Just ahead was a small coppice of trees. Although they could not yet see her, Sapphire's screeches could already be heard, carried on the breeze. Fear shot through Eve, and she broke into a sprint.

"Eve...wait! It could be a trap!" called Caleb. His new vampire speed was a blessing as he ran to catch the girl he loved. On reaching the trees, Eve was met not by a screaming Sapphire but an army of vampires and two black witches. The rest of her group arrived moments later.

"Great," Eli mumbled and shifted swiftly into his blue jay form, hiding in the branches of a nearby pine. Jericho was disgusted by such cowardly behaviour. He would be having a word with Eli later if he lived long enough.

"So, you're the Light Carrier who should be dead. Well, we can rectify that now," leered a vampire clad in leather armour, his fangs fully extended. Jeers came at Eve from the men behind him. Clearly, he was in charge here. The witches stood impassively at the side of the group. Their eyes travelled lazily over the new arrivals and widened in shock when they spied Caleb.

"Where is the Protector? I know she is here. I heard her screams," Eve said, squaring her shoulders and looking the vampire in the eye. His muted aura was a dull red. It was the witches that answered.

"The Protector is not here. We knew she could not accompany you across the lake, so we took a chance, and it seems to have paid off. She has not arrived yet." They spoke in unison, which gave Eve the feeling of hundreds of spiders running over her skin.

She is not here. Her relief was short lived as the leather-clad vampire leapt towards her, fangs bared and claws extended. Eve was not prepared, but thankfully Jericho was. Launching one of his knives, he slowed the vampire enough to get in front of Eve. Slightly winded from the shove, Eve regained her balance and removed her dagger, ready for the next attack.

The fight was bloody, and it was clear that, even with Caleb's new abilities, they were no match for fifty rage-drunk vampires. Thankfully, the witches seemed to keep out of the fray. Jericho was bathed in crimson; some was his own blood, though most of it belonged to the enemy. He looked for Eve and Caleb. Finding them both close together, he called, "We cannot win this; there are too many! We must retreat!"

Looking over, Caleb nodded in agreement as he shot a deflecting charm at two charging vampires, causing them to crash into each other. Suddenly, Eve found her feet taken from under her as she was dragged along the ground. Half buried rocks bruised her back as her captor continued to run at supernatural speed. The others had not seen her capture; she was sure of it.

Sapphire where are you? We are under attack! Please help us if you can hear me.

Eve felt the connection flare and knew Sapphire was still alive. What worried her was...why had she not been waiting on the bank for them? Thankfully an answer was swift, *I am coming dear one. I waited on the bank for you, and I saw you disembark the ferry, but, try as I might, I could not come to you or make you hear me. Dark magic must have been at work. I know where you are. I can see the battle; the spell has been lifted. Hold on Evangeline, I am coming.*

Minutes passed as Eve continued to be dragged. She could feel a warm wetness spreading along her back; she was bleeding, and that was never a good thing around a vampire. It happened so fast, it took Eve's breath away. One moment she was being dragged along on her bleeding and bruised back, and the next her kidnapper was on top of her, fangs bared and ready to strike. There was no way she could fight him off. She hoped it would be quick and relatively painless. Eve looked into her attacker's eyes. She would show no fear. Death held no secrets for her.

"You are brave, Light Carrier, but it will not save you now," the vampire snarled, extending his fangs even more until they were almost two inches long, their sharp points glinting with venom.

"I am ready to die. Can you say the same, vampire?" Challenge laced her words, masking the heartbreak due to the fact that she still hadn't told Caleb she loved him, even after her second chance at life. Eve was sure they could fulfil the prophecy without her. After all, they had the stone now. Then she remembered that the stone was in her pocket. The knowledge crushed her.

"There shall only be one death today, and that will be yo..." He did not finish his sentence. Sapphire had arrived. Silent and deadly, she had glided down and sunk her sharp talons into the vampire's back and lifted him off and away from Eve. Sitting up, she saw her circle, and then the vampire was falling. His scream was short-lived as he landed with a splash in the lake of the dead. Taking a moment to assess her injuries, Eve waited for Sapphire to return to her.

You are hurt, Evangeline. Stay here. I shall go and assist the others.

No, I must go with you. I have the Stone, and I do not want to be left behind. I am fine, really; it is not as bad as it seems.

Clicking her beak, Sapphire knew there was little point in arguing. Eve would simply walk back if she did not take her. Sapphire extended her wing, and Eve smiled and climbed onto her back. They saw the men almost right away; they were retreating, but the vampires were not letting up. From the air, it was clear that they were herding Jericho and Caleb towards the lake. If any of them fell...

Then it happened. Jericho lost his footing. He tried to right himself, but it was too late. Sapphire dove down, and, in one graceful move, she rescued the two men. Eve let out the breath she had been holding. For a horrifying moment, she had truly thought that Jericho was done for. Moments later they had landed.

"That was far too close," Jericho said. His breathing was ragged from the fight.

"You're telling me. Even with my extra abilities, we were outnumbered," Caleb panted, flopping down on the mossy ground and taking deep breaths and rubbing his palms, which were sensitive from all the spell casting. From out of nowhere, Eli appeared. Apparently, he had emerged from his hiding place. Eli said nothing. He was wounded, a broken arm, which had happened while he was in his bird form. Jericho felt vindicated. Hiding, it seemed, had not saved the coward from injury. Eve, however, went to him to see if she could help.

"Leave me. It is my own fault; I should have been more careful." Eli snapped, jerking away from his sister's touch. Hurt but not wanting to show just how much, Eve returned to Sapphire.

Thank you for your help, we would be very few in number had you not arrived when you did.

Sapphire's jewel-bright eyes regarded Eve. A single tear welled and then gently over spilled her eyelid and made its journey down her feathered cheek.

Why are you crying? We are all safe, my friend. There is no need for your tears. Eve was shocked to see Sapphire cry; it made her uneasy. Sapphire was the one constant in her turbulent life. She was her moon: not always visible, but there just the same.

The great Protector did not answer. She merely opened her large wings and waited for Eve and Jericho to climb on. Caleb quickly grounded himself ready to fly a ley line. Looking over at Eli's broken arm, Caleb muttered a charm to mend the break so that Eli could at least transfigure into his bird form and not be a burden to his sister. Eli looked over at where Caleb was standing preparing to launch into the sky and nodded his thanks. He knew he didn't deserve this kindness. Closing his eyes, he concentrated. It was only a moment before he felt his skin rippling, and then he was once again a bird, his beady eyes trained on Eve for instruction.

We will make the journey to the Fortress of the Damned now, dear one. This will be the greatest challenge you have faced and a defining moment in your life.

"We travel to the Fortress of the Damned. I admit, I have no idea where that is or how we get there. It is not on my map," Eve explained to her comrades. Jericho and Caleb looked defeated. It was clear from their expressions that they didn't know how to reach the fortress, either.

Sapphire, do you know the way to the fortress? We have no guide or map to get us there. Eve stroked the owl's white feathers that crowned her head while she waited for their connection to flare with a response. She was surprised that an answer was not immediately forthcoming. This, along with the tears, was leaving an uneasy feeling within Eve. Sapphire was not herself.

I know how to get there, in theory. However, it is not easy to enter, and we would need to fly a great distance to reach the entrance to the Darkness's realm.

Eve was sure that her friend was holding something back, but she did not wish to question her further. It was clear that Sapphire was ailing in some way, and Eve did not want to add to her burden with questions.

Realising that the vampires were regrouping and approaching them once again, they knew they needed to hurry. They were about to take off when Jericho turned sharply towards the lake. The Ferryman approached. This time, his passenger was the princess. She was dressed for traveling and for battle. A sword hung in a bejewelled scabbard at her right hip, and throwing knives adorned the leather straps that crossed her torso. It was clear for all to see that Winter was prepared.

Alighting from the vessel, Winter was almost immediately at Caleb's side. Eve blinked a few times. Vampire speed was something she was going to have to get used to.

"I would like to join you on your journey. If the offer is still open, that is? I am skilled in many forms of combat; it would be an honour to aid you." Winter bowed slightly at the waist, pleased that she had gone to her father directly after the group had left the castle.

She had explained all that had happened and of the trade she had arranged. King Fredrick had been shocked by the events that he had partaken in but had no memory of. When Winter had finished her tale, Fredrick knew that she must join the elf on her quest. The stone had been left to her, and so she should stay with it and ensure the safety of the Light Carrier, Evangeline.

"Of course, you are welcome to join us, though I am not sure how you will travel. Sapphire can only carry two of us at a time." Eve smiled at her new companion, pleased that she was with them. It felt right that she was here, like the puzzle was complete. Winter looked crestfallen. Her shoulders drooped. She was desperate to stay with her mother's stone for as long as she could. Sighing, she turned to head back to the jetty to call the Ferryman back when she suddenly had an idea.

"Where is it you are traveling to?" she asked, her eyes bright with poorly concealed excitement.

"We travel to the Fortress of the Damned. I must confront and destroy the darkness," Eve replied, eyeing the slowing approaching vampires. They had managed to manoeuvre themselves in such a way that Eve and her party were surrounded on three sides with the lake at their backs. They needed to leave before it was too late.

"Would your protector be able to carry me in her talons for just a few miles? I know a way into the lands surrounding the fortress you speak of. It is not well known and it is not far." Winter asked, pleased that she was able to offer assistance so soon. Eve asked Sapphire if that was, indeed, possible. She eyed their enemies the whole time. They were cutting it fine; time was running out.

"Yes, she says that would be possible, but we must leave now. Your kinsmen are not fond of us, and I would rather not have to fight our way out," Eve rushed as Sapphire began to rise into the air. As Winter leaped into the air to be caught by Sapphire, Caleb shouted that he needed a direction. Winter pointed south, and Caleb vanished into the sky. With Eli at her side, Sapphire beat her powerful wings. They were finally out of harm's way...for now.

CLEAR WATER VALLEY was now under the control of Nimayaorin. The ghouls had possessed the most influential witches of the realm. Those who dared to oppose the new rules were killed. Nimayaorin was pleased with the swift capture and obedience of the witches; it gave him great pleasure to have them kneel in his name.

Lervirion would be rewarded for his skill and cunning. His execution of the raid had been simply flawless. Nimayaorin had spent many an hour watching his orb of revelation. The witches belonged to him now, and soon every other realm would too. He wondered how his vampire assassins were faring; he hoped they had caused the Light Carrier pain, knowing it was unlikely that they would manage to kill her. He stood and glided to the locked cabinet that housed his only physical weapon. The lock opened with a click. Reaching in, he withdrew an athame, its pewter handle embedded with Quartz, the perfect amplifier to any curse or poison he would cast on the silver blade. Taking his weapon to his throne, he placed it hilt deep between two of the bones that made up the right arm of the throne, which placed it within easy reach for when his guests arrived.

Soon it will be hilt deep in the chest of the Light Carrier and not in some old bones, Nimayaorin thought as he watched the quartz flash with white fire reflected from the candlelight. The wait would soon be over.

Chapter Twenty-Three

The flight took no time at all, Winter had directed them to some rather bleak scrubland. It was bare and completely devoid of colour. Eve felt closed in; the stale air seemed to press down on the group. Eli remained in bird form and perched on a nearby rock. Winter scanned the land before her while absentmindedly rubbing her shoulders. The vampire knew she would heal in a few minutes, but she felt sore from the tight pinch of Sapphire's talons.

"Which way? It all looks very much the same," murmured Eve. She was suddenly feeling very tired. With heavy limbs, she dragged herself over to Caleb. Each step felt like she was wading through thick mud.

"Winter, I think we need to speed this up. Eve is acting very strange," Jericho cautioned, watching Eve fall into Caleb's arms. He was practically holding her up. It was clear that both Winter and Caleb were unaffected by whatever was causing Eve's malady. Hoping she was not suffering further side effects of her resurrection, Jericho went over to Caleb to seek his opinion.

"I feel fine, how about you?" Caleb asked as he supported Eve's slim frame. She was still awake, but every so often her eyes would turn a dull sludge green and roll in their sockets before closing completely. It was then that Caleb would gently shake her, and the process would begin again. Jericho was worried. This was not the time for sickness. They were so close to fulfilling their task.

"We keep heading south. The gate here has been closed, so we must reach another - and quickly. We do not want to be here when darkness falls," Winter called over her shoulder, still scanning the barren landscape. Having no argument with the plan, they began to move out. Caleb passed Eve to Jericho, who then once again climbed onto Sapphire's back. Then they took to the skies. They travelled for hours, the gloom of the sky getting progressively darker.

"I'll run this time. It's not far, and I think we will move quicker if Sapphire isn't having to carry me," Winter said. The others agreed, too worried about Eve to care about how Winter chose to travel as long as she was fast. Winter insisted once more on keeping to a fast pace. She had meant what she said; they did not want to be out here in the open once darkness fell.

"What's that?" Jericho called, knowing Winter would hear him just fine.

"I can't see anything from down here. How far ahead is it?" Winter called back.

"Looks like a spilt in the land... about three miles ahead."

The ravine, Winter thought, and a shudder passed through her. They were heading in the right direction, but the thought of passing into the land that nightmares were made of was not something she relished. Being a vampire was one thing, but the thought of the creatures so vile that even hell didn't want them caused Winter to shudder. Calling back that they should head straight for the ravine, Winter once more picked up the pace.

Eve was drowsy. All she wanted to do was sleep, but she knew that it was important that she didn't. Jericho kept her talking, which helped, and the rapidly cooling air was enough to stop her from getting too warm leaning into the Miscurt. Sapphire began her decent. Extending her talons, she made the perfect landing fifteen feet from the fissure.

"This is it. The only other way I have heard of to get into the Wastelands of the Soulless and reach the Fortress of the Damned. I must warn you, this is by far the most perilous entrance that exists,"

Winter explained to her new comrades, casting a worried look at the still listless Eve.

"If there are other gates, why not just head to one of those instead of this hole in the ground?" Eli countered, his hair sticking out at odd angles due to his swift shift back into his elfin form. Winter patiently explained that, yes, that would be ideal and then held up her hand to halt Eli's interjection.

"We simply do not have the time to hunt for gates that may or may not still be active and open. It's getting darker by the second; we need to be off this land now!" Winter was almost shouting by the time she finished her explanation, her eyes flashing with icy fury.

They simply didn't have time for questions. Could Eli not see how the land was affecting his twin? Was he incapable of heeding a warning, even when it had been given several times? Winter's anger fizzed in her veins. Eli could well be a liability. She would have to keep a close eye on him and make sure he did not jeopardise this mission.

They all approached the edge of the ravine. Looking down, they were greeted with a terrifyingly narrow path that was hewn from the rock face. The bottom was nowhere to be seen. Eli immediately began to protest.

"I am not allowing my sister to travel down that!" he all but screamed while pointing at the path. Winter had had enough.

Walking up to Eli and staring up into his puce countenance, she let rip, "Eve has no choice, you moron! Look at her! This place is leaching away her goodness; her soul is under attack, and she has lost a lot of blood. We have to be off the land, as I have told you repeatedly, before darkness falls, or we will be facing worse than a long drop and a broken neck at the end of it. In fact, you will be wishing for it if we do not leave now!"

Eli stood stock still. His mouth opened and closed several times. Never had he been spoken to in such a manner - and by a female! A cutting retort sprang to his lips. However, Jericho clamped a meaty paw hard onto his shoulder and squeezed.

"I think you should consider holding your tongue, or you may find it cut out. Do not presume to know your twin. Eve has and always will make her own decisions," he growled at a now pale Eli. Clearly, he wasn't so brave when faced with a male opponent. "The Fae have made you weak, boy. If we live through this, I suggest you accompany me to Olia. There is time to make a decent warrior out of you, yet. That is if you are not afraid of a challenge?" Jericho growled, applying more pressure to Eli's shoulder. Eli let out a squeak but held his ground

"I thought so. Let's go. We are wasting time we do not have on your ego." Releasing his iron grip, Jericho returned to Caleb and Eve and lifted her into his arms.

They were almost at the start of the path when the last of the daylight faded to black. It was quite a shock. There was no inky blue that gently melted into the black of night. This was an instantaneous change, like an extinguished candle. Everyone stopped - everyone apart from Winter, that is, who just kept moving. Suddenly the blackness was pierced by eerie clicking, like many small joints popping to a drum beat. A blue light appeared in arcs across the blackness. When it made contact with the ground, it hissed and crackled like embers in a fire.

"RUN!" cried Winter as she moved more swiftly through the infinite gloom. Jericho began to run with a groggy Eve bouncing off his chest. Eli passed him. Even in the pitch black, he could smell his perfume-scented clothes. Rolling his eyes, Jericho kept going, hoping he was not about to run off the cliff edge. Caleb was bringing up the rear. He had called for Sapphire and cast an orb of fire that levitated a few inches away from his upturned palm, but she was nowhere to be seen. He assumed she had taken to the skies.

Owls are not great on their feet.

He cast the orb further away to discover what was creating the blue lights and the noise. What he saw was beyond reason. Spiders - giant arachnids - with their thick legs covered in white hair, scurried in all directions. As he watched one, it spotted something in the darkness. Its multiple pink eyes flashed in the meagre light of his orb. Then, without warning, it reared up on its four rear legs and shot bright blue liquid from between its pincers. After this display, it scurried in the direction in which its attack had been directed. Its jarring run made Caleb's skin crawl.

He realised then that it was not light, it was fluorescent acid! They needed to be as far from these beasts as possible. Recalling his orb, Caleb, turned and ran to catch the rest of the group, sending his light source ahead of him to illuminate their path.

Winter was waiting for them at the junction where the rocky path met the barren landscape. She hoped they would arrive soon. Her acute senses were in overdrive. She knew all too well what lay out there in the dark, waiting to devourer them. The smell of burning scrub and the occasional meaty odour indicated that the 'scourge of the scrub,' as they were known to her people, were out and attacking. At last, someone appeared before her. Unfortunately, it was Eli.

Wonderful, she thought. *Now I have to wait with the one creature I wouldn't have minded getting consumed.* Sighing, Winter nodded to him and then returned her gaze to the direction he had run from, willing the rest of them to arrive. Jericho, who was still carrying Eve, was next. He looked hot, and his eyes were showing signs of tension. Running full tilt carrying an almost dead weight could not have been easy.

"Caleb is right behind us. I saw his light orb. Thank goodness he cast it; I was inches away from death without even realising!" Jericho puffed. Winter walked to him and looked at Eve. She did not smell near death, and though her soul was sick from this land, she would recover once they entered the pathways.

Caleb appeared, waving his arms frantically,

"Run, run, go, go, go!" he shouted as he fired defecting charms over his shoulder. The sound of hissing acid was uncomfortably close. He reached the group and began to herd them towards the path. "Come on, we need to move! Winter was right; we do not want to be caught by what's out there," Caleb urged, moving forward while still shooting the charms back towards the unseen danger. He wished he could 'un-see' them! Those eyes were going to be forever etched on his mind.

"AARRGGGGGHHH!" His yell seemed to go on forever. One of the spiders had managed to dodge his charm, and its acid was burning through his thick leather boot. The heat was intense. Once it reached his calf, it was going to render him immobile, of that he was completely sure. As the first caustic droplets touched his skin, Caleb let out another yell, this time, to urge his friends on. There was no saving him now; he could try and hold these beasts off and ensure the rest of them made it onto the path. The burning was growing; he could feel the skin on his leg melting away as the acid began working through his muscle. Caleb thought of his sister Grace and his father; he would never see them again. Then he thought of Eve. He wished he had had the chance to kiss her, just once. Gritting his teeth, Caleb continued to fight off the beasts that would soon claim his life and then consume his flesh.

Sapphire had taken flight as Caleb had hoped and was frantically searching for her companion in the dark. Their connection was sluggish, no doubt due to Eve's lethargic state. Then she heard it - Caleb's yell of pain. Quick as lighting, she headed in the direction the sounds had come from. What she saw once she was close enough was both horrifying and a relief. Eve was safe. She was in the arms of Jericho and already on the path. Caleb, on the other hand, was surrounded by the creatures and severely injured. His life would be extinguished in moments. Sapphire once again opened her connection with Eve and spoke to her dear one: *Evangeline, I have fulfilled my part in this quest. You have become who you were destined to be. My last piece of knowledge to you is this: When it all seems lost, use the power of three and victory shall be yours. You have my heart, dear one, so I shall always be with you.*

Closing the connection, Sapphire swooped down and scooped Caleb up, taking him to the safety of the junction as jets of blue acid followed her into the sky. Winter was still there waiting for him. On seeing his injury, she quickly ripped her hoodie and bound it above the burn. She then looked at Sapphire, and was horrified by what she saw. The great Protector must have been in agony. Huge areas of her plumage were burned away, and her white skin was red raw. Even as Winter observed, Sapphire's skin broke down, and the muscle and sinews became visible.

"You are, indeed, a protector; I will never forget your sacrifice this day," Caleb said as he watched the creature he had come to respect burn before his eyes. Nodding her snowy head, Sapphire turned and opened her great wings and took another volley of acid. Tears streaming down their faces, Winter and Caleb crossed the junction and entered into the relative safety of the ravine. Turning back, they watched as Sapphire's wings became nothing more than bone. There was no blood. The acid was cooking her flesh wherever it touched.

It was becoming too gruesome to watch, but Caleb made himself look out of respect. Sapphire, the great Protector, once a majestic white giant with the jewel blue eyes, was dragged to the ground by five of her attackers. Caleb couldn't watch them devour what was left. Wiping his eyes, he turned away from the horrific scene, breathing through his pain.

"She never cried out," whispered Winter as she wiped her eyes on her sleeve. "Come on. We need to get you further down the path so I can check your leg," she said, helping him to his feet, Winter supported Caleb as they made their way slowly towards the rest of their party.

Eve had regained her sense by the time Winter and Caleb reached them. Caleb was all set to break the sad news to her. When he was close enough, he reached out to her. Eve looked at him with watery eyes and smiled a heartbreakingly sad smile.

"It's alright, Cal, I know. She spoke to me before it happened." Eve reached into the bag and removed a kerchief and wiped at her eyes. She would mourn her friend later, once she had fulfilled her quest. Jericho watched her with pride. How brave she was; a true warrior, even in the face of great loss. He was sure all of Orea would be speaking her name for generations to come.

"Caleb is hurt. We need to deal with his leg before we go any further," Winter said to no one in particular as she began rummaging through Caleb's bag, Eve went to Caleb and looked at his wound and then his aura. Despite the severe burn to his calf, he was not in mortal danger, which was a blessing. Eve could not bear losing him as well.

"It's alright, I can heal it myself. Winter, could you pass me the lavender? You will find it in a bundle." Caleb pointed to the pocket it could be found in and waited. Once he had it, he asked Jericho to hold him still and once again created an orb of fire. This time, he used it to burn the lavender. Its heady perfume filled their senses. "Now hold me still. Eve, please can you crush this over the wound and repeat the words I speak?"

Nodding, Eve did as she was asked. Caleb screamed but managed to rush out the incantation that Eve repeated. Once the last word had passed her lips, she was amazed to see that the skin on Caleb's calf was already re-growing. Panting, his eyes wet with unshed tears, Caleb explained that in a few moments he would be healed enough to walk without being a hindrance to the group.

"Good. We have to move soon. We may be away from the scourge, but there could be something worse waiting around the next bend," Winter said grimly. Faces set with determined expressions, the group readied themselves for the next challenge.

Chapter Twenty-Four

Down and down they travelled. The path was narrow and crumbling in places. Eli hadn't said anything since his confrontation with Winter. He was sandwiched between Jericho and Eve, with Caleb behind her and Winter at the rear. As much as he loved being with his twin, Eli was beginning to wish he had remained in Gloria under the care of the Royals.

Jericho halted abruptly and raised his arm to motion the others to do the same. Turning, he indicated that everyone was to stay put while he checked the path ahead. After they nodded their agreement, Jericho eyeballed Eli and then disappeared around the next corner. The silence was eerie; no one dared to move. Minutes passed, and Jericho had not returned. Eli was becoming twitchy, as he was now at the front of the group. Not wanting to shift and leave his sister to face whatever may come, he stayed where he was. Sweat trickled between his shoulder blades. He was not built for battle and bloodshed.

When Jericho eventually reappeared, everyone expelled the breath they had been holding. Thankfully, he seemed to be alone and uninjured. Beckoning them to follow him, they all continued along the path. After a mile or so, the path ended and opened out to form a platform of sorts. Keeping close to the wall, Jericho led them behind a cluster of large boulders. Once they were all hidden, he relayed what he had discovered.

"Not far ahead there is a bridge. The bad news is that about two-thirds of the way across, there is a huge gap that is impassable." Jericho watched as his comrade's shoulders drooped. He needed to continue, and quickly. He could see Eli getting ready to complain, and even though he had been lucky to not encounter any creatures so far, if Eli started creating a fuss it would likely draw unwanted attention. Holding up his palms to show he hadn't finished, Jericho continued.

"Now, I had a look for a way across, and it is true that there is no way to reach the other side. However, by chance I looked down, and twenty feet below the opening, there is what I believe to be a portal."

"YOU WANT US TO JUMP OFF A BRIDGE AND FREE FALL TWENTY FEET IN THE HOPES THAT THE PORTAL IS ACTUALLY ACTIVE! AND IF IT IS, WE WILL FALL INTO WHO KNOWS WHAT!" Eli exploded. The sound of his voice echoed off the vast stone walls. Wincing, Jericho really wanted to knock the selfish elf senseless.

Instead, he and Caleb exchanged a look. "Eli, if you do not desist, I will have no choice but to silence you myself," Jericho warned, his voice low but full of promise. Eli opened his mouth to reply. Thankfully, Caleb was ready, and, shooting Eve an apologetic look, he muttered a quick incantation. Eli's mouth moved. His eyes bulged and he clutched his throat. He tried again to speak, but nothing happened.

"I warned you, Eli, we cannot have you shouting in here. Do you want to bring whatever guards this place out of hiding? So until I can be sure you will keep quiet, I am afraid that Caleb will continue to keep you mute," Jericho explained to a brick-red Eli, who glared at the two males and began to think of ways to get revenge.

"Enough fighting. Your auras are glowing so brightly with your anger and becoming so muddled with rage that I am feeling quite ill," Eve groaned, holding her temples and closing her eyes against the harsh colours surrounding her friends. Taking some deep breaths, she managed to regain her composure. The pain of losing Sapphire was so fresh; all of her senses were in overdrive. Feeling ashamed of his outburst, Eli moved towards Eve and put his arm around her. Eve squeezed his other hand and begged him to do as Jericho asked. He was the most skilled in combat in the group, and he was pointing out the only real option they had. Nodding solemnly, Eli removed his arm and returned to his place.

"So, are we clear? We are to execute this as quickly and as quietly as possible." Jericho waited for them all to nod in agreement. Satisfied that he had their attention, he ran through the order of the drop. Eve wanted to protest. Seeing as she was the one that had brought everyone else into this, she felt that she should be the one to jump first. Another heated discussion followed this, this time between Caleb and Eve. Jericho was becoming irritated; they were wasting time, and he still wasn't completely confident that they were alone down there. Every minute wasted was one a potential threat had to sneak up on them.

"Enough! You will jump after me, Eve, followed by Caleb, followed by Winter and with Eli at the rear. Are you all clear on this? I am not changing the plan for anyone, since, as you pointed out, Eve, I am the most skilled in combat, and regardless of what you think you should do, I will be keeping you as safe as possible," Jericho hissed, waves of agitation radiating off him.

"Of course, Jericho. I'm sorry," Eve mumbled. Getting ready to move out from behind the rocks in single file, they moved as silently as possible. It was now or never. Jericho led the group to the bridge. Thankfully, nothing appeared out of the dark to attack them, but he was all too aware that this could change any moment. Halting the others, he motioned for them to follow him, though at a distance, so that their weight was evenly distributed on the old planks of the bridge. Making eye contact with each of them, Jericho gave a slight nod and then began to make his way to the break in the planks. After ten paces, he felt Eve join him. By the time he had reached the gap, everyone was standing on the slightly swaying bridge. Caleb was levitating just above the planks to ease the load on the rotting planks, which Jericho was thankful for. The protesting ancient wood would not hold up for long.

Turning to face Eve, he held up his paws, opening and closing his splayed fingers once to indicate that she was to count to twenty before following him. Eve nodded and mouthed 'see you soon.' Jericho gave a small smile, and then, without dwelling on the possibility that this could literally be his last adventure, he jumped

It was an unpleasant feeling to free fall - not knowing what was waiting for you at the end of it. The air whistled past Jericho, causing his ears to sting with cold and his eyes to water. The gaping hole seemed to rush towards him, eager to swallow him whole. His descent seemed to last for hours, though in reality it was but a few moments. Relief coursed through him when he finally saw the shimmering swirls that clearly identified this was a portal and that is was, mercifully, active. Thank the Goddess. Taking a deep breath, Jericho passed into another realm.

Eve let out the breath she had been holding. Up until Jericho's form had made contact with the portal, she had still been in doubt about what that blackness below was. She watched as it shimmered and rippled with pale light as her friend passed through it, both comforted and worried her in equal measure. What exactly was waiting for him - for all of them - on the other side?

Suddenly remembering that she should be counting, Eve started from five to account for the time missed while she had been lost in her thoughts. As she counted the last few numbers, she turned to look at Caleb; he looked pale, his fear for her written all over his handsome face. Gifting him with a smile, Eve turned back and jumped.

Jericho was eternally thankful that he had great reflexes. After exiting the portal, he found himself facing a very solid-looking stone path. He managed to turn himself feet first just moments before impact, his bent knees taking the shock. He then rolled away from the landing zone. Taking only a moment to check for any broken bones or injuries and happy to find that there were none, he moved back towards where he had landed and braced himself to catch Eve.

Moments later, Eve appeared through the portal and managed to at least turn herself the right way up, ready for Jericho to catch her. They landed in a heap on the hard stone. Quickly extracting herself from him, Eve jumped to her feet and offered her hand to a slightly winded Jericho.

"Sorry about that. I didn't think I was that heavy," Eve blushed while Jericho braced his hands on his thighs and took deep breaths.

"It's not your fault; I should have braced myself more effectively," he wheezed. "Best we stand back and let the others pass through. They will all manage just fine without our intervention."

Sure enough, Caleb, Winter, and Eli appeared, and each used their special abilities to land quietly and safely. Once everyone was present, Jericho took a better look at their surroundings. They seemed to be on a grey stone path that was poorly maintained. Great slabs had cracked and others had crumbled into rubble. It wound its way down the boulder-strewn hill and disappeared into a black mass, which Winter informed them was sure to be snare weed. Met with inquiring faces, Winter explained that snare weed was highly deadly. Its thick black stems were covered in hundreds of bruise-coloured thorns. If the thorns broke the skin, they would inject a neurotoxin that would render the victim blind, or would, in some cases, cause vivid hallucinations, leaving the victim helpless for any creature to pick off.

"Sounds like we should maybe avoid that way, then," Eli piped up.

"Oh, that's not all. Snare weed is intelligent. It remembers every countermeasure any past traveller has used against it and sets its own traps," Winter concluded, her pretty countenance marred with worry lines.

"We don't really have the option of going around it, Eli. Look, it stretches for miles in both directions. You may be able to shift into bird form, and I may be able to fly the ley lines, but there are none of those down here. And, Jericho, Eve and Winter possess no such powers," Caleb said to Eli, knowing it was not what he wished to hear. Eve scanned the gloomy vista before her; the entire place seemed to be void of all colour and life, apart from the snare weed. Beyond it, the road continued, and she could just make out what she thought was a pair of large gates embedded in a black wall. In all, the distance was no more than four miles.

"This is what we must do: Eli, you can shift into a bird and fly ahead and scout out the snare weed and what lies beyond. The rest of us will make our way along the road and meet you before we enter the weed," Eve said, taking charge of the situation before her twin lost his nerve again. His voice had only been given back to him at Eve's request; she could feel his discomfort. Everyone considered her plan.

"It's a good a plan as any, as long as he actually comes back," Winter replied, her eyes like ice chips on Eli.

"I would not abandon my sister. I shall stick to her plan and relay all I see to you when we rendezvous."

Rolling her eyes, Winter bent to refasten her boots. Jericho couldn't deny that it was a good plan, though he too had his doubts about Eli's valour.

"Eli, you should leave now. It will give you more time to scout the area as we make our way down. Anything dangerous, you head straight back to us, understand?" Jericho ordered. Eli agreed and very quickly transformed into a black bird and took off.

"We need to move, but remember, we stay together," Caleb murmured taking Eve's hand. They followed Jericho out from their hiding place, with Winter bringing up the rear. They cautiously began the descent to the barrier of snare weed.

Eli flew as fast has his wings would allow. Swooping low over the snare weed, he could see that there was no easy path through. It was going to take a lot of patience and teamwork to get through it. Soaring back up into the bruise-coloured sky, he pondered how portals and this whole realm worked. How was it possible to have a sky underground? All of this was giving him a headache. Continuing on, he observed precisely... nothing. The road continued for a few miles until he reached a huge portcullis that was embedded into the thick black walls of what could only be described as a fortress.

The wall was an imposing structure, made from onyx. It rose at least twenty feet into the air. Eli pointed his beak upwards and began to flap vigorously as he tried to reach the top. The air was frigid at this altitude for such a small bird, and Eli's wings were becoming numb. When he was all set to give up, he spied a grotesque gargoyle a few feet above him, and with one final push, he reached it. Collapsing on its freezing onyx head for just a moment, he used his vantage point to take in the surrounding lands.

What he saw made his little heart flip-flop in his breast. To the east, and heading his way fast, was a vast army. He could not tell what creatures made up the mass, but he was very sure that they were not going to be friendly. Glancing up, he saw he only had another five feet to go before reaching the top of the wall. However, remembering his promise to Jericho, he took one more look at the army and took off, heading back the way he had come.

With his descent aiding him, Eli made it back in double quick time. He could see them; they had almost made it to the weed barrier. Taking a risk, he shifted into a large vulture, which had a larger wingspan. He was soon just meters away from them. Eve's red hair flashed like a beacon in the barren surroundings. Landing rather heavily, he quickly turned back into his elvish form and jogged to meet Jericho, who was heading the party,

"There… is an army coming… from the east," he gasped, still breathless, his lungs burning from the cold air.

"How many?" Jericho asked, his calm tone at odds with his clenched fists and tense posture.

"Hard to say… a legion, maybe two? All I know is that when you get through that," Eli rushed on, pointing to the mass of black foliage behind him. "There are going to be a lot of creatures waiting to kill you."

Chapter Twenty-Five

Eli took a moment to catch his breath and smooth his hair into a more respectable arrangement while Jericho paced, muttering to himself. They all knew that there was no way to avoid the army that was heading toward them. Going back was not an option, either.

"We have no choice; we have to get through the snare as quickly as possible and get the fortress behind us so our enemies cannot force us back into the thorns," Winter said, halting Jericho in his tracks. She knew it wasn't a great plan. At this point, however, it seemed the lesser of two evils.

"I don't see how that will help us. Surely, staying this side of the weed will be the best option," Eli muttered to no one in particular; he knew they thought he was a coward, and maybe he was. Battle training was not something that was offered to him at the palace. Turning to him, Winter explained that, although that would seem like the best option, creatures of this realm were immune to the toxin on the thorns; they would simply crash their way through or spread out along the far side, making it impossible for anyone one to pass through.

"Winter is right. We have a chance, however small, of getting to the fortress if we make it through this ahead of the army," Eve injected. She looked at her friends and knew that she was asking more than she should of them. "I can't ask you all to risk your lives again. I will slip through, myself. There is a good chance that I can get through unobserved."

"Absolutely not! There is no way you are going through this only to face an entire army alone!" Caleb protested, his eyes flashing with determination. "We are all in this together, and we shall see it through to the end." Taking Eve's hands, he gazed into her beautiful eyes. "I love you. I thought I had lost you once, and it nearly killed me. Where you go, I go."

Eve was lost in Caleb's blue eyes. The words she had been longing to hear for so long had now been said, and with such conviction that it took her breath away. Caleb loved her. Her heart swelled with happiness. "Cal, I..."

"Sorry to have to break this up and all, but the army is getting closer, and we still have to navigate our way through that," Winter stated, crashing right through the tender moment with a hard dose of reality and pointing to the black and purple mass before them. Blushing to the tips of his ears, Caleb dropped Eve's hands and muttered something about checking that his pack was secure before he bent down and became very interested in the buckles on his bag.

Eve looked over at Jericho, who was smiling at her. Picking up her own pack, she headed over to the dense plant and began to search for a gap big enough to fit through. Precious moments ticked by as each of them searched for any semblance of a path. Eve knew this plant was an effective barrier; its pulsing brown aura gave a very clear warning.

Suddenly, Winter called everyone's attention. Finally, she had found a way through, and it looked big enough to allow Jericho to pass through as well. Deciding quickly that Eli would shift into a shrew and scout ahead for them, the rest organised themselves into a line. Gingerly, they began to make their way through the organic barrier.

It was dark within the confines of the weed. Caleb cast some witch fire for each of them. The orbs of blue flame hovered at waist height. The weed looked even more forbidding in the eerie light.

"Remember, try not to touch it. We don't want it to attack. At the moment, it is tolerating our presence. However, that could change at any time," Winter reminded them in hushed tones.

"Very comforting, thanks," Jericho replied, rolling his beetle black eyes to the heavens. He wondered, not for the first time, how had he ended up in such a motley crew. Eli, for once, was proving his worth; his small form allowed him to shoot ahead and then return and use his tail to direct the group to the next passable section. They were about two-thirds of the way through when Winter suddenly hissed. Everyone stopped immediately. Caleb dropped Eve's hand and drew his athame.

"We need to pick up the pace. Can you hear that?"

"No... wait, is that thunder?" Caleb asked.

"It's the army; they are getting closer. We need to move," Winter hissed back, her fangs partly extended. Shuddering, Jericho gave a low whistle. The next moment Eli appeared, his whiskers twitching.

"The army is getting closer, as no doubt you heard. How much further until we clear this infernal plant?"

Eli gazed up at Jericho. Holding up one tiny paw, he turned tail and scampered off back into the dense plant. Thankfully, they didn't have to wait long for his return. Eli squeaked to announce his return. Thumping his tail ten times, he then pointed back into the weed.

"That is good news, thank you," Jericho whispered to Eli and then turned to the others to relay the results of the reconnaissance. "This..." he said, gesturing to the bulbous coils around them, "will cease to be a problem in a few feet."

Sighing with relief, they all moved forward, following the tail of Eli. Caleb waited until the weed began to thin before extinguishing the orbs. The sound of the army was getting louder, like rolling thunder. Finally, they cleared the weed and breathed the slightly dusty air of the open plane.

"The wall is not far. We need to get as much distance as we can between us and the weed before the army spots us," Jericho instructed as he tightened his pack and checked his weapons. Agreeing, they all began running towards the wall. Eli had shifted into a raven and was continuing in his role as a scout. He was to call twice when the army was just beyond firing range. The ground was grey and dusty. They had decided not to run on the path; it was in even worse state this side of the weed, and they simply could not afford for someone to trip.

The wall rose up before them. Its complete blackness seemed to suck the very light out of the atmosphere. Half a mile from the imposing portcullis, they heard Eli's call. Picking up the pace, they ran as if the devil himself was chasing them.

The first volley of arrows peppered the ground three feet behind them, far sooner than they had anticipated. The very ground seemed to vibrate under them as the soulless legions gained on them. More arrows rained down. Their tips were barbed, designed to cause massive internal damage. Caleb cast a shield over the group, but it wouldn't hold forever, and they still had some distance to go before they reached the portcullis.

The general had his orders, and he followed them to the letter. The enemy was within his sights. Turning to his second in command, he ordered him to take his small contingent and herd the group toward the portcullis.

"You may kill all but the Light Carrier. Go now, our master is waiting for his prize."

Saluting, the demon broke away from the heaving mass of the army, calling his soldiers to follow. The scorpions they sat astride moved at a terrifying speed, the sway of their massive twin tails adding to their momentum.

"Today we shall claim victory over the light. Show no mercy!" Luranthor shouted to his men, who, in answer, raised their bows and swords.

Eli saw the small group break away from the huge mass of bodies and swooped down towards Jericho; he needed to warn him. Landing a few feet in front of the fierce Miscurt, Eli quickly shifted into his elfin form and ran towards him.

"A small contingent of demons has broken away, and they are heading right for us. There are bowmen and swordsmen, and they are astride scorpions!" he panted, his face a sickly grey colour. He decided right then that if he lived through this, he was becoming a recluse and cultivating flowers. Jericho knew they didn't have long. Slowing his pace, he ordered everyone into a huddle.

"We will have company very soon, and they out-number us. Now we have to split up. I will hang back and hold them off for as long as I can; the rest of you must head for the entrance," Jericho explained in a rush.

"I will stay with you. With my ability to shift, I can be a terrible nuisance," Eli said, surprising everyone. Jericho nodded and was about to break away when Winter also announced that she would stay and hold back the oncoming demons.

"I haven't had a good fight in quite a while; I need to keep my edge," she added nonchalantly. Eve was torn. She knew there was a high probability that they would die. She also knew that this was the only chance she would ever have to destroy Nimayaorin and possibly save all of Orea.

Thanking each of them, Eve and Caleb broke away from the huddle. Caleb somehow managed to scoop Eve up and ran for the entrance, his newly acquired Vampire abilities aiding him, and soon enough they were within a few feet of the iron portcullis.

Jericho, Winter, and Eli prepared to face the demons. They all knew they might not live for much longer, but each believed that their sacrifice was worth it. A dust cloud appeared one hundred feet away. Within moments, the first of a dozen scorpions appeared, their black bristly exoskeletons making loud clicking sounds as they ran. The giant pincers, that would cut a creature in half, snapped menacingly. Sat astride them were Demons; their yellowish skin was covered in tufts of black hair and putrid boils. The leader held aloft a huge claymore. Its blade was tarnished with the blood of its many victims. He pointed the blade at the trio and sent up a battle cry.

"By the Goddess, we don't stand a chance!" Eli squeaked, his eyes out on stalks.

"Now is not the time to lose your nerve! We need you to blind them. Just watch the scorpion tails; one sting would kill a giant," Winter informed him, lisping slightly as her fangs extended fully. She grinned at him and winked. Taking courage in the fact that he was doing this for the greater good, he shifted into a hummingbird and headed directly for the leader of their would-be assassins.

"If we get through this, remind me to thank you," Jericho said to Winter. Smiling, she looked over at the Miscurt.

"Don't worry, I will."

The battle was fierce. The demon archers fired volleys of barbed tipped arrows. One of them grazed Winter's left bicep. Thankfully, she healed within moments of it tearing through her flesh. Hissing, she leapt at the archer. Her claws slashed at its chest leaving deep wounds that oozed its defiled blood. Growling in pain, it reached for her. Grabbing hold of her ankle, she was whipped back and forth like a rag doll.

"Jericho... Eli... a little... help," Winter yelled as she swung about wildly by her ankle, the joint screaming in pain.

"I think I will let Kane here give you a sting. You will be more fun to play with then, little vampire," the demon chuckled as he held Winter up towards the scorpions' tail. "Go on, Kane, give her a taste of your venom."

Kane's tail swayed hypnotically before Winter, the sharply curved stinger wet with venom. Closing her eyes, Winter waited for the bite of pain and the burn of the toxin. The demon laughed as he shook her. Then there was a whoosh, and the laughing stopped suddenly. Just as Kane thrust his stinger towards Winter, she was dropped. Rolling away from her attacker, she was just in time to watch Kane pierce its demon master's midsection with such force that the tip burst through his chest, pumping venom over his own head. Winter had never heard a scorpion scream. The sound was shrill and haunting, and she was sure it would torment her dreams for the rest of her existence.

Jericho watched as Winter dropped to the ground and rolled out of harm's way. His throw had been excellent. His knife had embedded itself to the hilt in the demon's skull. He had killed eight of the creatures so far, nine including the one that attacked Winter. He had not managed to avoid injury completely. A large slash on his thigh bled freely, and the ground beneath his feet was fast becoming slick with his blood. Thankfully, once the demon was dead, the scorpion turned and fled the battle.

Another mounted demon was headed straight for him, sword held high, its muddy eyes manic with blood lust. Jericho prepared another blade, ready to dispatch the creature, when he was knocked off his feet and into the air. He landed heavily on his shoulder. He heard the sickening crack of it dislocating and then felt the mind-numbing pain that came with such an injury. Clutching his shoulder, he scrambled to his feet. If he were to die, he would face death head-on with a blade in his hand and a smile on his face. The demon who he had aimed for was fighting with Winter. He watched as she sank her claws into its chest and ripped its heart out. Out of the corner of his eye he saw another demon, this time on foot, charging him. Jericho threw his knife, but it was deflected by the sword blade. The demon smiled.

"Is that the best you can do, little mouse?"

Jericho knew he was going to die. He had a few blades left, but with the demon approaching so quickly, it was unlikely he would make the killing blow. Reaching for another blade, he tossed it into the air, watching it spin and summersault. As the perfectly balanced hilt landed in his paw, he threw it with all the force he had at the demon. It sailed through the air. The demon swung his blade to deflect the shot. Its hideous features rearranged themselves from an expression of gloating superiority to one of shock and then pain.

Jericho had known he had little chance of making the head shot, so he had thrown the blade at his opponent's feet. It was a tricky shot but one he had practiced many times. The now screaming demon was anchored to the dusty ground by his left foot. Walking over to his felled opponent, Jericho unsheathed another blade from his belt, tossing it lightly into the air and catching it as he approached.

"Well, I guess my best is good enough for a little mouse wouldn't you say, parasite?" Jericho inquired as he placed his foot on the hilt of the blade sticking out of the demon's boot and applied pressure. The demon screamed again and dropped to the floor, clutching its leg.

"You can kill me, but it will make little difference. The master will get what he wants, and you will still die. Foolish mouse, caught by the cat and doesn't even realise." The demon laughed manically up at Jericho, its eyes wild, strings of spittle clinging to his blackened teeth.

"Either way, you won't be here to see it," Jericho replied as he swiftly sunk the blade of his knife into the creature's temple and twisted. "And I will have my blades, back," he added as he retrieved both, the one from its head and the other from its foot. Turning, he saw Winter running towards him, her mouth and chin covered in blood.

"Where is Eli?" she asked. Looking over Jericho and noticing his shoulder, she moved in front of him. "Let me fix your shoulder. We need to find Eli, and you are a liability with one arm."

"I think I handled myself quite well thank you, Princess. But some help with this would be appreciated. We are too far from the wall for me to fix it myself. Rolling her eyes, Winter placed a hand on his bad shoulder and held tight. She then took his hand.

"Hold my shoulder and brace against me. I am going to push your shoulder back while bringing your arm forward. It's going to hurt like hell."

Jericho did as he was asked. He took a deep breath, and then there was the sickening crunch as his shoulder relocated into the socket. For a second, the world titled with the blinding pain.

"You are all set. The pain will pass in a moment. We need to find Eli. Eve and Caleb have passed through the gate," Winter explained as she scanned the battlefield for their companion.

They found him motionless a few feet from the demon leader. As Jericho looked over the creature, he saw that Eli had succeeded in his attack. Where its eyes had once been, were now two bloodied sockets, the brownish clumps that splattered his cheeks the only remains of his sense of sight. Winter quickly made her way to Eli. He was still in the form of a tiny hummingbird.

"He is breathing, just knocked out," she called to Jericho, who was just removing one of his knives from the blinded creature's temple, a quick and efficient kill.

"Pick him up; we can worry about reviving him later. Right now, our primary concern is getting into the fortress before a scout comes and brings the rest of the army." With Winter cradling Eli in her hands, they ran for the gate, just as the first volley of arrows peppered the ground at their heels.

The Army had arrived.

Chapter Twenty-Six

Eve tried hard not to look back as she and Caleb squeezed their way through a gap between the wall and the iron bars of the portcullis. The sounds of the Scorpions scurrying around the battlefield made the tiny hairs on the back of her neck stand to attention. She couldn't afford to think about what was happening out there now. The most important thing was to stay alive long enough to return the Stone.

"Cal, we need to be quick. Can you see anyone in the courtyard?" Even her whisper sounded loud in the confines of the vaulted arch that made up the frame for the massive iron barrier that was now at their backs. Caleb reached back, took Eve's hand, and squeezed before he let it go. Then he moved forward to get a view of the courtyard beyond their shadowed hiding place.

The vast open space was deserted, which was both a relief and highly suspicious. *Surely the guards would have heard the commotion happening right outside the walls and mobilized?* Caleb thought to himself. Taking a deep breath through his nose, he used his new acute senses to pinpoint where the next threat was. Nothing jumped out at him. *This is too easy*, he thought and returned to Eve.

"The courtyard is deserted. We need to be ready for surprise attacks and traps, though. This all seems too easy to me."

Eve nodded and drew her dagger. Taking her free hand, Caleb led her to the entrance. They waited for a moment just to be sure that the coast was clear. There were several arches around the edges of the marble-floored space, each one potentially hiding a threat. Eve allowed her mind's eye to open, hoping this would aid them in their choice of direction. The place was devoid of life, as Caleb had said. However, there was an energy pulsing like a beacon behind the double doors opposite them and off to the right. Pointing with her dagger, she indicated the direction in which they needed to move in order to get the doors opened with minimal effort. The first thing about their new surroundings that hit them was the heat. The very atmosphere seemed to boil. Steam covered everything in a misty blanket, concealing any traps or enemies. Caleb tugged on Eve's hand, and they walked as quickly as they dared, eyes on the floor. Suddenly, the steam seemed to become thinner, as if the heat had sucked all the moisture from the air. Glancing around, Eve saw they were on a wide marble gantry that overlooked a steaming pool of reddish sludge, the smell of which was only just permeating the air. Gagging, she turned to look ahead. Before them was an imposing structure, its crenelated turrets jutting like broken teeth into the churning sky. It was then that she realised they were still outside.

If it wasn't so horrifying and hot, this place could be considered beautiful, she thought. Tugging on Caleb, she pointed to the keep ahead. "That's where we need to go."

"I really wish it wasn't. Stay close and keep the Stone out of sight," he muttered as they ran along the gantry towards the entrance of the fortress's inner sanctum.

They had almost made it when a huge form appeared from a doorway, an axe held high as it charged them. Eve had seen the creature's aura flare seconds before it appeared and yelled a warning to Caleb. Thanks to his improved speed, the axe only removed a few strands of his hair. Turning, he grabbed Eve and all but threw her towards the entrance of the keep.

"Keep going! I will catch you up!" he yelled as he dodged another swing of the axe. Caleb blasted the creature with white fire, which momentarily blinded Eve; its brilliance illuminated the vast space and their attacker.

Grimmer stood before them, his scarred features contorted into what Caleb imagined was his idea of a smile. His huge war-axe held high, Eve suddenly had a flashback from her abduction, those terrible eyes flashing in the moonlight as her capture ran through the night.

"Caleb, that's the creature that abducted me in Gloria!" Eve yelled just as Grimmer swung the axe at Caleb's mid-section. He missed his mark, embedding the axe in the marble pillar, just past Caleb's left hand. Taking his opportunity, Caleb muttered a charm, which caused the axe to burst into flame. Glimmer's leathery palms melted to the handle in seconds. His growls of pain and anger sent chills through Eve, while the acrid stench of his corrupt flesh melting made her heave.

"I shall enjoy ridding Orea of his existence. It is the least I can do after he caused the one I love so much pain!" Caleb growled as he punched Grimmer with a swift uppercut, causing his head to snap back with a sickening crack. He then kicked him full in the chest, causing the demon to land on his back. An unearthly cry escaped his bloodied mouth as his hands were ripped from the super-heated axe, his skin hanging in charred ribbons. Caleb didn't stop there. He kicked him again and again, all his hatred for this creature manifesting itself as pure rage. Eve couldn't watch; the look in Caleb's eyes was one she didn't know.

Allowing the celestial world to become dominant, she looked again at Caleb, and her heart sank. His aura was becoming muddied with jagged bolts of black and muddy brown. He was losing himself in hatred.

Rushing back to his side, she spoke to him, hoping to save him from his darker nature. The vampire side of him was taking hold; she couldn't allow that to happen. "Caleb, stop! If you must have him dead, then make it clean. Yes, he hurt me, but he is just a pawn, in this deadly game his master is playing. Our time is running out! Please come back to me! Become the man I know you are: the man I love."

His chest heaving, Caleb turned to look at Eve. His eyes were dark with hate. Tentatively, she reached for his hand. Very slowly, she brought it to her face and held it there; his rough palm cupped her cheek. Eve watched as, slowly, Caleb returned to his sense. His aura calmed and cleared to its usual brilliant yellow.

"I will never leave you. I swear it, Eve. You are my world. Where you go, I go," Caleb assured her, his eyes never leaving hers. Suddenly, there was a harsh, jagged sound from behind him. Turning, he saw that Grimmer had managed to prop himself up on one elbow and was laughing.

"Ah, you poor dull creatures. You really believe that you will get to live your happy ever after?" His gravelly voice echoed off the columns. "You will not live past the next hour. Everything you have done has been a waste. My master will kill you all and suck the marrow from your bones. Love has no place here; you are already dead. You just don't realise it yet!" Grimmer laughed, blood dripping from his mouth.

Caleb removed his hand from Eve's face and turned to face Grimmer. Reaching his hand back, he gestured for Eve to hand over her dagger. Placing the hilt in his hand, Eve hoped that he would do the honourable thing and make the kill quick and clean.

"Whether we die this day or live for a hundred years, we will have lived and died knowing love, loyalty, friendship, and hope. You will not live more than a few moments more. I pity you and your kind, taken in by a madman and fed lies all your days. Look where it has gotten you." With that, Caleb thrust the blade into Grimmer's heart and twisted the hilt.

Pulling the blade free, he bent forward and wiped it on the edge of his shirt, then handed it back to Eve. As they walked away from the body, Caleb heard footsteps approaching fast. He tensed and turned to face whatever came through the mist.

"Now that's a welcome - a flaming axe and a dead partly-roasted higher demon. Really, you shouldn't have," Winter quipped as she and Jericho appeared. Both were covered in blood but seemed in good spirits.

"Where is Eli?" Eve asked, immediately hoping he was right behind them. *He isn't dead,* she told herself. He couldn't be; she would have felt it. Winter reached into her pocket and held her hand out to Eve. Lying in her palm was a tiny jewel coloured hummingbird. Its green plumage rose and fell rapidly, reassuring her that he was, indeed, alive.

"You should be proud of your twin. He took on a demon officer in this form and blinded him. He was instrumental in our survival," Jericho said, his eyes sincere.

"When will he change back? We need him now more than ever," Eve said, hoping someone had the answer. Caleb assured her that Eli would come back to his senses soon, and then he would be able to shift back. Taking comfort in his words, Winter once again returned Eli to her pocket, and the foursome headed into the keep.

As soon as they entered the vast entrance, Eve knew where they had to go. Her nightmare came back to her full force as she ran along the high-ceilinged corridors, the others running behind her. Finally, when she thought her lungs might burst from her chest, Eve rounded the final corner. There before her was the vast copper doors from her dream. The intricate details were just as she remembered them. Walking towards them, Eve found she understood the message mapped out in the design.

"I know what I must do now," Eve murmured as she ran her hands over the cold copper surface. The others looked on expectantly. Caleb had a sinking feeling. He had seen these doors in Eve's dream and knew that this was a significant moment. This should have made him happy. However, he sensed this whole venture had been too easy. From entering the fortress to reaching this point... something was amiss.

"Eve, I think you should come away from there; something isn't right," Caleb said, reaching for her shoulder.

"It's okay, Cal. I know what I need to do..." Eve didn't finish. Just like in her dream, she was suddenly in the presence of a great evil. Its cloying scent filled the chamber. "Everyone run! This is up to me now," Eve called as the others faded from view. The darkness had come for her.

Nimayaorin manifested before Eve, his form fully cloaked.

So foolish, to be standing in the home of death, he thought as he gazed at the one being capable of destroying everything. She was such an unimpressive creature, so small and breakable. He was going to take great pleasure in killing her and then each of her companions.

"Welcome to my home, Light Carrier. Although you won't be staying long, it was kind of you to bring me the stone and so much fresh meat to enjoy."

His voice was like ice. Eve's skin crawled at his closeness. Holding her head high she looked into the blackness of Nimayaorin's cowled head. She was not going to show her fear to this creature. Placing her hand on the hilt of her dagger, she waited.

"Where are my friends?" she demanded, surprised by how calm she sounded. He circled her, watching how she turned with him, her hand gripping her weapon. *She believes she has a chance!* he thought with a chuckle. *Hope is a dangerous thing.*

"Well, I would be less inclined to be worrying about those who cannot help you and more about yourself. Although, you shall be dead soon, so maybe there is no point in worrying at all," he answered, stopping between Eve and the vault.

"I want to know where they are, Nimayaorin. NOW!" Eve yelled, drawing her dagger and pointing at his heart. Suddenly, Eve could see her friends. Even Eli had come around and was standing five feet away. They seemed to be unharmed.

"They are, for the time being, alive. I shall be killing you in front of them. I thought it would be poetic - darkness extinguishing the light."

Eve had had enough of his taunting. She lunged for him, dagger raised high, ready to pierce whatever remained of his heart. She was fast, but her aim was off, the blade sinking into Nimayaorin just below his clavicle. He roared with pain. Gripping her by the wrist, he twisted hard. Eve saw stars; the pain was unbearable. She could feel the bones twist and then break under his strong grip. Despite trying not to, she cried out. How he wished he had brought his athame. It was still stuck in this throne. Still, using his bare hands had its pros. He could feel her bones breaking.

Caleb was losing his mind. He watched as Eve screamed and grappled with the Darkness. If he could just get to her, he would tear Nimayaorin to pieces. Turning to the others, he saw that they all felt the same.

"We need to break this enchantment, and fast. Eve is no match for him alone," Eli groaned, his eyes wet with unshed tears. Caleb turned back to the invisible wall before them and began to chant frantically, his eyes never leaving Eve.

Nimayaorin was relentless in his attacks. Breaking bones and tearing flesh had become second nature to him over the years. Now he was somewhat of an artist; he could break and tear a creature to ribbons and yet keep them alive for weeks. It seemed the prophesied Light Carrier would be no different. That disappointed him. Reaching down, he grabbed a fist full of her silken tresses and heaved her up to his eye level.

"Poor little girl, so far from home, full of dreams and silly ideas. Do you still think you can beat me? You are nothing more than a weak elf, a gardener, and a dreamer. Your kind are all the same - so full of their own self-importance that they believe they can achieve anything!" He spat the words out as though they offended him. Eve's head was beginning to swim. Her broken wrist was throbbing, and her tormentor's putrid breath was making her nauseous.

"I am not afraid of you; I pity you," she replied, her eyes defiant. "I have seen your past. I know what happened to you. It was wrong the little girl...." His eyes blazed with rage.

"Do not presume to know anything about me or my past, elf. It was your people that did this to me, yours and those filthy witches! All because I was born a halfling... hardly my fault. They beat my sister to death, and they took my brother! I never found what became of him... he raged. "I do not want your pity! I want your blood!"

At that moment, there was a smell of burning ozone as her friends broke through the barrier and headed for her. Weapons ready, they ran towards Eve, retribution radiating from every pore. The darkness would not be allowed to win.

"I see our time is up." With those words, Nimayaorin gripped Eve's shirt and launched her across the short distance towards the casement windows.

"NOOOOOOO!" Caleb and Eli yelled. As Eve's broken body made contact with the glass, it shattered, exploding outwards. Eve seemed to hang in mid-air. Then, she was gone. Eli ran for the window, pushing past Caleb as he went. He didn't stop. Once he reached the gaping hole, he leapt, disappearing after his twin.

"Well, that saved me a job. One less to kill," Nimayaorin mused. "I am growing bored of you all, so if you are going to attack, please do so. I can end your pointless lives, and then I can return to the task at hand."

"It would be our pleasure," growled Caleb as he threw curse after curse at the darkness. Nothing touched the creature, though it kept him busy while Jericho and Winter positioned themselves. The first of Jericho's blades stuck Nimayaorin in his mid-section. The second and third followed quickly. It wasn't long before a pool of blood began to appear from beneath his cloak. Yet he continued to lunge and slash at his opponents. Winter managed to get behind him; she gripped him around the throat, choking him. Unfortunately, his groping claws found their mark, and she dropped to the floor, deep slashes marring her pretty face.

"I will heal, but let's see how pretty you are, Mr. Tall, Dark, and Melodramatic." Winter yanked at the hem of the cloak. There was a snap as the clasp gave way, and the heavy material slithered to the floor. They were now face to face with pure evil.

Chapter Twenty-Seven

Eve watched as the tower wall zipped past her at an alarming rate. This was not how it was supposed to end. The Aurora Stone pressed heavily on her chest. She had come so close, and yet she had let anger cloud her judgement, and the whole of Orea would pay for her mistake.

She thought of Sapphire, who had given up her life so that she might succeed - such a waste. She thought of all her friends back up in the tower and of her twin Eli. She had only just found him. Now she would never get to know him. The sound of screaming reached her. The shrill voices were coming from beneath her. *I can't look. I can't bear to see who or what is down there*, she thought as images of her mother filled her mind. How she would miss her.

The descent seemed to last forever. Eve closed her eyes and allowed Caleb's face to fill her mind's eye. *We never got to share our first kiss*, she thought sadly. The screaming was getting louder; it would be over soon. Reaching into the neck of her shirt, Eve gripped the comforting weight of the Aurora Stone and waited to die.

The inhabitants of the pits watched in horror as a young girl fell towards them. They hoped she was already dead, because if she hit the ground alive, she would be forever trapped here with them. At least the dead had peace. Suddenly, another body could be seen falling. This one appeared to be facing the ground. Then, before their very eyes, the second person shimmered and changed into a large barn owl. Keeping its wings pinned to its sides, the owl sped downward towards the girl, closing the gap second by second.

The screaming from below was replaced by complete silence; Eve was sure she must have died. Suddenly she felt the warm body and the steady beating of wings. *I must be dead. Sapphire is with me!* Opening their special connection, Eve reached out to her friend.

Sapphire, I have failed. We are both dead, and the stone lies around the neck of my broken body. I am so sorry that your sacrifice was in vain.

I never figured you as a quitter, Evangeline. It does not become you.

Eve opened her eyes in shock. *Eli?*

Yes, yes, it's me. I must say, I quite enjoy this form. I make almost no sound, and my vision is excellent. But enough about me. We have to get back up there; you have a prophecy to fulfil, friends to save, evil to defeat... you get the idea.

Eve laughed, *I have never heard you say so much, Brother.*

A ripple passed through Eli. *Yes, well, when I am scared to death, I talk far too much. Please, can you hold on? We need to hurry.*

Eve carefully turned herself over so she was sitting astride her brother's golden back, gripping with her knees as he pointed his head upwards and flew back towards the tower window.

Eve arrived just in time to see Winter pull the cloak off her enemy. What she saw was even worse than the images she had witnessed in limbo. Nimayaorin was unidentifiable as the creature he had once been; he didn't resemble anything Eve had ever seen. The years of dark magic, hatred, and cruelty had eaten away at him. The result was the twisted, mutilated being before her.

Turning his scarlet eyes on her, Nimayaorin stretched his lipless maw into what, for him, passed as a smile, his razor-sharp teeth and blackened gums fully exposed.

"Wow, you really are gross," Winter stated, her quivering voice betraying her as she spoke. It highlighted the fear that gripped her. The abomination that stood before Winter ignored her completely. Instead, he addressed Eve.

"I see you have a nasty habit of avoiding death. Well... I guess if something is worth doing..."

Eve had no time to react. He directed a curse at her, and she had no way of protecting herself. Caleb, thankfully, was waiting for an opportunity to do this creature some damage. He cast a counter curse, knocking the creature back into the copper doors. Once his balance was off, Caleb quickly ran to Eve and cast a protective bubble around her. Turing back to face Nimayaorin, Caleb sent a volley of curses at the creature, who, to his utter amazement, brushed them off as if they were nothing.

"What are they teaching you these days? If you are going to curse someone, boy, you need to mean it, body and soul!" Nimayaorin tsked. As he propelled himself forward with lightning speed and gripped both Caleb and Eve by the throat, the protection spell shattered. "It may interest you to know that the whole of your realm is under my control. As we speak, they are marching towards Hermoria. They will kill each other until not one of them has his soul intact, then the void will take them."

Jericho, Winter, and a now elfin-shaped Eli could only stand and watch as the creature smashed Caleb's head off the marble wall and dropped him. He crumpled like a rag doll, blood oozing from a large gash on his crown. Nimayaorin positioned Eve in front of the copper doors and began to read the ancient message inscribed there.

"What lies behind these doors must forever remain locked away from the worlds.

Kept hidden from the dark forces that shall rise up and wish to destroy and conquer.

Only the light can destroy its contents. Only the Light Carrier's blood and the stone of the morning can forever seal this Evil within this tomb.

If it should be opened, the stone bathed in the Light Carrier's blood must be cast into the void, or Darkness will be the victor over the realms, and the void shall swallow the sun."

"Rather poetic, don't you think? It is my favourite story," Nimayaorin added, his voice smooth and eloquent despite his disfigurements. Reaching out with his claws, he slashed Eve's cheek and watched as beads of blood pearled on the surface of her lily-white skin. His tongue snaked out of his own accord, wanting to taste. Remembering that she carried tainted blood, he managed to stop himself.

Gripping Eve, roughly he pressed her bloodied cheek to the cold copper door. Suddenly, the doors began to glow, the inscriptions outlined with light. As each section was illuminated, more details were revealed. A recess that Eve had not noticed before became all she could see. It was the exact shape of the stone hanging around her neck.

That is where I must place the stone to end this, she thought fervently. Reaching into her shirt, she gripped the cage the Stone was housed in and pulled it apart, her fingernails ripping in the process. Holding it tight, she slowly removed her hand that was clutching the stone from beneath her shirt and waited. She would only get one shot at this. Nimayaorin was still delivering his soliloquy, his attention not directed at her. With all her strength, Eve threw herself at the other door and reached for the recess. She almost had it when, suddenly, pain lanced through her broken wrist once more. It had gone mercifully numb, but now it felt like hot pokers had replaced her marrow. Screaming in pain, she slumped against the doors, the stone still gripped in her good hand.

Nimayaorin released her broken limb from his claws and dropped Eve to the ground. She had barely made contact with the floor when he kicked her, sending her skidding across the floor, the wind knocked out of her. "Nice try, but you are no match for me. I will have my revenge." Turning to the glowing doors, he extended a claw and slashed his palm, placing his own defiled blood over Eve's.

Nothing happened for a moment, but then the doors began to vibrate. The images glowed and turned darker, as if the light had burned too hot and scorched the metal. Then, there came a series of loud clicks; each one sounded like a death knell. Jericho was at Eve's side when she had regained her breath, but her arm was badly broken. He didn't know what else to do at that moment, so he held her close. Winter knew that Caleb wouldn't be out for long. His halfling status enabled him to heal at an accelerated rate. As she watched, she saw his colour return and his eyelids flicker. Quickly leaning forwards, she whispered in a low tone.

"Stay down until I give the word."

Eli was rooted to the spot. This was not how it was meant to be. However, something told him it wasn't over yet, so he, like the others, waited.

There was a groan, and then the doors flew open. The temperature instantly dropped. Even from the other side of the hall, it was clear that the vault was empty. It was completely black inside, so dark that the dimensions were indeterminable.

"YESSSSSS!" Nimayaorin hissed, raising his skeletal arms over his scarred head. "The void shall devour all. Even as I speak, chaos reigns across Orea!" Moving away from the doors, he muttered in a guttural language, and a large orb appeared. The scene within it was one of bloodshed and death. Witch fought with elf. Demons could be seen slaughtering anyone whom they came across. "I shall build a new world, a world built on power! A world that thrives on blood and pain. No one shall feel joy or love again!" As he spoke, the oily blackness began to seep out of the confines of the vault.

Eve knew they must do something before it reached them. She could already feel a slight pulling at her soul. She opened her mind's eye and was shocked to discover that, whatever the void was, it was soulless.

Eli, can you hear me? She opened their connection and hoped that he could, despite being in his elfin form.

Yes, what should we do? I am assuming you have a plan... well hoping actually.

Calm yourself, Brother; I know what we must do. But we need Caleb. Can you signal to him without being seen?

I can try, but I think he is still knocked out. Eli closed the connection and uttered Winter's name under his breath. He knew she would hear him. Looking over, Winter wiggled her eyebrows, silently communicating that she had heard, and she silently inquired as to what he wanted her to do.

Eli glanced at Nimayaorin. He was deeply absorbed in his own rapture to notice much else, but he didn't fancy attracting the demon's attention at such a critical moment. Instead, he simply mouthed.

We need Caleb.

Nodding, Winter leaned forward and touched Caleb's hand. Within seconds, both he and Winter were with the rest of the group. Eve quickly explained what they had to do.

"We need to combine our powers to defeat him, once and for all," she whispered looking pointedly at Eli and Caleb. "I am pretty confident that the two of you can use me as a conductor, and we know that Eli amplifies my powers, so this is what we are going to do…"

"Are you sure this is going to work?" Eli asked, his palms sweating.

"No, but we have to hope. It's all we have left," Eve replied. Nodding in agreement, the trio slowly stood. Eli and Caleb moved to Eve's sides but remained two steps behind her. They then each held her shoulders with one hand and had gripped each other by the wrist behind her back. Eve lifted her hand, clutching the Aurora Stone to her bloodied cheek and smearing its perfect surface with blood. *I really hope this works!* she thought.

Closing her eyes, she asked the others to begin channelling their power into her. The heady rush of pure energy was enough to knock her off her feet, but knowing this really was their last chance, was all that kept her standing. When she opened her eyes, she saw her skin was once again glowing, as it had been on her return from limbo. Her vision was a mixture of her usual sight and her soul-based sight, her sixth sense. The room was a fire with colour and light. Lifting the stone to chest height, she opened her hand and watched in wonder as the stone absorbed her blood and was now all the colours of the dawn. The morning stone: *Aurora*.

Nimayaorin spun around. He had felt the spike in power and wondered what little parlour trick the children were going to try and distract him with. Could they not see he had already won? In a few moments, the void would fully awaken, and all hell would break loose. However, what he saw held him to the spot. The light was blinding. Raising his arms to shield his eyes, he tried to see past the glare.

"You are of the darkness, the blackest of night.

You are the monster that goes bump in the night.

Darkness only has limited power.

It cannot survive where there is light."

Eve's chanting made his blood turn to ice in his veins. How was it possible? This was old, older than magic, older than time itself. How had she invoked the ancients?

She has the stone!

It was as the chant finished for the third time that Nimayaorin felt the power of the light hit him. It burned like righteous fire through his veins, killing the corruption and filling him with hope. It sickened him. He stumbled, the light of Aurora consuming him as it had done all those years ago. How he wished they had killed him then. After all, they had taken everything from him. Skin blistering, Nimayaorin stumbled again, his feet becoming entangled in his discarded cloak.

"NOOOOO!"

With his anguished protest still hanging in the air, he tumbled into the void.

"Is it over?" Winter asked tentatively. She wasn't sure if it was safe to approach the three of them. After a few moments, Eve's glow became less, and Caleb and Eli let go, breaking their trifecta.

"Yes, Nimayaorin is gone forever, but the void is still open," Caleb said. His voice was strained from the effort of what they had just achieved. "We need to close the vault and lock it with the Stone."

Jericho was the first to reach the doors. He might not know much about magic, but brute force was something he excelled in. Reaching across, he gripped both doors and pulled them towards himself. His biceps bulged and sweat began to dampen his fur. Try as he might, the doors didn't move an inch.

"Maybe if we all try - Caleb and Eli on one door Jericho, and myself on the other - Eve can be ready to insert the stone and then..."

"No," Eve said, cutting Winter off mid flow." That won't work. The void is activated. The only way to stop it now is if I jump into it with the Stone."

"Well, that isn't happening, not after everything you have been through. I only just found you! Please let us try!" Eli begged, his eyes pooling with tears. Eve smiled at her twin, and, stowing the stone in her pocket, she put her good arm around him.

"It is the only way, Brother," she replied, her own tears spilling silently down her face. Caleb was not going to let her die. He swiftly moved to her side, reached into the pocket, and took the stone, immediately moving away from her towards the doors. Eve turned to him, her eyes beseeching.

"I won't let you die. I can't go through that again, and you have sacrificed enough for all of us and for Orea. I will go in your place; your blood is already within the stone. The conditions have been met."

Caleb swallowed back the tears that threatened, and, knowing this was to be his one and only chance, strode over to the girl he loved. Taking her in his arms, he gazed into her beautiful turbulent eyes. "You have my heart, Evangeline," he whispered. Then, bending forward, he touched his lips to hers. It was bittersweet; their first kiss was also to be their last. Releasing her, he stroked her cheek.

"Give me a smile to take with me; this is going to be the ultimate adventure." His shaky smile and bravado were poor covers for his fear and heartbreak. Eve gave her best smile and tried to step towards him. Caleb knew he would give in if she touched him again. Quickly he glanced at the others. "Take care of her... Ooof!"

Caleb doubled over, the wind knocked out of him. As he fell onto his side, he dropped the Aurora Stone. It lay on the ground, inches from his face, its orangey-pink colour changing to red and golds and back again before a huge paw swooped down and picked it up.

"That's quite enough, Caleb. I will not allow you to do this. It will be my honour to undertake this task. Be brave, Eve, and tell our story to all of Orea!" With that, Jericho drew his short sword, and clutching the Stone close to his chest, he stepped back into the void. The last they saw of him was his face, a huge smile cast upon it, his sword arm erect, the blade held high. Just before he was completely consumed, they heard his fierce battle cry;

"For Orea!"

Epilogue

Eve would never forget the events of that day. Indeed, she would never forget any of it. After Jericho's sacrifice, they had searched the fortress for a way to free the souls in the pits. Caleb managed to decipher an old text in Nimayaorin's Book of Shadows, and the thousands of souls inhabiting the pits were able to pass onto the realm of the dead. Amongst them were Eve and Eli's parents. Eli had insisted on cataloguing each soul so that their families could be informed and memorials held. It took weeks. By the time the last soul had passed on, Eli's hand was sore, and his eyes burned from concentration. The final document was enormous - a complete account of every soul they had freed.

They half expected to encounter demons willing to defend the fortress. Then, Winter realised why they hadn't. Their lives were tied to the darkness, so once he was gone, they, too, perished. It was completely surreal to know that they had won. Winter wanted to leave the corpses to rot, but Eve said that, unlike the fallen creatures that lay strewn like macabre rag dolls all over the fortress, they were honourable, and, therefore, they would build a funeral pyre and cremate their fallen adversaries. Winter rolled her eyes and muttered something about a waste of time and how gross it was to lug about dead demons, but she made her way to the nearest one, hauled it over her shoulders, and turned to Eve with a fanged smile. "Where do you want it?" she asked sweetly

The huge funeral pyre burned for many days. Eve watched as the flames danced and thick acrid smoke billowed in dark, ominous plumes overhead. Though the scene was horrific - so many dead being burned - it gave them all a sense of peace. The enemy had been defeated, and now they could think about the future.

Before they left for the return journey home, Eve wanted to search for the box she had seen in her vision of the young man. After much searching, she finally found it locked away in a dusty room. Picking her way carefully across the broken furniture, she saw the box sitting on an upturned urn. Picking it up, she gently wiped the dust from the lid.

Caleb found her there a short while later. He had come to tell her that they had found the portal room and could head directly to any realm they wanted. He stopped short when he saw the box.

"What's that?" he asked.

Eve looked over at her true love. How lucky she was to have him after all the trials they had been through. Both had been changed, and, yet, they remained the same in each other's eyes. Maybe love truly was blind. Eve didn't care. He completed her, and she was never letting him go.

"It's a memory box," she replied. Caleb knew whose memories were enclosed, and he wondered why Eve was still holding it.

"Please tell me you are not going to open it?" Caleb asked. He had had quite enough excitement to last him several lifetimes.

"No, I'm not going to open it. I am going to take it to the border between our realms and bury it. He and his siblings were halflings. It seems fitting they be buried there." Not quite understanding, but willing to accept what she said, Caleb closed the distance between them and took her hand.

"Come, we need to get home; your mother will be waiting for you," he reminded her, stroking the back of her hand with his thumb.

"I can't go home just yet. We need to return to Gloria and make sure Bobby is returned home. I also need to inform Maximus and the Protectors of the loss of two of the bravest creatures I have ever known, and tell them how, without their help, we would not have succeeded." A single tear escaped and rolled down her cheek. Caleb then explained that Eli had already left for Gloria to find Bobby and inform the Royals of their victory. He would then travel to Olia under the protection of the Royal guard to deliver the news to Maximus and the Protectors.

"I know you would like to go yourself, but, right now, Hermoria is in ruins. I think we need to get there as soon as possible and help where we can. Winter is waiting in the portal chamber; she didn't want to leave for home without first saying goodbye."

Agreeing, though reluctantly, Eve allowed Caleb to lead her to the portal chamber where Winter was waiting for them.

"So, I guess this is where we say goodbye. It was an experience, I guess. Maybe now that I have helped save the world, my father might lay off me getting hitched for a while!" Winter laughed. Eve smiled at her new friend. She was always making jokes when the situation became emotionally charged or difficult. Walking over to her, Eve embraced the vampire princess.

"Thank you for everything. I know what it cost you to come here, and I am so sorry I could not return the stone to you."

Winter just shrugged. "It's okay. I got to battle the ultimate evil, sire a halfling, and score major brownie points back home. I know my mum would be proud, and that is all that matters." She smiled at her two new friends. Then, turning to the midnight blue portal, she gracefully leapt into its swirling depths.

"I know we will be seeing her again," Caleb said, chuckling, "if only for her sense of humour!"

Eve suddenly remembered something: the moonstone! Maximus had said that it was a key. Turning from Caleb, she ran back through the fortress to the copper vault, her bag banging against her hips as she ran. Once in front of the copper doors, she removed the moonstone from its hiding place. She looked over the door's intricately carved surfaces. Where was the hole for the stone? There had been one for the Aurora Stone, so surely there must be one here somewhere! Caleb shot into the room, looking ready for battle. Seeing that there was no danger, he walked over to Eve and put his arm around her waist.

"What is it? What caused you to dash back here, of all places, so quickly?" he asked. Eve showed him the moonstone.

"Maximus told me this was also a key, and I thought that since the stone of the morning opened this, perhaps the moonstone might lock it forever," she replied, feeling a little foolish for thinking such a thing. Caleb stared in wonder at the girl he would have died for. She was completely right! Taking the stone from her, he held it against the seam of the doors. "Cal, what are you doing?" Eve asked. Smiling back at her, he just continued to stand holding the milky stone to the doors. Eve then realised what he was doing, but he was missing a vital part of the key, her blood. Drawing her dagger from its sheath, Eve bit her bottom lip and drew the blade across her palm. Moving quickly, she placed her bloodied hand over the stone. The result was almost immediate. The moonstone glowed with a beautiful pearlescent light. As it drew in Eve's blood, the light turned a rose pink. "Beautiful." Caleb muttered.

"Let the stone go, Cal. It knows what to do. I can feel its need to change, to become what is was destined to be," Eve said. Not questioning her, Caleb removed his fingers from the stone. As soon as he had, it began to melt, filling the seam of the door and then finding its way into the carved surface. They watched in awe as the doors turned from copper to silver. Eve sighed.

"The prophecy has been fulfilled. Take me home, Cal."

Holding hands, Eve and Caleb made their way back to the portal chamber. Together they walked across the room to stand before another portal. "This one is green like the new leaves of spring," Eve said. She made sure the box was secure under her arm. Then, turning to Caleb, she smiled and said, "So, I guess you are the first suitor I have ever brought home to meet my mother."

Leaning down to place a chaste kiss on her soft lips, Caleb replied, "I will also be the last!"

With that thought hanging between them, Eve and Caleb stepped into the portal.

THE REBUILDING AND subsequent building of memorials of all who fell during the Battle of the Darkness took many months. During that time, Eli made his first visit to Hermoria and helped his kinsmen rebuild their homes and their hope. Gwen was overjoyed to have Eve return to her. As promised, she baked a huge cake, which Eve ate a hearty portion of. She was so thankful her mother had survived the conflict.

Gwen had had the foresight to gather all the children of the village and flee to Reena's home, where they had been safe. Though she was pleased to have saved so many young, Gwen was plagued by nightmares of all those who had died. Caleb was a great distraction for her. She kept hinting about weddings and being a grandmother. Eve and Caleb just smiled. Maybe in time, those things would come, but right now they just wanted to live in the moment.

One month after their return, Eve received a missive from Olia. It was a request for her and Caleb's attendance at the memorial of Jericho and Sapphire. So, once again, Caleb and Eve prepared to enter the realm of the owl riders, only this time the trip was a lot quicker. They travelled by ley line, and knowing where they were headed also helped.

Maximus seemed much older than the last time they had seen him. The great Miscurt was greyer, and his eyes had lost some of their sparkle. The ceremony was to be held on the lakeside, Jericho's most treasured place. It was where he had taken Eve to meet Sapphire almost two years ago. There were many Protectors there to honour both Jericho and Sapphire. Maximus took the stand and spoke of a great warrior, leader and warm-hearted kinsman.

"We shall all miss Jericho's presence here. You could not have wished to know a better creature than him." Eve was moved to see tears pooling in the Miscurts eyes. Taking a breath, Maximus continued, "It is hard to lose one you are so fond of. It is harder still, to lose your only son. I wish I had spent more time showing him how much he meant to me." With that, Maximus broke down.

Eve rushed to his side, "I am so, so sorry; I wish we had known. Please, just know that Jericho died as he had lived, with a smile on his face, a sword in his hand, and hope in his heart."

Maximus looked into Eve's ever-changing eyes and gave her a watery smile. "You are a good girl. I am pleased to have met you, and I know my son would not have laid down his life for someone unless he thought them special. You will always be welcome here, both you and Caleb. "

"Thank you. We will visit often. And, if you permit it, we will regale your mighty people with Jericho's quest to save, not just Olia, but the whole of Orea." Maximus nodded his thanks and then left to speak with others who had attended. Eve moved towards the Protectors. She just wanted to tell them how sorry she was and how much she missed dear Sapphire. Before she reached them, she felt one of them prod at her telepathically. Opening the connection, Eve allowed the words to flow freely.

Please do not be sad, Light Carrier. Sapphire met her destiny. We are honoured to have been a part of your quest and know that you and Sapphire shared a special bond. Hold that bond close to your heart, and she will never truly leave you.

Eve just nodded, her tears choking her, and turned back to where Caleb was waiting for her. Taking her in his arms, he kissed the top of her head. "Let's go home."

"Yes, I know. We are expecting Eli, Bobby, and Winter any day now, so I want to be prepared for their arrival," Eve said, some of her sparkle returning at the thought of seeing her twin and the vampire princess. Caleb chuckled. "Yes, I cannot wait to hear all about how many brownie points she actually scored saving the world. Now hold tight."

Eve gripped her soul mate and felt the bottom fall out her stomach as they shot upward to catch the emerald green ley line that would carry them home.

It is important to remember that even though this battle of light and dark is over, there will always be another enemy of the light. But no matter how mighty the army or how terrifying the foe, the light will always prevail.

Darkness cannot survive when light is cast upon it.

Aura colours and their meanings

This is my interpretation on the colours. There are many sites online, but, for the purposes of the story, these are the ones I have used:

White:
New Energy, Truth, Purity
Yellow:
Mentally Alert, Optimist, Happy.
Green:
Balance, Growth, Change, Love of Nature and Living Creatures.
Purple:
Wise, Compassionate, Visionary.
Brown:
Greedy, Self-Absorbed, Closed Mind, Negative Energy.
Black:
Unforgiving nature, Past Life Problems, Unreleased Anger, Grief.

Author Biography

Alana Greig is a thirty something, mother of two and happily married. She lives in on the west coast of England and loves to spend time at the beach.

Alana, predominantly writes fantasy. The Aurora Stone is her debut novel; she has other projects soon to be published.

Once Upon a Reality, is a collection of short stories based on old classics will be released September 2017. Alana co-wrote the book with international bestselling author Erin Lee.

Work is also underway for Alana's second novel; PULSE. Which is based on Princess Winter from The Aurora Stone.

When Alana isn't creating new worlds, she loves nothing more than to curl up with a cup of tea and lose herself in someone else's.

Printed in Great Britain
by Amazon